The Burglar's Baby

Katharine Ann Angel

2QT Limited (Publishing)

First Edition published 2015 by
2QT Limited (Publishing)
Settle, North Yorkshire BD24 9RH
www.2qt.co.uk

 Katharine Ann Angel  @katharine59

Typeset by Robbie Associates Ltd
Illustrations: Angela Allen
Graphic Design: Dale Rennard

Printed in the UK by Lightning Source UK Limited

A CIP catalogue record for this book is available
from the British Library
ISBN 978-1-910077-73-3

Contents

'We make men without chests and expect
from them virtue and enterprise.
We laugh at honour and are shocked to find
traitors in our midst.'
C.S Lewis, *The Abolition of Man*

Acknowledgements

Thank you to everyone who read, proofed or edited *The Burglar's Baby*; for your invaluable insights, suggestions concerning the 'details that matter,' and your constant encouragement. Special thanks to Dave Lamin, Kirsty-Jane Lamin, Andrew Gardner, Will Newton, Amanda Cross, Alan Greenwell, Charis Smith and Rebecca Townley. Thank you, Angela Allen, for your beautiful artwork. Thanks, Dale Rennard, for the graphic design – it has been great to work with you again. Thank you, Karen Holmes – I'm so glad you are, in your words, 'a pedant; finicky about sub-clauses and punctuation.' It makes you a very good editor. Thank you, Catherine Cousins, for your constant support and patient advice.

Finally, thanks to those readers who wrote saying how much they loved Hugo Quin in *The Froggitt Chain* and asking me to write him into another story. You will understand this quote from the essay 'Losing Control: Memoirs of Middle Age' by Karen Holmes: *There was always some sort of transport to get me out of a fix. Failing that, I walked.*

For Joel, Sam and Ethan

Finally the Truth
The truth about 1999 as dictated by Duncan Wilde, January 2nd 2016

What doesn't thrill isn't worth remembering. I think it was my dad who said that, but whoever said it was dead right. When I'm too old to care what others think, my idea is to relive (in my mind) some of the crazy stuff I did in my youth. I'll mumble, 'I lost Steve,' or 'I stole a baby,' they'll exchange knowing glances and tap their temples and whisper, 'Poor guy doesn't know what he's saying.'

But for now, only this Dictaphone will hear my story. Back in 1999 I coped with normal life by believing my own lies. But 'normal' being a pretty wife, two daughters and a job in IT, bored me rigid. Deep down I craved the old excitement and often wondered how or why I ever let it go.

'Normal' included nights managing an international 24-hour IT support line for Direction Data, before the firm decided on a massive shake-up. No problem, I thought. My boss forewarned me about the cuts: 'Don't you worry, Duncan. You're an asset to the company. Your job is secure.' Two days later he summoned me; 'Mr Wilde, we're letting you go . . . you're a good guy. You understand . . .'

As I left, I was that livid I lifted some random wallet off the desk of a colleague. I'd never nicked a thing before. Not as an adult. And it wasn't for money because I'd inherited plenty.

But they owed me. Later that evening, I admit to a minor panic thinking CCTV might've picked up on me, but after a week with no police at my door, I got a thrill. A vague awareness of triumph. But like the disobedient vicar who skived his Sunday service to play golf and played a hole-in-one, I couldn't tell a living soul of my success.

However, I did almost blurt to Julia that I'd lost my job and I don't know how I kept my mouth shut. After such a massive blow, I deserved a spot of freedom. I rewarded myself by going out wherever, five evenings a week without question. Ignorance is bliss as they say and Julia was blissfully ignorant in the belief that I was at work.

Initially I chatted to strangers in bars, but what nagged on at me was the thrill of that wallet, that frisson, a delicious rush that hit me right in the 'feels' from the feet up. I wanted more. Initially it was mere fantasy, something to entertain my frustrated mind. I imagined breaking into houses, this way or that: shinning a drainpipe, slipping into a house, pocketing some insignificant trophy then returning home nonchalant, like I'd been to work. Some evenings I stayed home, telling Julia my hours had changed, but that wallet . . .

So began an entertaining, um, hobby. Not getting caught, or almost getting caught, gave me the most phenomenal shot of adrenalin. By nature I'm no thief, but by habit I became one.

I did thirteen break-ins before Toby, the one Julia found out about. She was livid and threatened to leave me but then she reverted to type and amateur-psyched me. Said, 'If you ask me, you've got suppressed grief. I warned you to get therapy about Steve.' After Toby, I finally admitted that I lost my job months ago which, to Julia, explained my suspicious behaviour. She persuaded herself I'd cracked up but that with patience and understanding I could be fixed. She had this idea that I could become a motivational speaker and helped me set up an impressive web page. I've got the gift of the gab. They say I'm a natural. People part with good money to hear me go on about leadership, so I suppose I should be grateful, but even as I speak my demon 'boredom' rears its ugly head!

I'm past climbing drainpipes for a laugh but I am toying with something. I'm thinking of sabotaging one of my 'How to be a Born Leader' lectures. I'll switch on this Dictaphone and play this confession full volume. It'll be worth it to see the shock on their sycophantic faces when they realise that their all-knowing, self-assured guru was, and still is, a pathetic coward.

Recently I've had trouble sleeping. I get jittery. It's time for my brain to dispose of the gunk. I told myself, Duncan, if you can't talk to a human being, an actual, heart-beating, oxygen-inhaling human, then speak to a machine. So here goes.

In the time it took me to ski from the crevasse to the foot of the mountain, I convinced myself that what happened wasn't my responsibility. The fall killed him. I flatly refuse to accept he survived the fall then froze to death because of me on some God-forsaken ledge.

Nearly two decades later, I've begun to dream that Steve survived, at least for an hour or two. He is lying motionless, face-up, white as a ghost. In my dreams I dare to take a closer look, hoping he's dead already because that would be a mercy (for me). But suddenly he opens his eyes wide, like he's in shock, looking for light, praying for a saviour – and his prayers might have been answered if he'd been skiing with Luke or Moh or Yasin instead of me.

Spreadeagled against a vast expanse of sparkling, dripping whiteness, Steve would have searched for any sign of hope. He'd be expecting a stretcher to be lowered towards him. A simple stretcher and a man (most likely the reliable Yasin) and a rope, and that's it. Oh, and high above the crevasse this rope is secured to an ice axe, which in turn is secured by Steve's brother Luke, who is shielding his face from the biting down-draught of the blades of the high-altitude rescue helicopter, from which a haul-line descends; a merciful heavenly hand to which Steve reaches out . . .

Our three sets of parents had voiced concerns that their sons shared a strong death-wish but they knew how seriously we'd absorbed the law of the mountain: to keep a sharp watch on the weather and stay close to one another. We were in our early twenties, in no rush to assume the responsibilities of actual manhood, the nine-to-five job, a selfless relationship, raising our own offspring, paying a mortgage, taxing the car, blah, blah, blah. Unlike our anxious parents, we boys never imagined the worst. We couldn't foresee the inevitable disaster because we lived only to feel our spirits bursting out through our rib cages.

Our gang of five were two sets of brothers: Steve and Luke, Moh and Yasin, and yours truly. We'd done school together from Reception to Year Eleven. Officially none of us learnt music but as teenagers we formed a band and spent hours pretending we were called this or that (The Skiddoos, The Infamous Five, Wild Speed). I was the drummer because I had the best sense of rhythm. No way could I be like Luke who played the bass obsessively and annoyingly, and I definitely couldn't sing like Yasin. Yasin couldn't sing either but we assured him he was a natural, and he was the only one audacious enough to combine the depths of 'don't care' grunge with actual diction. He also composed some meaningful lyrics.

Second only to our music (if you can call it that) was one-upmanship. Competitiveness ran in our blood. We compared test results, the size of our biceps and how high we could mark the urinals. We argued over which girls paid who the most attention and how many shots we could down in a night. Obviously we were as stupid as stags without antlers but we believed we were beyond brilliant.

Each winter throughout our secondary school years our parents took us lads, plus my younger sister Emily, skiing abroad. We disdained the nursery slopes, vying to be let loose on something more challenging. Our skills evolved until we were eighteen and began to travel – lads only – to new resorts where we progressed to increasingly daring and more exhilarating pistes. Evenings were spent drinking and talking about who was faster, crazier, who'd leapt off the highest rock, skied the most dangerous route or survived the wildest tumble. One of us would start, 'What would you do if . . .' and we'd compete for the most heroic-sounding response. I bragged that I'd stand by the guys in good times and bad, building trust and confidence so they could rely on me to keep them calm in a crisis. We agreed that if today you help out your partner, tomorrow he will help you if you are struggling.

One night, Steve asked, 'What would you do if we all were caught at the edge of an avalanche? Everyone gets hit bad. All unconscious – except you – and one of us is buried alive?'

I can't for the life of me remember what the others said. Come to think of it, I rarely cared what their boasts were as long as mine sounded just great. My mouth said something like, 'I'd phone for help if my phone was still working. Press my locator thing. I'd find my inner, untapped resources and with superhuman strength I'd . . .' and off I went, spouting on and on about artificial resuscitation, digging hasty snow-holes in which to place my mates safely out of the wind, wrapping them in foil blankets, shoving them close together for warmth and all the time talking, reassuring them that help was on its way. Fortunately for us, the avalanche never did happen.

Steve and I were the worst for crazy schemes, such as our ridiculous plan to wing-suit off Everest, so we were tagged The Adrenalin Brothers. To bring most dreams to reality demands a level of discomfort for the dreamer and no one likes being uncomfortable. Of course dancers, distance runners and endurance athletes willingly embrace deprivation and pain because they know that by enduring agonies – early bedtimes, correct diet, hours of training – they can forge amazing new experiences. The pain we suffered for our obsession with extreme skiing was financial debt (the bank of Dad and Mum), some muscle fatigue, much cold and, for my part, more fear than I ever let on.

I told myself that fear was more about respecting the mountain but on reflection I'm not so sure. Even so, our Everest fantasy did morph into something spine-tingling – several trips to Verbier, a premier resort for extreme skiing, renowned for its off-piste slopes with many areas snow-covered all year round.

What attracted us, apart from the stunning glaciers, were the countless Brits and Scandinavians who spoke our lingo. Stress-free socialising. To top it all, Verbier pulls in royalty and only the year before Luke swore he'd seen Prince Harry with some other guys disappearing behind a sea of cameras. Then Jules, who reads those posh magazines, pointed out a bunch of toffs from the Swedish royal family. She made us laugh by brazenly flirting with an older man – one of their party – but we couldn't tell their princes from their servants.

Skiing is a great leveller. I eyed up the Prada-wearing socialites queuing for the lifts alongside us ordinary mortals. Mortals like Steve, the strong, usually silent type; a short muscular guy who'd been born with a hare-lip which lent him (now I'm being soppy) a certain endearing vulnerability. Everyone liked him but he didn't suffer fools gladly. He could be easily irritated by other burly blokes on the chair-lifts talking too loudly, exaggerating their skiing prowess. Steve could eyeball them with such contempt they'd instantly shut up. I like to think they were embarrassed by him.

Then what happened? Luke, Yasin and Moh turned serious. I suppose they grew up, disappearing off to London and Southampton to study medicine, economics and marine-biology. They jacked in skiing and abandoned our music just like that – like it meant zilch. I fumed because I hadn't seen it coming; nevertheless I bullied Steve into yet one more adventure. I also begged Julia to join us but she point-blank refused saying (okay, yelling) that it was about time I grew up. She was in a crazy frame of mind, talking marriage and what have you. I was wild about her – even so she was a distraction who could wait until I was properly ready for the very real terrors of settling down. And I wasn't prepared to chuck away one last 'Steve and me' buzz-fest. Not yet.

So we travelled our familiar route via Geneva, taking the Saint-Bernard Express from Martigny to Le Châble, then caught a cable-car up to Verbier, and all the while my heart beat brutally in anticipation of those fast-approaching adrenalin shots.

On that first day I felt sick to my stomach. It was nerves. A perverse stage-fright that I never could master but I told Steve it was something I ate and he was pretty good about it. Almost too chilled, in fact. Maybe he felt the same way. Maybe he daren't tell me how he too was sick with excitement and fear because although, professionally speaking, in terms of height Verbier is relatively tame, only fifteen hundred metres above sea level, some of the stunts we were imagining were pretty wild.

On day one, Steve let me down. Said he felt queasy. Something he ate. It never occurred to me that my burly mate might have something on his mind; that he might have his own internal plans and worries, and back then, I'd never have thought to ask him if he was okay on a deeper level. I mean, he was Steve. Just Steve. So instead of skiing we agreed to take the cable up to Mont Fort, over three thousand metres up, to inhale the awesomeness and remind ourselves how small we were. From Mont Fort we absorbed the enormity of the Alps, the breath-taking panorama encompassing Dom, the Matterhorn Cervin, Dent Blanche, Dent d'Hérens, Grand Combin and Mont Blanc massif, each mountain peak gnashing at the too-blue sky like the open jaws of a patient yet deadly alligator. Behind our goggles we screwed up our eyes against the powerful sinking sun.

I'm recording a ton too much detail which is my way of holding truth at arm's length. Even to voice the words 'losing Steve' scares me witless, so I dread to think how I'm going to tell the whole story but hey, I'll keep going.

We hung out at the summit of Mont Fort until it began to grow dark and hunger reminded us to head back to our chalet. But before we boarded the final cable car, Steve started romancing gruffly about the clarity of the evening stars that blazed in the velvet sky. His voice caught as his throat constricted, so he had to whisper and I could hardly hear his poetry. Then, incredibly, as if we were watching a blockbuster on some gigantic 3D wrap-around screen, we saw, away and below us, huge flattened thunderheads looming over lightning bolts that snapped like guitar-strings and burnt the clouds orange.

'This is living, Duncan,' Steve gasped, breathing it all in, and it crossed my mind that he was the genuine article. He loved this whole thing far more than I ever could. Steve was here because he needed to be. I was here only to impress the gang and to pretend to give my life some kind of meaning.

'No point in being alive if you don't live,' Steve said, more to himself than to me.

After that we spent three days on-piste, pretty much behaving ourselves. The previous year, at the insistence of my parents, we'd employed Will Hoyle, a fantastic guide from London who was fluent in French and a holder of the Patente Suisse License. Will was the same age as me but with tons more experience, so Steve and I booked him again. He liked to repeat what he called 'Will's Wisdom': 'Safety is my second name. Make it your first one. Or die.' We'd smirked but he wasn't laughing.

I clipped on my skis and instantly felt supercharged, trusting them to be energetic, springy, to hold their edge fantastically well on every turn. This year my muscles were stronger, my whole body more flexible and my belief in my improved ability spurred me on.

On the Wednesday evening Steve asked Will to lead us off-piste. He'd overheard some guys whooping at the bar, reliving their death-defying day and Steve wanted what they'd had. He seemed greedy for it all, the exhilaration, the sheer stomach-dropping fabulous terror that had me shaking in my boots.

The next morning we were stoked, steeling ourselves to face a new side of the mountain. The night before, knowing the weather forecast was perfect for some risky take-offs, I'd been so jittery I hardly slept. Will had warned us the Hidden Valley could be lethal with its submerged rocks, felled trees, crevasses, steep runs and ever-threatening avalanches, so of course we accepted his strict advice: 'All kit is essential, if only to limit the time rescuers are forced to endure as they locate and dig out your body. And you never know – they might get to you in time.'

Will led the way to the lift and we trudged after him, relishing this huge commitment to an unknown outcome, although obviously we envisaged a safe return.

We dismounted the lift. After that it was a long, hard trek to the summit of the Hidden Valley. The sun sparked off the snow-crystals, threatening to blind us if we removed our goggles. Finally we stood shoulder to shoulder, The Adrenalin Brothers, in a silent celebration of the beauty and power of the mountains. Will talked us through the planned route, checked we were fine, then we gave him the thumbs up, ready to go.

Oddly, when I looked to Steve for some sort of moral support (an encouraging nod might have settled my stomach), he was totally focussed on his own game and seemed to refuse to acknowledge me. As I hesitated, needing his reassurance, Steve swooped silently away, not along Will's precise tracks but creating fresh parallel grooves through powdery, virgin snow. Everyone likes to be the first over pure ground. I was left with no choice but to follow.

Our speed gathered as we negotiated areas of impacted ice towards a giant outcrop of rock, a natural half-pipe full of hardened snow. We swept through it then flattened our bodies into the wind, flying forward as far as possible until we touched down. The faster we sped, the more alert we were forced to be.

Steve passed through the channel behind Will several seconds before me. He must have managed it brilliantly because as I flew through the gap, scanning the terrain for a safe landing spot, I momentarily caught sight of him far below, cutting sharply to the left. Losing concentration, I dipped awkwardly as I landed, white shards spraying up in my wake and almost immediately I was forced to avoid a huge branch, half-submerged across my path.

I glanced up to check where Steve had gone and noticed Will way ahead, down to my right. I presumed Steve would materialise, deciding that somehow I'd missed seeing him cross to the right again but then I spotted him, very, very briefly, far further to my left than he should have been. I had to focus. There were not many fallen trees at this altitude but still, I had to keep my wits about me. Another glance and I caught Steve swerving expertly, zig-zagging alone. Will must have slowed a little because his fluorescent gear was clearly visible several hundred metres below me, exactly where he had told us he'd go.

Then Steve vanished.

Steve vanished and in a flash I knew he'd fallen through a crevasse. I heard a distant cry, a short, 'Aagghh!' My last memory of Steve is seeing him sweep across the snow-duvet and then, as if some invisible demon had yanked down a white sheet slung between two beds, he disappeared. And that's all I can say.

My brain screamed, 'Brake!' and I almost yelled 'Steve!' I imagined myself inching in Steve's direction. We had transceivers strapped around our chests so I should have switched mine on. But I did not. I did not brake. I did not shout out. I did not stop. I don't know why I kept moving but my indecision meant I'd already descended a further hundred metres or so.

Will must have slowed a little because I was closing on him quickly. Perhaps he braked because he'd also heard Steve yell. I convinced myself that 'Will the professional' would handle the whole thing far more efficiently than I ever could. I expected to draw alongside him at any second but then I realised he'd only slowed to glance back, seen me approaching and turned to picked up speed, zig-zagging towards the distant white roofs of Verbier village.

'Steve! Steve!' I was six years old again. My little sister fell off a wall. I heard the crack as her skull hit the ground. I saw her pale face and the way she lay on the pavement staring up, neither moving nor crying because she was dead. Straightaway, I ran home down the long street, all the time shouting, 'Help! Help! Dad! Mum!' I beat my fists on our front door because the back gate was locked. On tiptoes I pressed the doorbell urgently. 'Mum?' I cried as loud as my little lungs could muster, but no one answered, so I sat down on the doorstep and thought about last night's episode of Doctor Who because halfway through my dad switched it off, saying, 'This'll give you nightmares.'

I was still sitting on the step when my parents appeared, along with my sister who was not dead but skipping. After all my panic and running and shouting no one had needed me after all. Everyone went indoors and that was that.

I ground to a halt. Will was leaning against a tree trunk, nonchalantly waiting. Flushed and panting, I longed to collapse face down, to cool my skin in the mashed snow. Instead I smiled at Will.

'Wow! That was amazing, incredible! Best ever.' I started to look round. 'Where's Steve?' I said, aware of a wobble in my voice. It was as if I'd shocked Will with a thousand volts because he stood up straight, immediately alert.

'What do you mean? He was ahead of you all the way.'

'Yes, he was. I watched him follow you. He was with you all the way.' My mouth was dry but the words spilled out smoothly enough. Calm. Nothing untoward. Will immediately had his binoculars to his eyes, scanning the mountain: top, bottom, left, right. I blundered on, gabbling rubbish. 'Once we were over the worst of the mountain, through the cut, I relaxed. Steve and you, well, you were so focussed, in your own world. I just . . .'

Will was on his phone, talking fast, giving co-ordinates, ordering search and rescue. I was already convincing myself that Steve had beaten both of us down. Maybe he'd skied straight to the toilets because he couldn't wait. Any minute now he'd walk back up towards us, grinning. I pretended to survey the mountain, lifting my goggles and screwing up my eyes. I could do with a brandy. I began to push myself with my poles, over the snow and away from Will, but he shouted, 'Duncan! Where're you off to? Stay here. Don't go anywhere.'

'I must find Steve!' I yelled back, feeling desperate, truthfully desperate. If Will so much as guessed I'd seen something terrible, there'd be a never-ending inquisition. Why didn't you stop? Shout? Phone? Activate your transceiver? Idiotic, guilty fool. Back on the slope Will had briefly checked on our progress. He'd seen me heading on down and, because of that, he'd assumed all was well because it had been my responsibility to watch for Steve. I glided back to the tree and unclipped my skis. Then I slumped down, placed my head on my knees, and waited.

Above me I heard shouts, commands, men directing other men. Someone official told me to stand up (which I did), and he drilled me about what exactly I remembered. Where? Are you sure? I held my story. Steve was well ahead of me, a bit behind Will. Will, the excellent guide. Yes, of course he took us through all that safety stuff. Many times. We understood it all. Please don't blame Will.

I tried to look shocked, and I was shocked, but in the turmoil

I was struggling to navigate the fine line between acting and reality. Someone told me to go inside and get warm, so I obeyed. No one needed me. No amount of shouting for help, standing on tiptoes or ringing any doorbells would bring Steve back, skipping towards me like my little sister as if nothing had happened. I was just some rich guy on holiday while everyone else was working, responding to an emergency.

In the café I purchased a hot chocolate, then I sat rigid, moronically staring at MTV. But I could not forget. I cannot forget.

Later, they found Steve. He'd fallen thirty metres through a hidden snow-bridge. Much later, a high-altitude rescue helicopter lowered its line and lifted Steve's body towards the heavens; a dark sarcophagus floating in the palest blue sea.

'Dark sarcophagus! What am I saying?' Duncan tosses the little black recorder across the room. It hits the wooden floor, skids beneath the locked sideboard and in the dark space he hears it crash against the skirting board.

Duncan stares at the space, half-expecting his confession to rebound into the light, to shout out, to accuse him of leaving everything far too late, so that when the so-called truth finally emerges it is fuzzy and pixelated, memories confused by too many lies and layers. *Maybe it is time to make some sort of recompense, to begin, little-by-little, to donate my hidden stash of the Nowik-Judas money to charity. Or to Toby. I could try to trace Toby.* Duncan's heart races at the audacity of the thought because there is absolutely no way he'd ever dare leap from that particular rock-face.

Duncan checks his watch, clears his throat, and steadies himself against the wall. 'No one needs to know about my pathetic life,' he says out loud, as he departs for the university to deliver the final lecture in his leadership series. *'Self-esteem and How it Affects Motivation.'*

Lisa 1
October and November

Rats forage in the bins that scatter the ginnel behind a string of terraced houses in Lancaster. On this chilly autumn evening a young woman rummages with them, competing for pickings of limp pizza, congealed cheese and anchovies and the dregs of a can of lager. Tonight she retrieves a recently discarded pillow, mottled and lumpy, but still dry.

The woman has no gloves. Her walking boots are worn thin, lined with two pairs of socks. Her hoody is zipped to her neck, the hood cocooning her head, protection from the cold and any unwelcome, prying eyes. It is her security, a cloak of invisibility in place of a roof. From a distance she hopes people perceive her to be male. Close-up? There is no close-up; no one comes near.

She raises her shadowed eyes to examine the row of rear windows and is satisfied that no one is watching. She examines the final bin, the one behind the disused post office. The gate to the yard behind the post office hangs uselessly as a broken arm. The woman steps over the threshold. Where the concrete path meets the red-bricked terrace there are two adjacent doors framed by a single, flat-roofed porch. The left door is bolted and barred but the right is slightly ajar. Above this open door is a grimy, cracked window set in a rotting wooden frame. *Well, if no one lives here . . .*

The woman pushes it open. Without hesitation, she shuffles

across the threshold into a suffocating, musty hallway. She turns to close the door against the empty world, fumbling in the dark with the sliding lock-and-chain, but it is broken. Exhausted, the woman closes her eyes. Clutching the pillow to her stomach, she slowly leans until her forehead rests against the door.

I'm home from college. My key turns in the lock and I am free to enter. I fill our kettle for a brew. I check on Mum and as usual she is snoring on the sofa in front of the chattering TV. The chicken casserole that I chucked together first thing this morning is in the slow-cooker and it smells delicious. I close the door to my bedroom, lie back on my duvet and send a few texts. I check Facebook and arrange to meet Gareth later.

A narrow flight of stairs beckons the woman upwards. The stairs are carpeted, threadbare, stinking of mould. She ascends laboriously: one stair, rest. One stair, rest. Inhale. Exhale. Another stair then another, until a small landing opens into a large, curtainless room.

Light from the street falls on a sagging armchair and a mug-ringed table. A naked light bulb hangs limp from the high ceiling, beneath an ornate central rose. Against one wall, a grubby mattress curves like a sandbag flood barrier. There are three magnolia walls, streaked grey with fingerprints and damaged where cupboards and shelves have been removed. Paler rectangles boast of removed pictures and an oval shape – a mirror maybe. The main wall is papered, embossed with pink camellias, pearlescent daisies and lime-green leaves, and the damp corners curl like petals. At one end of this room is an excuse for a kitchen; two cupboards then a gap for an oven, then a sink over another cupboard. A drawer gapes open to reveal oddments: a bread-knife, scissors, cloths and paperclips. The only other room is the bathroom without a door. The woman pushes the flush on the toilet and jumps back at the unexpected noise. It works! Water. A gift.

Best not try the light, she thinks, because two sash windows at the front of the house overlook the busy A-road and opposite is the Texaco garage, busy even at night. Immediately to the right, traffic lights control the crossroads and behind the traffic lights is a small supermarket, beyond which is the Hala council estate that sprawls uphill and stops abruptly where a road bridge spans the M6; a gateway to the rolling Lancashire hills.

The young woman summons enough strength to shift the mattress to the centre of the room. She eases back, hands on hips, to assess its position and decides she hates the floor space all around the mattress because it reminds her of a raft, wrecked and abandoned at sea. Again she drags the mattress until she is satisfied with its position, shoved flat against the pretty wall where she plans to sleep facing the camellias and daisies.

With a sigh, she lowers herself onto the mattress. She picks at the soggy laces to remove her boots and socks then examines her feet, wrinkly-white with blue patches where the dye from her socks has rubbed. She grimaces at her long toenails and runs her fingers along the edges of them, thinking she could bite them if only she could get them to her mouth but her tight, round belly is in the way.

On her first night squatting in the Penhala Terrace flat, the woman (*more of a girl, barely out of university*) sleeps against the wall of flowers and, for the first time in a month, she is unafraid. The cold is less cold than sleeping outside but, compared to yesterday, the hunger is hungrier.

Blue lights from a fire engine sweep across the wobbly, white tiled walls, and the sirens wail outside in the street in sympathy with the birth. Lisa kneels against the bath side, rising and falling on her knees as the contractions command, clenching the edge of the bath with her elbows and forearms. She wears only a huge T-shirt and unzipped hoody. Her head hangs forward and her brown hair, dripping with sweat, snakes downwards into the bath space. Less than half a mile away, eight-year-old Ryan is dying in a raging fire, the one that his four older siblings had ordered him to defend.

It is not yet the fifth of November, but who cares and what should be remembered? History is meaningless. Now is the season of cat-stinking-toxic-sponge-sofas, splinter-backed chairs and broken trophies; a heap of burning rot.

The brothers goad little Ryan, 'Get yerself under there. That's right. Go in that space under the table. You be guard and if anyone comes to set fire before time, shout at them, see. Tell 'em where to go.'

Today is a full week before the fifth, but the weedy Ryan worships the big boys and so he obeys. On the night before Hallowe'en, the child curls beneath the rubbish and falls asleep. That dark night a different tribe lights the pile and the youngsters lie in wait, excited, for the fire engines. Glowing embers rise on the warm air, swirling against the starlit sky and the children stare agape, in awe of the massive light they created.

They don't intend for Ryan to die. It is a simply a hazard of the estate.

Between each contraction there is a single minute's rest. Then wave upon wave of power. Lisa is beside herself. What to do? To stand or sit or lie or crawl? Even in her darkest moment, she dare not scream. Kneeling, she lifts her eyes to where the street

27

lights bounce off the tiles, where the blue lights had rippled and gone. She can see her own shadow on the wall and behind her another shadow stands: a guardian angel, hovering. *I am dying,* Lisa thinks, *but I must live for the sake of my unborn.*

She holds her breath and pushes down. Her knees press on the hard lino and, 'Let me die!' she cries out loud, alarmed by the sound of herself. She groans as she rests her mouth on the bath side. Her voice echoes as if caught in a cave, a dark space within dripping rocks, inhabited by bats and cockroaches and fear. She looks again at the shadowy figure on the bathroom tiles with its wide, wobbly chest. The shadow sways. A shiver trickles over the crown of Lisa's head and down her back.

'Paul?' she asks but it can't possibly be Paul. He'd never stand mute like that. Paul would be yelling obscenities about the blood and the mess. He'd be raising a fist or throwing something heavy, and anyway Paul hasn't the foggiest where she is – so who *could* it be? Who'd stand so silently? Who would watch without aggression?

The pressure mounts and gravity pulls and the baby crowns and the woman thinks her spine might split in two like some butchered turkey. Her forehead rests against the coolness of the bath-side as the contraction wanes. A powerful light, a beam of silver-white sweeps across the floor and up the wall, then returns to find the woman. The baby is emerging. The woman lifts her head, opening her mouth to scream. A large hand clamps over her mouth, pressing Lisa's lips hard against her teeth. Her eyes open wide and wild. A torch clatters to the floor and its light pours across the lino. A man's voice hisses urgently, very close.

'Shut up! Shut up! I'll kill you if anyone calls the police.' His breath is in her ear.

There's no way Lisa can fight him, so she bites down and

cannot let go. His blood is in her mouth and a strange, sweet smell invades her nostrils. It reminds her of scented candles burning. The man is not Paul. Paul would yell, but this man hisses through his teeth. The pain becomes greater than her fear and she snaps ferociously onto his hand, vaguely aware that the man is cursing and prising at her jaw with his free hand.

A cry cuts the air, sharp as a blade. Lisa looks at the place where her bruised knees press into the lino, where a scrap of humanity is attached to her by a thick, greasy grey cord, its skinny body squirming and glistening in the torchlight. Water falls, rushing and gurgling.

'Which one's the hot tap?' asks the man, because both taps run only cold. Lisa drifts down to where the floor is cool and at last she can curl within the cowl of her hoody, where she forgets to reach for her baby. She thinks she is in hospital because someone is moving about, a nurse maybe, sorting things out; the placenta, the mess, the . . . She opens her eyes and discovers an infant at her breast, wrapped in a towel. Her sleeping bag has been unzipped and spread over them both. The damp mattress feels so soft that Lisa dares to sigh, inhales, exhales, closes her eyes to see her mother at the sash window, waving, mouthing, 'Bye sweetie. Won't be long. Take care. Love you.'

Lisa opens her eyes but her mother has gone already.

'You want to know what it is?' A stranger is sitting in her armchair, rhythmically tapping his fingers against something wooden. Lisa can't actually see him so he may not be real. She merely shrugs.

'A boy,' says the man, matter-of-fact, without congratulations.

Lisa dozes while he wanders about, opening and closing cupboard doors. He is breathing through his nose, clicking his lips as he mutters to himself. He rattles her shoulder bag, spilling loose change and oddments of junk over the table. His jacket rustles as he rifles through her stuff in search of the usual target, a small but interesting trophy to mark this month's mission. Frustrated, he resorts to a bankcard, the only item remotely worth taking.

'Tell me your PIN.' The voice is far, far away, way beyond the ceiling, at the same time clear and close and expecting an immediate answer. Lisa feigns sleep, one arm wrapped around the back of the newborn. The man nudges Lisa's back with his trainer. 'I said, what is your PIN? The code. For the bank.'

From experience, a harder kick is likely to follow so Lisa pretends to wake, yawning, confused. She heaves herself onto one elbow, separating from the cocooned baby.

'I – don't – want – it,' she whispers, and her teeth are chattering with shock and cold.

'What?' He thinks maybe she said, 'Eight two one six,' but he can't be sure. He has to be sure. 'Say again?'

'The baby. I don't want it. Take it away.' She pushes the sleeping boy further from herself then she turns her back to face the wall, leaving him on the edge of the mattress.

'The baby? What would I do with a baby? Take him? Me? You're crazy.' The man jabs his finger against his temple. He squats down on his haunches and leans over the little one to breathe into Lisa's ear. 'The PIN and I'm outta here.'

'But I can't keep him,' she confesses to the wall, as car headlights sweep in waves over the ceiling. *They can search all they like but they'll never find me here.*

'And I'm going nowhere without your number.' Lisa senses the subtle switch in tone from irritation to danger, from feigned patience through gritted teeth to white knuckles clenched in rage. She recognises the emphatic *I'm*, the way his words are evenly spaced, neat, like they are typewritten. *I'm. Going. Nowhere.*

The man lowers himself onto the floor. He lies down on the carpet, then lifts his head and rests it on the edge of the mattress. His stubbled chin brushes against the unblemished head of the little one. He's in no hurry.

Lisa groans. She holds her stomach as she rolls back to face the stranger and she can tell he's wearing a black, woolly hat over his eyebrows and a scarf wrapped around his face, so only his eyes are visible. She stares boldly into his pupils and he returns her stare. For several long silent seconds they each search the soul of the other. Slowly he unwraps the scarf. It occurs to Lisa that he might strangle her with it.

'PIN number,' he repeats, his lips over-emphatic like she is stupid, or maybe because the light is poor. The tip of his tongue emerges, a thought, curling out over his bottom lip before retreating.

Lisa reads the threat. Her heart beats so fiercely she knows he can hear it through the mattress. She draws her knees up until they touch two tiny, icy feet. Beneath the cover she wraps her hands around them, feeling them curl and uncurl against her warm palms.

'Four nine two three,' she manages, though her mouth is dry.

'Four nine two three. It better had be. Four nine two three,' he repeats beneath his breath, then rolls back and up onto his feet in one movement, so athletic. Lisa watches as he lifts his empty, black holdall. So close, she sees the laces of his trainers, thick, woven strings of blue, yellow and black, fraying, yet knotted at the ends. He steps away. She hears his feet descending the stairs, the unlocking of the door and she realises he must have entered through the broken window, the one above the flat-roofed porch. The door clicks shut. He is gone.

In her dreams, Lisa follows the man down the stairs and, quick as a flash, she locks the door behind him. She fixes the broken window pane. She arranges blue flowers in a white vase. Friends arrive with gifts of clothes, toys and fruit. She decorates the nursery, hanging cream curtains with dancing blue elephants, and above the cot she strings a musical mobile with dappled rocking horses, and across the pale yellow walls she pastes a poster: A is for apple, B for baby, C for cat.

Lisa's thoughts wake before she does. *The baby slept through. It never cried. I'll make a nappy from a tea towel. I'll have to clean up. I won't cope. I can't do it. I don't need this baby. So hungry. I have to go out, get some food in. Milk. Bread. Clothes. Money.*

Money! Lisa's eyes spring open. She is lying on her side with one leg forward, hanging off the mattress, her big toe resting on the carpet. Dusty sunlight slides into the room, settling on the arm of the chair where the night-stranger had sat. Lisa considers the two hundred pounds in notes that is still safely tucked behind the back cushions. She stares at the space on the floor where the man's body had lain beside her, then the space in the doorway at the top of the stairs, the broken window, the bits and pieces scattered over the carpet, the kitchen drawers and cupboards hanging open. Always empty.

Lisa smiles, remembering how he'd taken her bank card but she'd fooled him and had given him the wrong PIN. Risky, but he'd believed her in the end. By now he'll be frustrated and furious, grinding his teeth, seething with hatred and revenge. Lisa's heart races faster and faster because, if he's anything like Paul, the man will return with an unholy vengeance.

Lisa reaches her hand out from beneath the cover and the chill air hits it. She pats the mattress. Panic rises in her. Something should be there. *What* should be there? Something is not there that should be there. Something. Someone? She sits up too suddenly, clutching her stomach. Lisa searches for a name but there is no name. A face but there is no face. A body but there is

no

body.

Julia 1
Friday October 31st

Julia reassures herself that her husband is still breathing. She reaches over to touch his back, to dispel what she admitted to be her 'worry' since her grandfather had died in the night and her gran had woken to the shock. 'Yes, I know it's irrational and I'm a silly old fool,' Julia had told Duncan, 'but the idea of waking up next to a dead body, ice cold in your own bed, horrifies me.'

Duncan had shrugged her off. 'But isn't that how most people want to go? To leave this world peacefully, all tucked up in bed?'

After working each late shift, Duncan removes his shoes by the back door, creeps up to the bedroom, drops his clothes softly on to the carpet and slips into the bathroom to brush his teeth. He never flushes the toilet. He squirts antibacterial soap onto his hands so there's no need for noisy taps. He controls his breathing soundlessly through his mouth as he lifts the duvet and rolls stealthily onto the king-sized mattress. Finally he releases his breath, slowly, slowly and Julia never stirs. Even so, she always wakes, interpreting the scent of him: alcohol, nicotine, perfume, diesel, sweat; the undeniable presence of others.

She's taught herself to stay silent. Before, she used to whisper endless questions: *How was work? Who was on duty with you? Did you come straight home or . . .?* But she gets it now. He doesn't need small talk in the early hours. He's a sensitive soul. Thoughtful. Julia smiles and dares to open her eyes. 'I love him.' He has his back to her. She watches his shoulders rise and fall until he is snoring and she can relax.

Julia wakes. She pats her bedside cabinet to locate her mobile for the time. Seven fifteen. Up time. School day. And a day of orientation for her new receptionist job at their local surgery.

After his nightshift, it stands to reason that Duncan hates to be disturbed in the mornings, so Julia dresses in the kitchen while making tea and porridge for the girls. There's a mug in the sink, sticky with the dregs of hot chocolate. Julia washes and dries it and places it where it belongs, in its own space. Julia checks the *to-do* list on the noticeboard. The girls will sweep the kitchen floor and tidy their bedrooms after school. They'll be home before Julia for the very first time but Duncan will be here, so they'll never be latch-key kids. Duncan likes to do the ironing so he can catch up with the American football at the same time. Everyone has their chores. It makes for a good family. Responsible. Independent. Interdependent. *We work together, rest together, pull together. We have it good compared to so many, so we mustn't take anything for granted.*

Julia touches a glossy white drawer. It glides open to display all she needs for her beauty routine: cleanser, colours, brushes. The kitchen is immense; the light is perfect for seeing her reflection in the mirror behind the door. It is Julia's latest acquisition, catching the colours of her angled-bob, salon-streaked in 'shades of autumn', extravagantly labelled Conker-Brown, Golden Leaves and Russet Dawn. She applies eye-liner, concealer, mascara, bronzer and lipstick which will need a second application after breakfast. Four-year-old Meg appears, dressed in her light-blue polo-shirt, a navy skirt and thick winter tights.

'Jumper?' says Julia, raising her eyebrows. Meg runs back upstairs clomping passed her big sister.

'Ssh!' warns Sophie, 'Dad's sleeping.' Sophie is seven, sharp-jawed, with brown plaits and pale freckles. She grins at her mother, fast and fiercely, to display her cleaned teeth, then she perches bolt upright at the table.

'PE today,' says Julia as she serves Sophie porridge laced with brown sugar. 'Mummy starts her new job this morning. Wish me luck!'

'Luck.' Meg pulls on her jumper and clambers onto her chair.

'Mum's going to be a septionist,' explains Sophie seriously.

'That's right, darling. Not that we need the money of course, but since Meg started school Mummy needs to get out of the house for something to do and working for a doctor is very important.'

'Will you mend all the sick people?' asks Sophie, 'and give them 'jections?'

'No. I'll make appointments for them and file all their notes and work on the computer. It's ever so exciting for me. And Daddy will pick you up from school on Tuesdays and Wednesdays because Mummy has to work 'til five on those days, but on the other days, I'll finish at lunch, so it will be me collecting you.'

'So who gets us today then? You or Daddy?'

'Now what did I say Sophie? I told you. Listen well the first time.' Julia wags her finger and raises her eyebrows. She re-examines her face in the mirror. 'Earrings!' she says and opens the jewellery drawer beneath the curlers. She selects her largest gold studs because she considers them glamorous yet not too showy.

'Is it Tuesday?' guesses Meg.

'Sophie will tell you,' says Julia.

Sophie's eyes dart to the calendar but she can't read it from here. Her cheeks flush because she really should know. Even a baby knows the days of the week. Then she sees her PE bag hanging by the back door and she remembers. 'No, silly billy. It's Friday. Mummy's day.'

'Plates go in the dishwasher. Why do I always have to remind you?' Julia waits as Meg carries her bowl across the expansive floor then waits as Sophie opens the dishwasher and carefully arranges the first items of the day.

'Reading books,' says Julia, as they gather their coats and lunch boxes, then, 'Gloves. It's a gloves and hat day.'

Sophie skips into the utility room to fetch these from the 'winter-clothes' cupboard. The girls head outside to wait by the new four-wheel drive, a Ford Kuga in Burnished Bronze.

Julia hesitates, keys in hand. She notices Duncan's vehicle, parked skew-whiff again, like he's past caring. He knows full well how she likes it, parallel to the Kuga, two metres between. He'd bought the three-seater Citroen Berlingo off eBay of all places and she wouldn't be seen dead in it. What in heaven's name possessed a man like Duncan to dispose of his beautiful BMW 5-series for this piece of junk? She didn't buy his explanation that he needed something less ostentatious in which to transport his drums and equipment to the odd gig.

'Anything posher and you attract unwelcome attention,' he'd explained. Julia had flinched jealously when he'd added, 'Anyway, Sophie and Meg love sitting upfront with me. We're the three mouseketeers!' Duncan never mentioned how crazily they act, how he lets them hang loose, rocking their heads to his CDs, scruffing up their hair and being silly-billies. He never nags Sophie for chewing her nails whereas Julia makes her sit on her hands.

Among the other mothers at the school gates Julia feels the need to defend her husband's taste in vehicles. 'My Dunky's more of a sporty person than a car person. And of course, he's creative, a musician at heart. He used to play in a band, but nowadays . . .'

'But he's so gorgeous!' they giggle. 'Your man doesn't need a flash car to buy *anyone's* attention.'

Julia checks Meg is correctly strapped into her child seat. She walks around the back of the car to the driver's door. Something in the gravel catches her eye. She picks it up. It is a simple denim purse with a scratched silver popper, dew-damp in the palm of her hand. 'Now where did you come from?' she says, raising her eyes skyward.

Few people ever visit their house, Four Valleys, so-called after an area near the ski-resort where Duncan and Julia had met – and the girls are fine without playdates; they have each other. On the odd occasion when Julia does socialise she prefers to hang out in the coffee shops or wine bars of Lancaster.

She would have tossed the purse straight into the wheelie bin but it's at the end of the drive, so she pops it into the pocket of the driver's door. She slams the door and both girls jump. *Don't wake, Daddy!* Julia accelerates, spinning the gravel and the car crunches out onto the road.

As the Kuga turns in front of the house Meg suddenly spies her daddy staring out of bedroom window. She lifts her hand to wave but he steps back smoothly, out of sight.

Duncan 1
Daddy's Cave

Two years earlier, Duncan had purchased one of those new soundproof isolation booths that musicians use to avoid driving their neighbours insane. It had cost him the best part of five grand, but *'If it's worth doing, then it's worth doing well,'* he'd smiled as he'd scrolled through the online adverts. The booth had arrived, a gigantic, white freezer-type of thing; ugly as heck.

Julia had been furious, forcing him to site it as far from the house as the wide drive would allow. She'd demanded that he plant shrubs around it but he'd gone one better and had a company erect a shed around the booth, concealing his monster in a utilitarian wooden cloak. This resolved an ongoing 'marital debate' about the *'interminable racket'* and *'sprawling dust-trap'* (according to Julia) of an acoustic drum kit taking up one whole room of the house.

'Just because some ageing rocker allegedly played those drums in the O2, it doesn't give you the right to ruin our lives with it. The walls shake! I can't think! At the very least, invest in an electronic kit and a pair of headphones.'

Duncan's attempt to explain the sentimental attraction of 'the real thing' had fallen on deaf ears.

To the delight of the girls, Julia christened the booth 'Daddy's Cave'. She quickly recognised its value. The slightest friction between them and Duncan would vanish into this space that absorbed his every mood: boredom, anger, excitement, creativity, nothingness. Beating the hell out of drums is a whole lot more satisfying than a trip to the gym.

Duncan wakes, irritated with himself for falling asleep for the best part of an hour. He'd intended to stay alert until after Julia had gone, *then* check on the baby then catch up on sleep. What if the baby screams? However soundproof the Cave might be, Julia's intuition might kick in and she'd start asking impossible questions. Duncan imagines his wife flying up the stairs, shaking him, alarm written all over her skinny face. He imagines sitting up, feigning ignorance, blustering, 'What do you mean, you think you heard crying in the Cave? That's impossible! Maybe a cat got in when I left the door ajar. You think you heard a baby? You want to call the police? Um, yes, okay. I suppose you'd best phone them.'

Usually Duncan stays in bed until at least midday but this morning he listens intently as his wife of ten years creeps out of their bedroom to wake the girls. He hears Julia brushing her teeth and padding along the corridor. He is aware of every click of the kitchen cupboards and the clunk as the dishwasher is opened and shut. He hears Meg crashing up the stairs and Sophie shushing her urgently. Seconds stretch painfully into minutes until the car doors slam and the engine of the Kuga growls.

Duncan leaps out of bed. He is beside the window in one stride. Too fast he pulls back a curtain and looks down –straight into Meg's eyes. Solemn as ever, his little girl waves up to him and Duncan slides back behind the wall, cursing his impetuosity. What if Meg says something? 'Mummy, I saw Daddy. Can I go and say goodbye to Daddy? He's awake, really, really.' No. Meg won't say a word. She's a quiet soul. Julia is always preoccupied. In any case, Julia would ignore her daughter.

Duncan doesn't get it, why his wife wants to work when there is no need. 'Other people might assume we're needy. What if they think we can't afford the mortgage or something? There's plenty for you to do without being chained to some doctor's desk.' The thought of Julia trying to impress an immaculate, know-all medic is beyond irritating.

Duncan tugs on his jeans and indigo sweater. At the back door he shoves his feet into his Nikes. It is a crisp, clear morning as he crosses the drive to the Cave. He stops to listen, checking, checking. Would it be possible to catch even the faintest hint of crying on the air? But Duncan only hears the sweep of distant traffic and the chattering of sparrows in the twisted beech hedge. He berates himself because his van is badly parked. Julia would have noticed and she'll definitely ask about it over the evening meal, so he'll need an excuse but right now he can't think of one. He'll straighten it up before she gets home. Maybe, after all, it's not such a bad thing that she's taken this little job because for the first time in years Duncan finds himself with guaranteed time, without the pressure of Julia questioning his every move.

'Open Sesame,' he mutters as he fiddles with the outer lock on the wooden exterior, then the inner lock on the metal door. He steps into the room. It is warm, if a little airless, and quiet – too quiet. Panic surges as Duncan crosses to the open holdall, tucked in the corner behind the drums. He squats beside the baby whose face is motionless; a tiny, scrawny, porcelain doll swaddled in a tatty, blood-stained towel.

'Wake up,' he whispers urgently, afraid of what he is finding.

The baby's pale lips are pursed, his eyes shut without the faintest flutter of lashes. With the back of his shaking hand, Duncan tests the tip of the boy's nose. It is ice cold. He feels the baby's forehead and a shockwave shoots up his arm. He almost falls backwards. His other hand flies over his own mouth and— 'No! Please God, no!' Then the delicate eyelashes flicker and the baby opens his mouth; the tip of his pink tongue quivers, triggering in Duncan a tsunami of relief. Unchecked tears flow down his cheeks as he yanks off his pullover, reaches out and with one hand scoops the baby and folds him into the pullover, drawing him in, to rock him against the warmth of his chest. *Two blankets are not enough. I need some proper warmth in here.* Duncan flicks on the convector heater and sinks down onto the floor, sighing, blowing out the nerves, to reassure himself as much as the little one.

Duncan considers Meg, his second daughter, who'd slept for eleven whole hours after her very first feed. The nurse had explained that being born ten days early meant she hadn't yet woken up properly; she needed a huge amount of sleep so there was no need to fret so much. 'Babies are infinitely more resilient than we expect.' Duncan had seen the news about an infant who'd survived five days abandoned in a drain. Even so, one can never be sure.

He compiles a mental list of his requirements: powdered milk, nappies, baby wipes, a baby-grow or two, blankets. *That can't be the lot. Surely babies need a fortune spending on them?* Duncan shakes his head trying to recall at what stage of Sophie's life they purchased the Moses basket, the cot, the buggy, the playpen, the Winnie-the-Pooh mobile, the mountain of miniature designer dresses, tiny tights, cardigans and sleep-suits. Hadn't Julia rushed out and bought everything the instant she'd discovered she was pregnant?

The little one in his arms sleeps on, so Duncan replaces him into the holdall, still cocooned in Duncan's sweater.

Bare-chested, Duncan unlocks the metal cabinet and takes some tens and a twenty from his stash behind the CDs, before nipping indoors for his jacket and car keys. It dawns on him that he has no proper plan and without a plan everything's likely to end in disaster. *That girl told me to take her baby. She did. What if she wakes up and changes her mind? What if she phones the police? Where did I park last night? In the lane, around the corner from the disused post-office, hugging the wall alongside the graveyard. I avoided driving through the town centre because of CCTV. I swapped the unlicensed 'night' plates for the correct ones as soon as I arrived home. All bases covered, but I need to get a rush on and use that bank card in case she reports it stolen. I'd have done it last night if it wasn't for the baby . . .*

'Four nine two three,' repeats Duncan. He writes the number on his palm in biro before heading back into the house. He ascends the loft ladder and heaves himself into the attic. He flicks the light on and grimaces at the stacks of plastic boxes labelled *A-Level Files; Toys; Ornaments; Books; Baby clothes 6 mths; Baby clothes newborn; Bedding* and so on.

Duncan dangles his feet through the open hatch and selects the box marked Newborn. From this, he takes three white baby-grows and a couple of vests and cardigans. From a box marked *Bedding* he removes a flannelette sheet, two crocheted blankets and a small, padded quilt made by his mother-in-law. Duncan presses his nose into the quilt; *Congratulations Mr Wilde. You have a beautiful baby girl.*

He exchanges the bedding box for the one labelled *Bottles/ Steriliser.* Ignoring the steriliser, Duncan takes six plastic bottles with teats and drops them through the hatch onto the carpet below. He ensures that the storage containers are left precisely the way he'd found them before lowering himself down the ladder. In the kitchen he rinses the bottles with boiling water. His mind lurches between images of formula milk, nappies and that obnoxious couple from *The O'Leary Show*.

They were Germans, or maybe Poles. Something like that. What were their names? He knows exactly when the programme was aired. It was the day Julia dropped the girls at school and returned home to wake him with the usual buttered toast and black coffee. For no obvious reason she'd started to whine on about wanting more from life, saying she needed 'to feel more valued by society like all the other mums at the school gate'. The whine had inexplicably evolved into a full-blown row, ending with Julia flinging her slippers at Duncan's head, coffee spilling on the duvet then Julia storming out and slamming the door. After only a few seconds Julia had returned, flinging wide the bedroom door, screaming that someone around here needed to take initiative and obviously it was, as usual, all up to her so she'd be making some changes around here. By mid-afternoon she'd applied online for a job as a medical receptionist to a GP practice in the city square.

Shaking with rage, Duncan had poured himself a whisky and, as a distraction, turned on the TV. A substantially-built female was leaning into the camera, pontificating to the nation. 'You see, these adoption agencies refuse *perfectly normal couples as potential parents*, while thousands of children languish in care homes. Poor little mites. And what do the social care about them? They should prefer for them to have loving parents. Like me and Erik.' The host, Terry O'Leary, clicked across the stage in his sharp black shoes and shiny blue suit, encouraging their distress. Duncan racked his brains. *What on earth had this woman said exactly? Something about having money. A lot of money.*

At the door of the Cave, Duncan hesitates. *What if the baby is awake? What if he's crying? Well, what if? I'm no good to him without milk and nappies. Dad used to tell Mum, 'Crying is crying not dying.'*

Duncan decides to head straight into town, bypassing the local shops where he might be recognised. He struggles to keep his foot off the accelerator, stay patient at lights and calm behind a learner driver. He pulls into Sainsbury's and commands himself to shop normally, but he can't help striding too briskly, randomly selecting fruit and veg to disguise his true intentions. Into the trolley he tosses a multipack of crisps and a packet of digestives, but by the time he reaches the self-service checkout he is scanning nappies, wipes, formula milk and cream for nappy rash. The scanner is infuriatingly talkative and bossy. Duncan grits his teeth and smiles at the assistant. I'm fine thanks. *This is fine. Everything is above board and paid for. Stop hovering so closely.*

His cheek twitches as he stacks apples and crisps over the baby things then, head down, he rushes towards the exit. On the corner a rotund man in a baggy sweatshirt bumps into Duncan, knocking the crisps to the floor and immediately his female companion dips down to retrieve them.

'Thanks, Elizabeth,' smiles the rotund man as the woman offers the crisps to Duncan.

'For Pete's sake, watch what you're doing!' Duncan curses, snatching the bag and rushing on. Then he checks himself. He must not be remembered negatively so he glances back and shouts, 'Sorry. I mean, thanks,' but the couple have gone.

Fifteen minutes later, the van crunches up the driveway. Duncan slams on the brakes and rushes to the Cave, locking himself in with the baby who is crying with a high-pitched desperation that bounces off all four walls. Duncan dumps the carrier bag, spilling the contents over the floor. He scrabbles through his purchases for the box of formula and picks it open. 'I should have boiled some water earlier – it would be cool already.'

In one corner of the Cave is a small sink set into a counter on which buzzes a mini-fridge for beer. There's a double power socket and a glossy narrow cupboard containing a *Mega-Dad* mug and a jar of instant coffee. Duncan's hands shake as he deals with all the paraphernalia and his teeth clench until his jaw aches and the kettle boils. The steam shushes and soothes the baby. Duncan fills a bottle with boiling water, then empties it. He tips more hot water over the teat, a rough attempt at sterilisation. 'Let's put the lot into the microwave for a couple of seconds – murder the evil germs.' But the ping of the microwave upsets the baby and sets him off wailing again. Duncan measures the milk powder and mixes it with more water from the kettle. When all is done he places the bottle into his *Mega-Dad* mug full of cold water. Finally, he decides to change his first nappy.

Duncan washes his hands and dries them on a cloth he uses for removing grease or dust from his drum kit. The urgency of the cries increases the tension between the man who is at once a tender, loving father, yet a furious, impatient bully, a self-centred egotist, a pragmatic *don't-mess-this-up-because-it-is-worth-the-effort* crook. Nevertheless, Duncan forces himself to be gentle as he unwraps the tiny boy, whose skinny legs are bandy and wrinkled with translucent skin over thin veins. The boy's fingers curl and uncurl like fronds on a fern, delicate and clean, each with a scratchy, miniature nail. Ten fingers and ten toes. That's what they say, *'As long as he has all his fingers and toes, who cares if it's a girl or a boy so long as he's healthy?'* But what if he's unhealthy? Who cares about the sex of a baby as long as it keeps breathing? Breathe, baby, breathe.

Duncan lifts both legs between the fingers of one hand, then with a damp cloth he dabs over the sticky body until it is clean enough. He fixes the nappy in place. The vest is baggy and he presses the poppers together. The stressed baby stiffens. Duncan struggles to push his tiny arms and legs into a baby-grow. When he finally succeeds, the sleeves hang long over the baby's hands and the infant face is puce with screaming.

Duncan tests the milk again. 'Maybe I could add a bit of cold from the tap? What's so dangerous about that? Millions of kids drink far filthier water and of course some die, but many live.' All the same, Duncan daren't risk it. This treasure must not become ill for, well, all the tea in China. Instead, Duncan runs cold water over the bottle, then shakes some milk onto the back of his hand and licks it. *That'll have to do.*

Duncan scoops the baby into his left hand so his head rests on the tip of Duncan's middle finger, then he touches the tip of the bottle to the baby's mouth. This shocks the baby and he thrashes his head about, messing with the teat, emitting ghostly, wobbly wails but no real tears. Duncan begins to hum long notes, deep sounds from his sternum that resonate towards the infant's face until the little one relaxes at last, accepts the teat and takes the milk. For now at least, peace reigns in the Cave.

Five weeks earlier

Duncan sprawled over the chaise longue in the snug, smarting from his morning row with Julia. Above the fireplace, the flat screen flickered, halfway through the daily *O'Leary Show* on which the audience heckled a couple of guests.

'For crying out loud.' Duncan stretched his bare toes trying to reach the remote that had fallen on the carpet. The remote inched closer as he focused on it. 'Come on, you sweet, sweet thing, come to daddy,' he muttered, summoning all his superpowers to move the little grey zapper without having to sit up. He yelled, 'Coffee, petal?' but Julia slammed the kitchen door hard enough to crack the eggs in the fridge. On the telly, a brash Germanic-sounding woman was leaning into the crowd to emphasise every clipped syllable.

'You know, when anyone wins the lottery you're all jealous. I told you already, we won almost two million. Of course we spent a bit of it here and there, on this and that – wouldn't you? But social services treated us so unfair. Cruel. Heartless. I tell you, for absolute zero reason they refused us to adopt. Can any of you say to me why? Nowadays the social advertise and advertise, they give out the message that no one cares what colour my skin, what race or sexuality, but I'm telling you when they come in your house, they judge you for breathing too loud. They say, "You only need a spare room and bit of love." And we've got three times that, haven't we, Erik? Plus, we're willing to pay thousands, aren't we Erik?'

The audience heckled, throwing verbal rotten tomatoes: 'Disgusting!' 'Deranged!' 'Immoral.' 'It's illegal to exchange money for any child!'

'Then the law is an ass and it should be changed.' The woman raised her chin, emphasising her superior views while O'Leary goaded her to rise magnificently to her feet, a ship in full sail; *Come on girl, do your stuff and bring O'Leary greater glory.*

The woman eyeballed the advancing camera while her husband shrank into his seat, clasping his hands tightly onto his lap, with his knees and ankles together. He nodded sporadically because if he didn't appear to support his wife there'd be merry hell to pay later.

Erik's vulnerability did not escape O'Leary who leered over him, raising his eyebrows, challenging his prey. 'Let's hear the story from a *man's* point of view.' The audience cheered and jeered in equal measure. The studio lights burned down on Erik's bald patch. He dared not wipe the perspiration from his brow, but managed to stutter, 'We'll pay anything to anyone for my Monika to get her dream. Whatever it takes.'

Duncan sat bolt upright on the edge of his seat. The woman was saying those words again; 'We won almost two million.'

The audience reacted in fury; 'So?' they cried.

Monika threw up her hands. 'I don't think they get my meaning, Terry. We won almost *two million pounds*, you see?'

'What's this about – what is your dream, Monika? Come to Dunky, darling. Let Duncan help you with your millions.' He flicked the screen onto another side, where each show was repeated an hour later. 'Let's start from the very beginning,' he said out loud. 'Nothing better to do today.' He stuffed his mouth with crisps and waited.

Beneath the studio lights, O'Leary's mouth slipped into a white U-bend beneath his tan-powdered cheeks, with no danger of any shine-on-skin. His mouth wrapped around the autocue as it rolled and each audience member stared at him, vying for the star's attention.

'*Why Were We Rejected?* Friends, today we are considering the most emotive of subjects, ahead of National Adoption Week, a time when the United Kingdom will again be bombarded with images of children crying out for parents. Yet, as you are about to discover, countless potential adopters are rejected. I am about to introduce you to five of these: a single mother, a homosexual couple and a married couple of – let's call it what it is – a certain age. Ha ha – I'm not so young myself! Each one claims to have been rejected by the system and today, *The O'Leary Show* dares to ask *why*?

'This audience is special because among them are some who were adopted and others who grew up in care feeling unwanted, rejected. I like to call them 'the never-chosen ones'. Britain, *Great* Britain, I invite you to judge these good people for yourselves. After you've heard the very compelling evidence, you decide. I wonder what you will do. Reject these good people or, given the choice, would you place a desperate child into their care?'

Duncan fast-forwarded until a caption rolled across the screen: *Monika and Erik – Too rich? Too foreign? Too old?* And there she was again, the rich, foreign, older woman, gabbling away, shrugging and huffing at the injustice of it all.

'We have everything to offer a little one – beautiful country home, top-of-the-range seven-seater vehicle and so much love.' She flung her arms wide, but the crowd hissed and booed and laughed. The camera zoned in on the prettiest girls and, on the back row, a man in a baseball cap, standing on his chair, apoplectic with hysteria.

O'Leary to Monika: 'Do you think your problem may be one of attitude?'

'My problem? Attitude? What are you suggesting? Do you accuse me, Mr O'Leary?'

'A baby is not a can of baked beans. You can't simply pick one off a supermarket shelf and take it home for supper.' He leant back, triumphant, his smug mouth arched tightly downwards. Winked. Smirked.

'She'd most likely eat it!' yelled the man from the back and everyone laughed.

'You'd have attitude if you'd been rejected only because of being a very tiny bit overweight, with a different accent. Racism,

I call it. Pure, evil, judgemental racism.' Still leaning forward, hands on hips, Monika shook her head and blinked back angry tears.

Duncan flicked the television off. *She may be fat and foreign but she ain't no fool, he thought. Every viewer is tempted by that juicy maggot wriggling on the end of her line. She knows how many greedy bottom-feeders are scavenging beneath the English sea and she only needs one to take the bait. But where would I find a baby in this skip of a country? And even if I did I wouldn't have the foggiest how to get it to those foreigners. That would be impossible. Beyond stupid. Irritating beyond words. A complete waste of time.*

Duncan kicked the TV and headed for the kitchen to wrap potatoes in foil to bake them for the evening meal.

Confident that his baby is sleeping, Duncan heads into the house to search for his laptop. 'I am a shark and I am biting! Time to take a walk on the Wilde side and do a little research.' He types *Terry O'Leary*, locates a list of his recent chat shows and scrolls down the various headings. Duncan selects '*Why Were We Rejected? You Decide!*' He listens again to the introductions then scans through the end credits. 'Why don't they mention the surname of guests in these things?'

One last scan through the introduction of Monika and Erik – how had Duncan missed it? O'Leary clearly announces, '. . . and they've driven all the way from Cornwall to be on my show today!'

'Cornwall?' spits Duncan, 'They may as well live in flaming Alaska!' Nevertheless, the baby has come to him and now he knows the county. With no time for cold feet, there are lies to be spun and a journey to plan.

Duncan mutters something they'd rattled off at D-DIT training, months before they sacked him: *No mountain is unconquerable — not if you see it as a series of molehills. One step at a time is all that is required to reach your goal.*

Julia 2
Out of Sync

Julia returns from work to find Duncan pacing the kitchen. She is desperate to relate every detail of her day, the new job, the weird people who coughed and wheezed, the thanks from Dr Roberts but it's obvious that Duncan's in no mood for small talk. Julia decides to focus on the needs of her husband;

'Are you okay, darling? You look stressed out. Is it something at work? Thinking about Steve? Remember what they told you at CBT, do what fills you up. Go bash your drums. Do something that lifts your spirits. You're the one who's always saying how drumming's such a good workout. Get yourself into that Cave and release those endorphins.' She ruffles Duncan's hair but he shakes his head and her hand drops.

'Stop fretting, woman. You start a new job and suddenly you get all high and mighty. Give over with the psycho junk. You're not my shrink!'

Duncan thumps upstairs two at a time. He has a vague idea that somewhere in the back of Meg's toy cupboard is Slumber-Bear, a teddy attached to a silk-edged blanket. Flick a switch and a realistic heartbeat thumps through it, enough to fool any baby into sleeping another hour.

Furious, Julia flies into the bedroom after Duncan. 'Did you just call me *woman*? Is that my name now? How dare you – and what on earth do you think you are doing in Meg's cupboard?'

Duncan jumps back and bumps his head on the corner of a bookshelf, setting off a wind-up clown that shuffles a couple of paces then falls over with a dying buzz. He splutters, 'Look at all this stuff. You spoil the kids. They've got far too many toys. Some of this should go to charity. It's time we taught them how to share.'

'Since when did you care so much about others? I thought your philosophy was "Charity begins at home" and "God helps those who help themselves". It doesn't add up, you turning all self-righteous, expecting our kids to learn something you'd never do yourself. Whatever's got into you?'

Duncan forces himself to soften his body language. He slumps back on the sheepskin rug and forces an insipid smile. 'You're right, darling. I think all that counselling's finally got under my skin. Made me question myself. Seriously, I do think it's working but I ask myself all the time, am I really a good enough dad? I'm so afraid of repeating history.'

'I've told you a thousand times, you are not the sum of your father. You'd never mistreat your own children. There isn't a cruel bone in your body.' Julia sinks down beside her husband and touches his hand. 'I love you. You're a good man. A hard worker. A talented musician. A caring dad – and it goes without saying you are totally and utterly gorgeous. The past is the past. Of course you're good enough.'

'Really?'

'Now you're giving me those puppy-dog eyes! How can I resist?' She kisses him on the chin and jumps up. 'It's my turn to fetch the girls. Come with me. It'd be fun!'

Duncan shrugs. 'Love to, but I'd best tidy up this mess before Meg sees what I've been up to. And I'll make a start on the spag bol so the flavours have plenty of time to infuse.'

'Fantastic! Thanks, sweetie. You're a star.'

'And you're my galaxy. My universe. . .'

'Don't exaggerate. Sun and moon will suffice. See you in twenty.'

Julia leaves Duncan leaning heavily against Slumber-Bear, whose heart is switched on, beating a calmer, steadier rhythm than Duncan's own.

Outside the school gates Julia assesses the competition, the mums and aunties and carers and glamorous grannies. When Duncan does the school run, which of those females does he approach? What does he chat about? Julia stalks up to her usual 'in-crowd', hovering on the fringe of conversations about weight loss and talent shows.

Children burst out of school and fling themselves at their mothers, hugging and chattering nineteen to the dozen. Behind them, Sophie, hand-in-hand with Meg, solemnly approaches her mother.

Sophie says, 'Hi, Mummy. We did percentages in numeracy.'

But Julia focuses on Meg. The girls immediately notice the scary, high pitch of their mother's voice. 'Daddy's decided it's about time we all learnt to share our possessions with the poor children of Africa. What do you make of that then?'

Meg hauls herself into her car-seat and allows Julia to strap her in. She says, 'There's poor children in England too. Miss Blakey says we have no idea because we are priv-lidged.'

'Privileged.'

'Miss Blakey says. . .'

'Miss Blakey isn't always right,' Julia snaps, turning the key in the ignition and forgetting to look in her mirror. Someone bangs on the rear window to warn her, 'Watch out for me!' and Julia throws a quick wave of apology. What is it with teachers that they have to be so *flaming right* all the time?

Sophie twists her hair until it cuts into the never-healing blister on the first finger of her right hand.

After tea, Duncan fills the dishwasher. He hopes he sounds casual. 'Work wants me to do a week away. I know it's unusual but they assure me I'll get paid extra for it.'

'Away? Why on earth?'

'Something to do with D-DIT taking on more staff in the south. They want me to oversee some of the new guys. Training days.'

'But where will you stay?'

'Hotel. Everything's covered. Remember, there'll be a fat bonus for us. How about an activity holiday? I fancy sky-diving – tandem!' He slaps a hand twice against his trouser pocket. 'Good, hey?'

'When?'

'Not exactly sure of the details as yet. Should know by the end of next week.'

'No.'

'What d'you mean, no?'

'What I mean, in case you haven't noticed, is that you're not the only one who goes out to work. What about the girls? Who'll fetch them from school? And what about ballet?'

'You've hardly started with – what's his name? Dr Flaming Know-all Roberts. And already your, um, your *job* has to complicate everything. Ask your mother.'

'You know she won't run around after us at the drop of a hat.

She'll lecture me about working while the children are so young. She'll go on and on about how much she sacrificed for me so I didn't have to be a latch-key kid.'

'There you go, then. She'll agree with me for a change. Your children need you at home. Come on, Jules – use your brains. Work it out. I'll only be gone a week and I might not need to leave 'til next Thursday. I was giving you plenty of time to plan, not start World War Three. Everything has to be a battle with you. If you want me to bring home a decent income, you can't expect me to pussyfoot around here all the time.'

'Fine.' Julia slams down her tea towel and storms out of the room. Julia can be dramatic but she cools down quickly. She is proud of Duncan's work as a first-line support-engineer and has learnt his job description by heart, enabling her to boast effortlessly: 'He works for Direction Data, an IT company that plans, builds, supports and manages IT infrastructure solutions to help five thousand clients achieve their business goals. They need technical know-alls that can sort out problems any time, night or day. My Duncan does the graveyard shift through choice so he can be home more for me and the girls. It's a round-the-clock business and Duncan hates to let a client down.'

Julia whirls into her dressing room to change into her tracksuit, ready for her work-out in the spare-room gym. She glances out of the window to admire the darkening autumn evening with its amber-daggered sky and mottled moon. Something catches her eye and she cocks her head to consider it. Her forehead wrinkles and she sets her mouth sideways until everything about her is a question mark. Why? He's done it again. His van is wonky. It's like he no longer cares about the small things, and when the small things are out of sync, the bigger things need closer inspection.

Lisa 2
Zig. Zag. Cut.

Lisa drags the armchair to the front window and perches on its arm. She needs to see people, ordinary humans who walk, drive, cycle, queue for a bus or trip on a curb, their very existence confirming that Lisa is one of them, a single, vital thread woven into the texture of this hour, the fabric of this day, whatever day it is on planet Earth.

She massages the soft place in her abdomen where the baby had grown. It feels deep and tender and bruised. As it shrinks back her uterus punishes her, clenching and contracting, and each time it happens the agonising, stabbing pain comes as a shock. Lisa reckons giving birth is suffering enough but to top it all, her thighs ache like she's swum the Channel without any training and suddenly she is starving but can't face shopping for food.

The loneliness of bearing Paul's progeny is over, superseded by the salt-searing scar of separation. Yet something good has happened. A kind of miracle.

An angel had visited during the night and taken the infant. Like a gardener who transplants the seedling that requires a larger pot with more nutritious soil and places it into the sunlight to grow strong and warm, so an angel had transplanted her baby. And this is good.

A double-decker bus grumbles, hesitating at the traffic lights, a dozen faces littering the windows of the top deck. Lisa shrinks back because you never know who is watching. Someone could so easily be the brother of a friend of the owner of the flat and they might know the flat is supposed to be empty. What if their eyes met hers? They might think Lisa is a new tenant and they might say something to someone and she'll have to move on.

I chose Paul because I wanted to yank my mother's rope. She warned me he was a demon but I blocked my ears. Mother's an alcoholic waster. What does she know about anyone else's demons? I exchanged my parents, my room, my whole future for the deceit of an older, single man. Man? Huh! He thought his nose was so important he had to underline it! I fell for a stupid bit of hair under his nose. What made me think his moustache symbolised masculinity, power and intellect? I imagined his physical muscles meant he had inner strength. And when he smiled at me with his perfect teeth and sharp features, I knew I was the only girl for him, that he loved me.

All those poems I wrote for him. Thank the Lord I never dared show him.

> *My universe is very small,*
> *There's only space for me and Paul.*

Lisa blinks and the bus has vanished. In its place is a cement mixer. A tattooed arm, tanned and crooked through an open window. A blue car. A red one. Silver grey. Silver grey. Silver grey. Lisa records the colours on a tally chart behind her eyelids. She recalls being in Year Six, when the top set had to stand on the pavement and count the number of vehicles that passed in exactly half an hour. Tick for car, lorry, bike, *other*. The cement mixer is other. As is the ragman's horse and cart. Every fifth tick, score a line through to form a group to make a bunch of asparagus. A kind of family. Mum, dad, two kids and oops, one extra. Put a line through and start again. Car, car, lorry, bike, other.

I am other, she thinks. I am the cross-bar over the family. The wonky one that doesn't fit right. They say the average family has two-point-four children, but I think, 'How can you have point-four of a child? That's not a whole person.' But now I realise that I am the point-four, less than half, and I cannot possibly be whole.

Lisa's mum's eyes glaze over so she is incapable of seeing her own daughter. She foams frothy whiteness from the corners of her mouth, dehydration from the drink. Once, when Paul happened to pop round, Lisa had offered her mum a glass of water but the shaky woman forgot to grip onto it and the glass slipped through her fingers, smashing to smithereens on the stone tiles. Water. Glass. Cut feet. Diluted blood streamed along the grout grooves.

Lisa had glanced at Paul, her eyes pleading, *'Get me out of here so I don't have to witness this mess,'* so he did. He took her away from it all, her knight in rusting armour.

'Where are you going?' Lisa is saying to Paul because it is eleven at night and he is heading out again. Lisa is wrapped in her dressing gown watching any old thing on TV.

'Out,' he says and the door slams. Paul will return when he returns. Lisa dares to phone her mum and her mum actually answers.

'Come home Lisa darling, he's bad for you,' she begs, but Lisa hates to hear her mother wheedling.

'Don't go on about it, Mum. I'm better off here. Has the post come?'
'Oh yes. Your results? I opened them the other day. You got a 2.1.'

'And you didn't phone to tell me?' But Lisa is happy. She scraped a 2.1. She had put in the hours and deserved the good grade, but what does anyone do with textiles? She'd scanned the list of criteria set out for textiles' students in the course handbook: 'You must demonstrate an aptitude for experimental craftwork, surface decoration or manipulation.' That describes Paul perfectly: 'surface decoration and manipulation.'

Her mother had been right.

'What should I do with your portfolio that's gathering dust under your bed, now that you've left home without a job?' Her words, sharp as pinking shears. Zig. Zag. Cut.

'Don't touch it, Mum! I'll come and get it when I get time.'

Lisa had been offered an interview for an apprenticeship somewhere or other, but that was well over a year ago. Why hadn't she attended the interview? Oh yes, Paul had forbidden her and given her a black eye. She cooked for him and cleaned and sometimes they went to The Three Mariners, close to the Millennium Bridge, where Paul might sit with Lisa but if he fancied someone else he'd ignore her, chat up the newcomer and not care less if Lisa walked home without him.

Lisa shifts her weight, leaning onto the sill. On the pavement below a young girl is pushing a double buggy, striding quickly in the direction of the city. Someone sounds a horn and Lisa sees a toddler, a boy, some ten metres behind, crying, trying to keep up. She longs to go there and save him, to sweep him into her arms and carry him. She wants to chase the girl and scream at her, 'What do you think you're playing at? Can't you see he needs you? Slow down. Hold his hand. He's a person with feelings, not a point-four to ignore.'

A car pulls up and parks on a double yellow. A grey-haired gentleman leaves the engine running and jumps out of his car. At least someone has their priorities right: forget traffic cops and rules and watch out for the children. The gentleman calls, 'Stop, wait!' He lifts the boy and carries him to his mother. The girl swings round, furious. She shouts, gesticulating, accusing the man of child abduction but calmly he stands his ground until the girl places her son onto the back-bar of the buggy. The girl tosses back her hair and stalks away with both arms wrapped around her child.

Lisa relaxes. 'Maybe my thoughts do control the world beyond. Can any good thing happen if I pray?' *My arms around my own son. My arms. My son.* Lisa closes her eyes. Candles flicker on a birthday cake. Lisa blows and they are extinguished. A bunch of little friends chatter like sparrows. *'What did you wish for?'*

'I can't tell you or it won't come true!'

A cluster of multi-coloured balloons bob against the ceiling, one for each year of her life, and Lisa hears them popping

     one

          by

               one.

Duncan 3
This is Business

It was easier than Duncan had anticipated, contacting the television station for information about Monika and Erik. He'd made notes on his iPad of their details, their appearances and their precise words. He'd scanned information on adoption and discovered a fascinating article by a real-life adoption researcher, a Mr Chris Simons, a genuinely caring man, very understanding and extremely sympathetic to the cause of the rejects, of whom there were apparently thousands. At least some of these people had been unjustly rejected by the social services, so why not Monika and Erik Nowik?

For the Wildes there had never been any worries on the reproduction front, no tears of empty frustration or heart-searching agonies over IVF or fostering or adoption or surrogacy. Eight years ago Duncan had accepted a January promotion so they'd agreed it was the perfect time to try for a baby. Sophie arrived the following October. Three years later, another January promotion was followed by a second October baby, Meg.

Duncan re-checks the infant in the Cave. He is bewildered by his own anxiety and his many straightforward, yet unanswerable questions: How long do babies sleep for? How often do they need food? How many nappies per day? When Sophie was born, Julia had been super-attentive, reacting to her every snuffle, so Sophie quickly learnt to manipulate her mother by crying ferociously for the slightest thing. Julia deciphered each complaint with super-confident diagnoses: colic; nappy rash; teething; hunger; over-tired.

'I was a spare part, not expected to comprehend or react, and back then it suited me fine. Now I wish I'd been more assertive. I should've insisted on being a hands-on dad.'

Duncan is attentive, but reminds himself that this is business. 'Like preparing a bird with a broken wing to be returned to the wild, attachment is futile.' Nevertheless Duncan cannot help being amazed by the little head resting on his finger-tips and the skinny legs that flop out over his forearm. The baby opens his dark eyes and stares at Duncan in silent trust. As the bottle empties, the baby's eyes flicker until they close and Duncan simply returns him to his nest. Job done.

The Cave insulation prevents mobile reception, forcing Duncan to leave the door ajar to call the number given to him by the woman from the television company. He jabs at the phone. His heart rate rises. He tries to swallow his own spit to wet his mouth.

At the first ring the woman answers instantly. 'Yes?' With relief, Duncan recognises the Germanic accent from the O'Leary show. Monika. Duncan steels himself to read from his notebook, a planned script. Even as he speaks he is aware he sounds staccato. Nervy.

'Hello, this is Mr Chris Simons speaking. As you are aware, I am an adoption researcher. The TV station forwarded me your details with your full permission.'

Monika interrupts, gabbling incomprehensible gibberish as Duncan continues reading. 'Concerning adoption, our team has investigated your application and believe you were unfairly ruled against. If you agree to discuss this, I plan to be in your locality towards the middle of next week so . . .'

'Make it Wednesday – soon as possible.'

'It is more likely to be Thursday afternoon, but as long as you won't be on holiday or abroad or anything untoward—'

'May I have your number, Mr Simons?'

'In due course. I won't let you down.' Duncan presses *end call*. The palm of his hand is sticky against the phone. He wipes it on his trousers and inhales deeply.

'That'll be your new mummy,' he informs the baby. 'Fresh air. I need air!'

Duncan flings wide the door of the Cave and steps out onto the gravel. Immediately he sees Meg standing alone, clutching the rag doll she'd inexplicably christened 'Moop'.

'Spinkles-you-made-me-jump!' Duncan gasps, defaulting to the family swear word they'd agreed on for the sake of the children. He closes the door behind him quickly.

Meg purses her lips and glares accusingly at her daddy. It's unnerving. She couldn't possibly have overheard anything and even if she had, what on earth does a four year old understand?

'Where's Mummy and why are you out the front on your own?' Duncan snaps. Meg remains silent, so Duncan drops his shoulders and softens his voice. 'Daddy's been composing some new music. Did you hear me?' He takes his daughter's hand and leads her into the kitchen where Julia is chopping carrots into batons for a stir fry.

'Oh, here come two of my favouritest people in the whole wide world,' she smiles, offering them sticks of carrot before turning on the radio.

Meg skips upstairs with the carrot stick, but at the top she suddenly flings Moop over the banister and watches as it flops down to the floor below.

'Poor Moop,' says Duncan, but he glares at Meg who glares back. Her mouth is set tight, like her mother's.

The music fades as someone on Radio Lancashire announces the news. Julia clatters around only half listening, but Duncan stands stock-still as if he's about to hear an announcement for the end of the world.

'Could you possibly bring yourself to help . . .' starts Julia.

'Shh,' Duncan hisses.

'Whatever's got into you?' Julia sidles up to him, the way he usually likes, caressing his cheeks with her cold hands. Duncan shakes them off as the weather report announces, 'Heavy rain is expected tomorrow with some areas on flood alert.'

'I'm so glad we didn't buy that place on the River Ribble, the one you fell in love with,' says Julia, backing away from her husband, wary of upsetting him.

Duncan manages a smile. 'Yup. If rain is the worst thing they can throw at us, we have no complaints.' He raises a bottle in her direction. 'Glass of the red?'

'Don't mind if I do.' Julia smacks her lips together, like she's fine. All fine.

'You know what I said about the conference next week? Well, I've been given a definite date. You'll be okay because I don't have to leave 'til Wednesday evening, so all's sorted where the kids are concerned. I asked the boss 'specially and he said, "No problem. Anything for you Duncan." So there you are – I put my family first. And I'll phone you all the time and be home before you can say tiddly-winks.'

Julia sniffs. Duncan's speaking too brightly and he can feel it but he can't help himself. The more he tries to sound natural, the less convinced he is of his own act.

Julia crashes a few pots around. 'Have it your way. You will anyway.' She calls the girls to eat and the family sit four-square around the kitchen table, all four corners pointing away from each other. The cutlery clatters on the plates.

'When am I getting a new mummy?' Meg asks loudly.

Duncan pales but Julia isn't bothered about his reaction. She turns on her daughter;

'Why do you want a new mummy? Am I suddenly not good enough for you?' Julia scrapes back her chair and stalks to the fridge. She snatches the yoghurt pots for dessert and drops one and the creamy mess smears across the shiny floor. Julia stares at it as if there is something far below her that she can't quite comprehend.

In the dark, Duncan lies back to back with Julia. She is breathing so evenly he knows she is awake.

'Hey, Jules—'

'Hey, what?'

'I was thinking – before Meg was born, you said if we had a boy you wanted to call him . . .'

'Toby. Why?'

'Toby? Really? You liked the name *Toby*? Toby. No wonder I forgot.'

'You forgot because you didn't agree with my choice. You went with Ben or James. Conventional. Every other bloke in Britain is Ben or James. But why bring that up now? I don't want more children. Meg's started school. My life is changing. Are you trying to tell me you want us to try for a boy? Because obviously, even if we did have a baby it might turn out to be another girl.'

'Don't be daft. Of course I don't want any more. It's nothing. I was only wondering.'

'But to be fair, if we ever *did* have a boy you'd get your choice of name, because I got my way with the girls.'

'Thanks. And you're right, there're far too many Ben's in the world. Toby it is.' Duncan leans over and kisses Julia on the forehead. 'I think I'll nip downstairs for a hot drink. Thinking about the long journey tomorrow night is making me all edgy and I don't want to disturb you by tossing and turning.'

Julia snuggles down. A cloud passes over the moon. Dark shadows ripple over the creases in their duvet. Julia is almost asleep when she hears Duncan outside crunching softly across the gravel. Her eyes open wide and she strains her ears, lying so still she can hear her own heart. There's no point rushing to the window. She knows her man is in his Cave.

'Toby,' whispers Duncan. The milk is the perfect temperature and the baby is content.

Monika and Erik 1

A Storm is Brewing

'Telephone!'

'I know I know. One of these days you can move your lazy butt and answer it yourself.' Monika slices the phone from its rest on the wall. 'Yes?'

'This is Alison Grey from the television company. I'm ringing to inform you that someone contacted us as a direct result of seeing you on the Terry O' show last month . . .'

'You mean two months ago,' Monika corrects, smoothing the green satin pencil skirt over her ample hips.

'Six or seven weeks.' Alison won't be pushed around or put right by anybody, least of all the type of guests she's forced to relate to for the benefit of Terry's fame. 'Is it all right to pass on your details to this man? I can't guarantee his identity so . . .'

'Who?'

'A Mr Chris Simons, an adoption research official. He says he believes you've been dealt with unjustly and wants to investigate your case. He is not making any promises. He wants to ask you a couple of questions. I checked him out online. We do background checks before we connect our guests with the public and everything appears to be in order. However, I must caution you that he could be a charlatan.'

'We'll do it.'

'Do it?'

'We will do whatever Mr Simons wants. I get your meaning. I understand you take no responsibility. Give Mr Simons our email. And our landline. Yes, of course give him this number. Mobiles are useless here unless you stand on the bed in the attic. We're thinking of applying to have a mast erected in our own grounds.' Monika laughs harshly.

She gives her husband the thumbs up but Erik rolls his eyes at her, shifts in his recliner and presses the TV remote aimlessly. The view through the French doors holds more interest. Erik shakes his head at the sun as it melts into a slick of tangerine and gently lowers itself below the sea. Monika's 'adoption button' has been hit and that unexpected phone call has triggered a lava flow of verbosity. A storm is brewing and Erik can't decide where in the world to take cover.

'Erik, didn't I tell you it was because they can't get us a precise racial match? I mean, what does it matter that we are Polish-Americans with a UK passport? Everyone's a little bit of this and a little bit of that nowadays, don't you think, Erik? Remember what that woman said, you know who I mean – that social worker cow – after we won the lottery?'

Monika alters her voice in an appalling attempt to imitate the social worker's Bristol accent. '"This event unfortunately sets your case back; winning huge amounts of money is life-changing. Your life perspective will alter significantly. We must satisfy ourselves that a baby is still your priority."' Monika stamps her foot. 'Sixty-five thousand children are in state care and they decide that not one single one of them is a match for us. I mean honestly, Erik, look at this!'

She sweeps her arms over the immense lounge with the French doors that slide open onto an Indian stone patio and beyond, a yawning salt-bleached lawn punctuated with wind-torn palm trees bowing towards the house. Two granite stone basins planted with fading montbretia spears frame the view of the Celtic Sea.

'I'll tell him.'

'Tell who what?' Erik is on the move. With his unkempt greying hair falling over one eye and his heavy-rimmed oblong glasses, he resembles a mature philosophy student. He is forty-two but shuffles in the manner of a weary, sighing octogenarian, wondering how on earth he came to be here, in *this* place, at *this* time, with *this* woman and her impossible dream.

'Tell Mr Simons. Are you walking away from me, Erik? I answer *your* question and you turn your back? Didn't I tell you already, I knew it was right for me to do much research? I'll explain to Mr Simons how we are one of those twenty-two thousand hopefuls who've been put off adopting by this impossible process. Erik, where are you going? Come back. Show your wife proper support.'

'Swimming.'

'Swimming? But how is it you can relax at a time like this?'

'Precisely because I can. Inform me when Mr Simons phones. Could be weeks. He won't phone today. It doesn't work like that. He'll have fifty clients. Or maybe he is like the rest of them, only after our money.' The bottle-glass door closes behind Erik and he pads down the corridor to fetch his towel.

'I should hope money is *exactly* what he's after. I don't care what Mr Simons says he wants.' Monika stands on tiptoe to examine her image in the immense mirror over the fireplace. She rubs a smudge of lipstick from her chin. 'So long as I get my baby.'

Erik is still doing lengths when Mr. Chris Simons phones Monika. After the call, the wobbly woman wearing flat, furry slippers rushes out onto the patio and vomits.

Monika and Erik 2
The Genuine Mr Simons

'But you can't possibly be ill, my darling. Mr Simons arrives in two days. What if he's doing a secret assessment? He must not think that we are incapable. We must look right. I thought to ask Pippa to do an extra shift tomorrow morning – a quick dust and polish, but you have to go all pathetic on me.'

'It's my achy bones. This terrible winter weather – always grey, always cold.'

'Always moaning.'

'We could've moved to the South of France.'

'We don't speak the lingo and you know I simply dissolve in that dreadful heat.'

'Say what you like but after this Simons fellow has done his bit, I'm out of here.'

'What do you mean, out? Out of where?'

'Exactly what I say. You only get one life and I'm not spending the rest of mine stuck in this monstrosity pretending to be something I'm not.'

'But my sweetest love, you are something; a very important man, a lord no less. Lord Erik Nowik. A millionaire landowner with a sea view. Goodness me, your mother would burst with pride in your achievements.'

'I hardly call winning the lottery, dumping my job and purchasing a personalised title printed on an online certificate an *achievement*, even if it is gold-embossed. Where's the Hedex?'

'If you didn't wash those down with port, they might actually do some good,' snorts Monika. She glances down the drive. *Oh, Mr Simons, come quickly to me. Bring me my little prince or princess.* 'And, my love, don't you forget it, that your lordship came with a plot of land in the Lake District.'

'Whoopee-whoo. A whole half-square metre, I believe. Bring on the dancing girls and pass me the cold flannel. Oh, my head!' Erik flops down on the sofa, shielding his eyes from the daylight and his wife's constant disapproval.

The landline sounds on full volume. Monika has her hand on it before the second ring. 'Monika Nowik speaking.' She affects an accent of coffee meringue laden with lemon and ginger, excessively sweet yet distinctly odd.

'Are we still on for Thursday?' Duncan dispenses with niceties. May as well get down to business. Nobody should mess with the life of a baby. He's checked on the internet about parental bonding and a newborn's response to the scent of its mother or something like that. Toby must *inhale* Monika Nowik. The sooner the better.

'Ooh, Mr Simons,' Monika cups her hand over the mouthpiece and nudges Erik with her thigh. 'What did I tell you? He is genuine. Will be here tomorrow.' Erik, with a cold flannel sticking to his forehead, sits up to listen to his wife affecting her best British accent.

'Any time. Early is best. Know the way, do you? Got the address? You can't miss it. Silver gates. Cattle grid. They'll be open, yes. Ten o'clock? Later, of course we understand. The kettle will be on. Nothing showy mind, we're simple folk. Take us as you find us.'

'Has he gone?' Erik's head pounds even after the codeine

releases a shot of morphine via his liver. His body is a human liquidiser into which he chucks various substances from alcohol to painkillers and pasties to antacids, which combine to create an internal cocktail, a smoothie to help keep him level-headed, a desperate attempt to counter the apathy that rises with each new dawn. 'Why must you do that stupid telephone voice?' he mutters.

'We must eliminate every possible hurdle so they give us my baby. What if they hate my accent? They might presume we are Poles.'

'He's *our* baby – and we are Poles. Well, half Poles. I'm also half German, born in Los Angeles and you moved to Poland from Austria in your teens. Anyway, so what if we were Polish? You don't need me to tell you, Poles are reputed to have an excellent work ethic.' Before the lottery, Erik had got out of the house, worked all day: a little banter with whoever sat beside him, a bite of ham sandwich at lunchtime, endless form filling online and on paper. Life like clockwork. The closest thing to an emotion he displayed was when a colleague had a birthday, which occurred most weeks; Erik faked congratulations whilst pretending to enjoy the obligatory cake. Initially, the lottery win had been genuinely exciting. All Erik's workmates spoke to him at once, reminding him of their names. Several invited him to bring his wife in for 'farewell drinks'. 'Will you leave work now that you're rolling?' was the commonest question, to which Erik had proudly responded, 'Nope.'

Erik left work after Monika purchased the lordship for his birthday and persuaded him to move to Cornwall. Embarrassed at the thought his colleagues might throw him one of those pretentious lovey-dovey-miss-you give-us-a-few-quid parties, Erik had slipped out of work unannounced. No one posted it on social media. No one cried. They didn't hate him, but he was only Erik Nowik, pronounced Novik. No one pronounced it with a V and Erik had long since stopped correcting their mistake. For years he'd known that, behind his back, they called him not so affectionately, *No Wick.*

Duncan 4
Taking on a New Beat

Cocooned in the Cave, Toby is surprisingly placid. As babies, Sophie and Meg had whined and wailed, grating on Duncan's nerves until he could barely conceal his rage, yet this tiny boy rarely whimpers. Even when he does, he easily relaxes and accepts Duncan's offer of a bottle.

Duncan secretes the soiled nappies in a black bin-liner. It is surprising how little mess this strange baby creates. When Meg was born, Duncan had been working night shifts so he'd slept much of the day. When he'd tried to help his wife with the parenting, Julia had criticised his 'cack-handed' efforts. She'd treated her daughters with kid gloves, over-attentive to the point of exhaustion, meeting their demands to the point of exhaustion. Then in frustration, she'd flare up and scream in their faces. Sophie had become passive and pale, with distant eyes. Duncan recalled that Sophie, because of her fine bones appeared frail, yet sometimes he'd seen a faint twitch in her cheekbone and he knew she was clenching her teeth, creating a tough little exterior.

Meg, on the other hand, imitated her mother's moods, screaming back at her with the same language however foul, only to be given a swipe across the face with the back of Julia's hand. Once Meg had fallen, narrowly missing her head on the open door of the dishwasher. Julia quickly knelt beside her and it was Julia, not Meg, who was sobbing, 'Oh, Mummy's so sorry, Meggie. She didn't mean it. Tell you what, for a treat, you can watch Octonauts.' Meg had spat back, 'You watch Octonauts yourself, fat pig.'

Duncan cups Toby's head in the palm of his hand. The tiny fingers instinctively wrap around Duncan's little finger. The vulnerability, the perfection, the trusting beauty, causes a bubble of air to catch in Duncan's throat.

'Hello, son,' he whispers. Toby's quiet brown eyes silently assess Duncan's face. 'We're going on a road trip, driving through the night. It's a bit of a trek, but you'll be fine.' Duncan softly sings, 'Twinkle, twinkle little star . . .' as he places Toby back into the holdall, smooths a folded blanket beneath him and tucks another over him. Anticipating the journey, Duncan selects CDs from his extensive collection. 'How I wonder what you are. . .' He decides on Emerson, Lake and Palmer because he can't get enough of Carl Palmer's expert drumming. For variety he takes Tchaikovsky and then Beethoven's Fifth. He selects drummer Warren 'Baby' Dodds on 'Sobbin' Blues', Joe Cocker's 'Delta Lady' with Jim Keltner on drums, and top of the pile is Led Zeppelin with 'Bonzo' Bonham again on drums. Stacked with CDs from hand to chin, Duncan slips out of the Cave and through the side door of his small van.

A golden retriever rushes to greet him followed by a hesitant middle-aged woman nervously calling a high-pitched, 'Heel! Oh, I'm so sorry. Heel, Goldie. Please don't be alarmed, she doesn't bite.' The woman is closing in.

Duncan sets his top teeth hard against the bottom row and fakes a smile that forces a clicking sound behind his back teeth. He resists the temptation to knee the dog in the chest as the CDs scatter across the floor of the van towards a black suitcase and a plastic box crammed with wet-weather gear. On a hanger, a grey suit swings over a couple of shirts.

The door of the Cave is open. Duncan panics. What if Toby cries out? The woman is halfway towards him and advancing. Duncan grabs the dog's collar. He yanks the over-friendly beast away from the vehicle and drags it towards its owner.

'That is *so* kind of you,' starts the woman, fixing the lead to Goldie's collar. 'I'm new to the area. I live in one of those semis beyond the park,' she holds out her hand to shake Duncan's. 'My name's Rachel Hook – call me Rae.'

Duncan stands tall, forcing himself to look her in the eye. He affects politeness. 'Right. Good. Fine. Duncan Wilde. Okay. Right. See you around.' Communication over, Duncan marches back up the gravel, slams the van door and vanishes into the Cave. He needn't have sweated; Toby is asleep.

There's an hour to kill before Duncan needs to collect his daughters, concoct their tea and be ready for Julia when she returns from work. He checks his 'Bude-list' and everything seems to be in order. It is a fair bet the weather will be foul, so Duncan takes a belt-and-braces approach, chucking in his walking boots as well as wellies, cagoule and fleece, smart shoes and tatty trainers. Extra socks. Two mobiles: the Blackberry that Julia sees and the Nokia pay-as-you-go for emergencies. A cardboard box marked 'Files and Reports' contains baby paraphernalia.

As usual, the family Wilde sit four-square around the kitchen table. Julia, bursting with her day, chatters details of every client, their appearance, attitude and medical complaints as far as she understands them. She keeps jumping up for whatever Duncan had missed in laying the table; pepper – 'We never add salt in our house;' – the jug of water; a napkin for Meg.

'Didn't you make this same meal last week? Spag bol isn't something I'd choose to make,' Julia gabbles. 'It's so unsociable. You have to concentrate on eating or you look a right idiot. Sophie, stop sucking it up. Filthy, disgusting!'

Sophie allows the pasta to flick into her mouth, spattering tomato sauce onto her cheeks. Meg smirks at her. *Mummy hates you now.*

'The flowers are beautiful, darling,' Julia says, admiring the mixed bunch in the cut-glass vase on the sill.

'We're celebrating Mummy's new job! Top of the range from a real florist – none of your supermarket malarkey. Only the best for my beautiful wife!' Duncan crashes the plates into the dishwasher. *The view from the edge is exhilarating; glistening ice and jagged rocks. His blood is a rushing fire through every vein. A familiar tune emanates from beneath his Adam's apple.*

'What's that you're humming? How sweet!'

'Me? Was I humming? Something and nothing. You know me. Always composing something or other, taking on a new beat. Yes, Sophie, you may get down, thank you for asking so nicely. Take an apple or a banana. All right, some grapes then. Homework?'

'We'll miss you sweetheart, won't we, girls,' Julia says, patting Duncan's arm but rolling her eyes at him as he passes. 'What time are you planning to get away?'

'There's no real rush – I'll set off later when the traffic's thinned out a bit. You'll be asleep when I arrive so I'll text you in the morning before the meeting.'

'Bude, did you say?'

'Yup. Near Bude.'

'Honestly, you'd think a major company like D-DIT would choose someplace more central like Plymouth or Truro.'

'True. But I'm sure they have their reasons. Probably financial.' Duncan turns to leave the room when Meg, still sitting at the table licking the lid of a yoghurt pot, suddenly sings at the top of her voice, *'Up above the world so high...'*

'Clever girl, Meggie – that's what Daddy's humming reminded me of!' Julia joins with Meg and, without noticing how Duncan pales, they chorus loudly together, *'Like a diamond in the sky, twinkle, twinkle little star...'* and dance across the kitchen.

The neighbours are setting off massive fireworks, and not only next door but all over the city.

'Hasn't anyone round here heard of the Fireworks Spectacular they put on at the castle? Why waste good money on damp squibs when anyone can get a brilliant display from the council?' Julia paces the room, wiping her finger along the tops of photo frames and ridges of furniture, checking for dust.

Duncan checks his watch. He daren't set off too early or too late. 'Sorry to miss the big event on Saturday but I promise next year I'll get us all wristbands for the best viewing area in town. Meg will still be small enough to sit on my shoulders.' He checks his watch again.

Julia stops sharply as if she has forgotten something essential or is about to make a vital announcement.

'Have you got your bag?'

'Here. And my toothbrush and my phone charger and my socks, all present and correct, sir!' Duncan salutes and clicks his heels together. He laughs. He hugs his wife. 'Glad you had a great day at work. You make me very, very proud to be married to a modern woman who can have it all, a fabulantastic *working* mum who keeps a fabulous house and a gorgeous husband. Call me Mr Happy.'

'Happy maybe. Mr Modesty? Certainly not.' Julia squeezes both his cheeks. 'And I'm proud of you too. D-DIT are lucky to share you with me, but then again, they pay you well so I suppose I can lend you to them for a couple of days. By the way, there's a new woman moved in up the road. Rachel, I think, with a golden lab . . .'

'Retriever. And she's called Rae.'

'You met her already?'

'Yup. Her dog near enough attacked me earlier this afternoon.' Duncan feigns a limp.

'Attacked? You poor thing, you should've told me. Are you really hurt?'

'That's my gullible girl! I'm fine. It ran up the drive to say hello. Totally ignored the silly woman. She had no control. Anyway, what about her?'

'I was going to tell you, she was the only one in the waiting room so we got chatting. I'm not supposed to – you know – chat to patients. Anyway, she told me her husband got made redundant so they've had to seriously downsize. Apparently they had six bedrooms and some stables before he lost his job. Such a tragedy, poor woman. I can't think of anything worse than having to move from this place after all we've worked for. Imagine if D-DIT let you go. . .'

'You're over-thinking again. Stop imagining what's never going to happen.'

'And you're such an optimist, Duncan. How'd you do it? Nothing ever fazes you. Sometimes I'm just a teensy bit jealous of my own husband!' Julia stands on tiptoes to kiss Duncan on the nose. Above her head, the clock on the wall ticks. Duncan watches the minute hand move one space. Check. Check mate. A couple more minutes chat should suffice.

'I've no complaints about what we've got – though sometimes I think a swimming pool would be a plus. I suppose the Jacuzzi is plenty enough to manage. If I really wanted to moan, I could say there's not a lot in life left to aim for and maybe I do get a wee bit bored now and again.' Duncan can't help adding, 'Anyway, I know how to get my kicks.'

'Oh yes? And how's that then?'

'That'd be telling.' Duncan winks. He taps the side of one nostril with his forefinger.

'We should go skiing again,' Julia says. 'But of course I don't mean Verbier. Let's try Chamonix for a laugh. Get the girls started on the nursery slopes. We don't need to do all that extreme stuff we were into before Steve. . .'

'Steve was an idiot. He didn't know his own limits.'

'Duncan, don't speak ill of the dead! And about Steve of all amazing people! He took a wrong turn. Had an accident. Going at that speed, it wasn't his fault the ground gave way. Thankfully you had the sense not to follow him.'

Duncan runs a finger across his own lips; *enough of Steve.* 'So in your mind, Chamonix is a good plan because you imagine me flying off another crazy rock would make me happy. Look at me! I'm unfit. I'd break my fat neck.' He snatches at a Bag-for-Life that Julia has loaded with beef sandwiches, chocolate, fruit, crisps and a thermos of black coffee.

'Yes, but you should . . .'

'I should nothing. It's obvious I'm decrepit. My lightning-quick reaction is less lightning, more glow-lamp. I'd be over the edge before you even got your skis on.'

'All the same, I can't imagine anything less inspiring for you than driving to Cornwall in November to sit round a table with a load of stuffed shirts talking computers, so you'd better hurry up and go and come back before I change my mind and keep you all for myself.' Julia arches her back and flexes her fingers, as if warming up for exercise. Somewhere in the back of his mind, Duncan hears a baby crying.

He doesn't remember kissing his wife or closing the front door or strapping the holdall with its precious cargo into its space behind the passenger seat of the van. The headlights guide Duncan on automatic pilot through the city and towards the M6. His mood is buoyant, invigorated, free as a youth in Verbier. *The view from the summit takes my breath away. I flatten my body against the bitter wind and, forcing my ski-poles deep into the virgin snow, I lurch forwards. Every muscle is controlled, strong, responding to my every command. The ice rushes under me. I skim over snow, sparkling blue and white stripes like a glitzy ad for toothpaste. Sunlit streaks rush towards me, beneath me, behind me. I imagine the half-pipe rock until it is the only object I can see, in all its terrifying glory. With no alternative but to find the gap, exhilaration courses through my body, the rock envelopes me; I leap and I am flying . . .*

Duncan 5

Lost Something?

Duncan is satisfied with his choice of a nondescript hotel near Bristol for a stop-over. Three hours of driving with Toby asleep in the back. Duncan texts Julia to say he's arrived and all's well. It is irritating when Julia instantly phones.

'Darling!' she says, 'You made good time. I've been worrying because the weather forecast says high winds. Those high-sided lorries could topple over any time.' Julia chatters on, with Duncan grunting in suitable places, anxious because Toby is stirring. The baby's hands are reaching out, translucent fingers stretching, wriggling, then his little face begins to contort, creating fretful whimpers, anticipating the big scream.

'Is someone with you?' says Julia, 'I'm sure I heard. . .'

'No. Oh you mean . . . it's only some guy with a baby. We're in the foyer. I'm not booked in yet. Thought of you first. Best go – I'm next in the queue. *Ciao* for now.'

In the windowless back of the van, Duncan squats on his roll-bag. He shakes two bottles of milk using pre-boiled, cooled water from a plastic milk container. Toby is crying, pitiful as a kitten, tremorous, then increasingly high-pitched until Duncan feeds him. After twenty minutes feeding, during which Duncan shuts his own eyes, Toby pushes his mouth against the teat and stares up. *What next?* Duncan gently massages Toby's back until the infant burps and relaxes. He changes Toby's nappy then zips him into a baby sleep-sack and covers his head in a white knitted hat. He wills Toby to sleep, but Toby is happy as an owl staring into the darkness, refusing to nod off for a further ten interminable minutes. Then it is all systems go.

Duncan lowers Toby into the holdall and shuts it. He leaves the safety of the van, his mouth so dry that he worries he won't be able to book in. As expected, the foyer of the Premier Inn is empty apart from the receptionist, a beanpole of a youth sporting a wispy goatee.

'Mr Chris Simons.' Duncan swings the holdall, keeping eye-contact with 'Goatee', praying Toby to stay silent. Duncan is given the key to room 17. Once inside, he places the holdall on the bed and unzips it. Toby is sound asleep. Duncan checks the shallow breath. Satisfied, he risks taking a quick shower. The hot water streams over his body, calming, almost joyful. For a few minutes he is lost in comfortable thought, until, 'Did I lock the van?' Duncan slams off the shower. He stands paralysed, his mind hastily reviewing the previous fifteen minutes. *I drove into the car park. I removed the keys from the ignition. I opened the sliding door. I sat in the back, texting Julia, feeding Toby, waiting for him to sleep. I closed the door. Did I press the fob to lock the door? Did I? Did I?*

He jumps out of the shower, dripping as he pats each pocket of his jeans, his jacket and the holdall. 'Come on, Toby, where did I put them?' He glances around the room in case he's chucked the keys – in Julia's words – *somewhere silly*. Cursing himself for having to leave Toby, Duncan moves the baby in the holdall into the wardrobe and closes the door as gently as his pounding heart will allow. 'I won't be long,' he whispers.

Not bothering with underwear, he drags on jeans, trainers and his indigo pullover, then nips downstairs. He asks the receptionist if anyone has handed in some keys. The receptionist smiles, anxious to help, briefly scanning the carpet, shrugging apologetically; *yes, no. Sorry. Not my job. No can do.* Duncan rushes out to the van, which thankfully has not been stolen. He peers through the window at the ignition. Nothing. His mind replays a 'chink' and Duncan hears himself dropping the keys, but in his anxiety to get Toby through reception without waking him, he'd ignored the sound.

The external hotel light casts shadows between the parked vehicles so Duncan decides to get his torch from the glove compartment of the van. He opens the passenger door and instantly grimaces at a stale, sweaty stink that hits his nostrils; an offensive whiff of cheap aftershave and greasy socks. The hairs on the back of Duncan's neck bristle. He grabs at the torch. Muscles taut, fists curled, he wheels around, ready to attack. But there is no one behind him. In the silence, Duncan stands perfectly still, hardly breathing, every sense on high alert.

'Lost something?' The voice of a man from the back of the van.

Duncan flicks on the torch and steps back. It is almost midnight. No one is around to help if all hell breaks loose. He steals himself to open the side door. Duncan evaluates the risk: Most likely an illegal immigrant. *Most likely he's more afraid of me than I am of him.* In a shot, he slides the door and it bangs open. Duncan shines the torch into the dark space. On the floor is a scruffy man, sitting bolt upright with his legs sticking straight out towards Duncan. The soles of his boots are muddied. On his head is a checked deerstalker hat with a furry flap over each ear and in one hand the man is jangling Duncan's keys.

'What the . . . ? My keys . . .'

'Found them on the gravel. Checked a few vehicles. Decided to wait here, knowing you'd be grateful.'

'Get out. You've no right . . .' Duncan raises his voice, drops to an angry whisper. The stranger doesn't flinch but cocks his head to one side. He flicks the keys into his other hand.

'All right, all right, hold your horses. Kick a poor man in the gutter while you sleep comfortably alone in your luxurious double bed. Extra blanket, have you?'

'Give me the keys,' Duncan tries to sound authoritative but something about this unkempt man unnerves him because he doesn't appear to be the least fazed at having been discovered. Duncan lowers his shoulders. 'Look here, I've had to leave my extremely young son alone, on his own, asleep, so I can't hang about all night chatting. I'm a reasonable guy so I'll let it go if you hand over the keys and move on quietly.'

'No extra blanket? No nice soft bed?'

'Get out of my van or I'll call the police!' Duncan snarls. He raises his fists, lowers his head and flares his nostrils but he fails to intimidate the man, who jangles the keys in the light of the torch.

'For what? Finding your keys. Being a good Samaritan? I could've waited here all night guarding your vehicle from – from tramps and thieves and despicable monstresses! I'm just a poor bloke without a roof over my head. Weather too wild for sleeping in the woods. As I said—'

'All right, all right,' Duncan lowers his arms, steps back, gulps on his fury. 'Thanks. I, um, appreciate you finding and returning my keys. Tell you what; I'll cover the cost of one room for one night, if that's what it takes to persuade you.' Duncan holds out his hand for the keys, but the man tuts and shakes his head.

'How can I be sure you won't go back on your word? I don't know you from Adam.' The man clasps the keys in both hands and shakes them like maracas. Duncan briefly considers grabbing the man's ankles and hauling him out of the van, dragging him over the gravel and thumping the living daylights out of him, but if the guy yells or fights it would alert security. Then what? *Toby.* Duncan grits his teeth. 'Get out. Let me lock this thing up and *then* I'll get you the room.'

To Duncan's relief, the man shuffles forwards on his backside. He is weighed down by some kind of army-issue rucksack and his faux-fur-lined khaki jacket flaps open to reveal an olive-green fisherman's waistcoat, with an over-abundance of zipped and velcroed compartments. As the man brushes himself down, Duncan slides the door shut. The man flicks the fob and the van locks. He shuffles towards the foyer, expecting Duncan to tag along behind.

As soon as they are inside, Duncan speaks to the receptionist in a voice pitched uncomfortably high, but whatever his opinion of the odd pair, Goatee maintains his professional equilibrium – anything to help.

'This man there,' Duncan nudges his head in the direction of the deerstalker hat, 'found the keys I told you about.' He clears his throat. 'So I, er, want to show my gratitude by covering the cost of a room for one night.' Toby is causing him speak too quickly.

'With breakfast,' adds the man, raising his eyebrows and winking at the receptionist.

'And what is sir's name?'

'Mr Wilde. Room 17.' Duncan shifts his weight. The receptionist checks the details on the screen.

'Sorry, you are mistaken. It appears that a different guest is booked into room 17.' *Another guest in Toby's room?* Duncan shakes his head; 'No, no, it is definitely mine. Here, check my room card.' Goatee scans it and nods, 'Yup. Room 17. How to solve the mystery?'

Duncan's eyes widen as he remembers. His businessman's voice checks in, deeper, steadier, more certain. Charming. 'Oh, I do beg your pardon. You see, I booked in under my work name. Like a writer has a pen name and Elton John's real name is Reg something or other, so my work name is Chris Simons. For a moment there, I forgot it myself.'

'Mr Simons. That is correct, sir.' Goatee acts as if he is the one who got it sorted. He turns to the man who is rattling the van keys, important as a prison officer. 'Here's your key card. Room 23: along the corridor and up the stairs. For fire purposes I need your name, sir.'

'Me? My name?' says the man brightly, tossing the van keys to Duncan, who catches them deftly in his left hand and immediately rushes off to check on Toby. 'Me? I'm Mr Quin. Hugo to you, Mr Simons!' he calls after Duncan. Mr Hugo Quin shuffles down the corridor in pursuit of a hot shower and a warm bed.

Lisa 3
Open Me x

For Lisa, one week passes through no-man's land, a place in-between, a time of not knowing where she is in the universe, or what to do or how to heal herself. She is dozing in the chair when she hears a purposeful rap on the outside door. Lisa sits bolt upright. What if it is the owner of the flat? The police? Her hair is stuck to her forehead and sweat immediately runs down her face.

She jumps up quickly, causing her blood pressure to drop, so she grabs at the wall and stumbles towards the bathroom where the mirror reveals an emaciated stranger; a female with greasy, lank hair and dark, deep-set eyes. 'Who's that?' Lisa squints and the stranger screws up her eyes, leaning into Lisa, until their foreheads are all but touching. Their mouths form a silent, 'Who?' A clunk downstairs makes Lisa blink, but the stranger stares unbreathing, inquisitive without accusation.

Lisa tears herself away from her reflection. She hurries downstairs, the soles of her feet stabbed by the scattering of wood-splinters, hairgrips, pennies and paperclips. A pile of junk mail has collapsed against one wall, on top of which is an envelope in an attractive kingfisher blue with a white daisy in one corner. In another corner is scrawled, *Open Me x*. To Lisa this simple thing appears so extraordinarily beautiful that she cries aloud, 'My baby! Please wait a sec, I'm just. . .'

She fiddles with the chain and opens the door but no one is there. She steps out into the world to look this way and that, to catch a glimpse of the deliverer. The cold air smacks her cheeks; its freshness catches her lungs. The rain had stopped, leaving rainbows of motorcycle oil swirling on puddles.

'Hello?' Lisa gazes along the terrace backs, but sees and hears no one. Her heart sinks. If it hadn't been for the shock of seeing herself in the mirror she would have been quicker. She scowls down and, seeing two human feet, she glares at the crowd of overgrown, dirty toenails. She commands one foot to lift and it obeys, so the girl accepts that this foot belongs to her. She steps backwards into the flat. The door clicks behind her and the girl sinks to the floor, until she is squatting, slumped against the door, exhausted. No tears fall.

After a while, Lisa musters the strength to rise, to bring the envelope upstairs into the light. She delights in its blueness, the pretty flower, the little x in the corner. By way of a ceremony she fills a glass with water and takes it to the armchair, where she eases back and takes a long drink. The water is wonderful, cool and energising.

Open Me x. No name. Lisa gently rips at the paper, unwilling to damage the daisy. She pulls out a postcard showing a photograph of the famous Ashton Memorial, an impressive dome on the hilltop of a Lancaster park, a landmark for motorway travellers. The memorial conjures up Lisa's childhood memories of hiding places, steep steps and incredible mosaics leading to a butterfly house, a place of wonder, of contemplation, with a marvellous view of Morecambe Bay and far beyond to the hills of the Lake District. It is a space for summer plays and fountains and picnics with the family. As a child in Williamson's Park, Lisa had ridden her bicycle without stabilisers, her real dad running behind her shouting, 'Go, go, go! You can do it. That's my girl! Everyone look at my girl – isn't she amazing?' He'd set his child free to speed downhill, thrilled by the look of shock and joy on her face.

Lisa pushes her father to one side and opens the card. She reads; *Hi. I'm Sam. I moved into 7, Penhala Terrace last summer but I hardly know any of my neighbours, so everyone is invited to a housewarming party on Saturday 8th Nov 12.30 – 2.30pm, for a light lunch buffet. Soft drinks. Good company. Let's all meet. Please come! Sam Martin x*

Lisa smiles. Tiny cracks split the corners of her lips. A party. And I am invited. Me. A guest of Sam Martin. But what day is it today? She checks her mobile but it is dead, without charge. Who is Sam? Lisa had known a Sam once, a boy in Year Twelve who everyone fancied; tall and geeky, bespectacled, with wavy hair and green eyes. She imagines that same Sam, all grown up and surrounded by books, candles dripping by the fireplace, with navy-and-white striped wallpaper. Was Sam's surname Martin? She couldn't recall. Lisa imagines him welcoming her to his house. *'I remember you, Lisa. Come in and meet the gang; join the party. Meet John. And Amy. Yes, this is Lisa. She also lives on the terrace. You've never met? That's why I'm throwing this party. Rashin and Maggie have lived here for fifteen years. Meet Lisa – you'll like her. She's lovely.'*

Lisa returns to her reflection in the mirror. 'You need to eat,' she scolds the stranger and the stranger nods. Yes. Food. Good idea. Lisa crosses the floor to the space beside the front window to watch as people fuel up their vehicles at the filling station. Everyone out there knows exactly what they are doing. They climb in and out of cars, walk to and fro, open and close the shop door, rummage in bags for bank cards to pay for petrol and papers, flowers and chocolate.

'Newspapers will have the date,' Lisa tells herself. She pulls a brown sweater over her pyjamas, which she tucks into her blue jeans. Over odd socks, she laces her trainers. She drops a hoodie over the sweater. Lisa is lost and secure within it. She splashes her face with water. She grimaces; *teeth next.* The minty toothpaste is overwhelming. Lisa spits into the sink and rinses. There's some small change in her pocket but she takes a ten pound note from behind the cushion. Finally, she takes a carrier bag from the kitchen floor.

The Outside is an unmanageable space of grey sky, moving air and the constant groan of traffic. Lisa drifts across the road, negotiates the garage forecourt and passes like a spectre through the garage shop. A couple of men stand back from her. She ignores their disapproving frowns. It doesn't pay to be over-sensitive. She purchases an i newspaper, some whole milk, a chicken sandwich and a Topic. The cashier crumples his nose and turns down his bottom lip like he feels queasy. Lisa pays and leaves without a word.

In the forecourt a couple of teenage girls are sitting on a low wall. They point and laugh; 'You stinking filthy tramp! Peeyoo. Pong!' but no one intervenes to protect Lisa. She shuffles across the busy road. A car blares its horn. 'Kill me, why don't you,' she says flatly, but no one hears.

The newspaper confirms that today is the sixth of November. It carries the story of Ryan Higson, a little boy who tragically died in a fire, ignited by kids a week before the night of Guy Fawkes. *Investigations are ongoing.* Lisa skims the news. 'I must have slept through the fireworks but that's okay because in two days I'm going to a party.'

Duncan 6
Beethoven's Fifth

The unfamiliar smells and sounds of the hotel disturb Toby, who wakes erratically during the night. Duncan responds to every murmur by rolling over and scooping Toby from his nest, whilst simultaneously shaking the pre-prepared bottle. Toby accepts the milk cold.

Duncan had intended to leave the hotel by six am before anyone saw him but Toby is so peaceful after the restless night that Duncan decides not to rush. Instead, with the TV news on low volume, he brushes his teeth, then climbs back into bed with a cup of strong coffee.

'What's the hurry, son? We've not hit any headlines. No one is looking for us.'

The departing guests cluster in the foyer, dragging their suitcases and smart clothes on hangers out into the cool sunlight. Duncan curses himself for his laziness as he weaves through the throng, anxious not to bump the precious holdall and wake Toby. In the back of the van, he wedges the holdall between the boxes and sleeping bag. A lingering odour reminds him of last night's intruder. Duncan congratulates himself on dealing with a potential disaster with minimal fuss.

'Breakfast in Tiverton, young man!' Duncan is cheerful as he leans over to ensure Toby's holdall is buckled onto a metal ring fixed to the side of the van. 'We'll be there in less than an hour.'

'Sounds perfect,' says a deep, familiar voice. Duncan jumps back.

'What the . . ?' Duncan quickly closes the sliding door, defending his baby from prying eyes. Too late! The front passenger door slams. It's the old guy from last night, cheerfully shoving his rucksack down into the footwell. Duncan tugs at the door handle but it is already locked from the inside. He presses his key fob but the man inside clings to the door with both hands and grins at Duncan, shaking his head as if Duncan were a naughty child who ought to know when to submit. Duncan rushes around to the driver's side. He is raging as he leans into the van and draws back his fist.

'I wouldn't do that if I were you,' the man speaks calmly. 'Did you sleep like a, er, a baby?'

'If you don't get out right now, I'll –'

'Set your baby onto me?' The man leans back in the passenger seat. He pats the driver's seat. 'Take a seat Mr Simons. Or is it Mr Wilde? You'd best decide quickly before you give yourself a heart attack. Or you could relax and listen to some smooooth radio as we travel. The choice, as they say, is yours.'

'What makes you think I've got a baby?'

'You mentioned him last night. Memory failing? That's stress, that is.' The man faces forwards, stubbornly rigid but for his eyeballs which roll in Duncan's direction.

Duncan slumps behind the wheel and wearily submits: 'What do you want?'

'I'm a travelling man, flying south for winter. You wouldn't leave a poor soul to walk a hundred miles – I get terrible blisters.

A simple lift is all I ask. It's not much.'

'No.'

'No, you wouldn't leave me or no, you won't take me.'

'Get out.'

'I could babysit for you.'

'I wouldn't trust you with my dog.'

'You don't have a dog.'

'How do you know?'

'There you are. You told me yourself. You didn't disagree that you don't have a dog.'

'I'll give you money to get out of my car.'

'I already have money, so no need to give me a penny, see?' says Hugo as he delves into one of his jacket pockets and waves a couple of twenty-pound notes in Duncan's face.

'So you could've paid for your own room last night, you. . .'

'Yes, but *you* paid so I didn't have to. Cheer up, sunshine. Get that ignition on. I'm freezing and it's not doing your boy any good. I've got a daughter myself. She's all grown up and married already, can you believe?'

Duncan drives, his mind racing with how to dispose of this leech. Hugo stabs at the buttons on the radio. An ostensible expert is explaining how best to respond to a disaster in the Philippines. Duncan switches it off and, at the same time, accelerates.

'Hey, I was interested in that. And you're doing ninety,' says Hugo.

Duncan clenches his teeth and speeds past a double wall of trucks.

'It's illegal,' adds Hugo. 'The angels only stay with you up to seventy. Then you're on your own because angels never break the law.'

Duncan swerves into the middle lane and slows to seventy-five, but only because he clocks a police car ahead.

'What I'm suggesting is, if you get stopped, a baby in a handbag is bang out of order. It's not in a proper car seat.'

'It's not a handbag. Anyway, what do you care?' Duncan's knuckles whiten on the wheel.

Toby frets, staccato 'Uh, uh, uh,' from the back and before long he breaks full-throttle into an ear-splitting wail. Duncan curses. 'Not again! It's less than two hours since I fed him. Where're the next services?'

'Surely you don't want to stop already? We've only just departed. Chill down mate. Monsieur Hugo to the rescue!' Hugo unfastens his seat belt.

'What d'you think you're playing at?' Duncan struggles to concentrate as Hugo clambers over the middle seat and dives headlong into the back of the van, catching his ankles by his walking boots in the narrow space between the seats.

'Get back here now!' Duncan tries to focus on the road at the same time as using his left fist to thump Hugo on his ankles, but Hugo pulls his feet through and lands with a clunk in the back.

'You got a dummy or something?' Hugo shouts above the piercing cries. He rummages through the bag and the boxes. 'Aha! Ready-made milk! Good one,' he says, triumphant.

'Don't touch the teat, man. You'll be full of germs.'

'What's his name?'

'Toby.' The traffic is thick and the hard shoulder is no place to pull over.

'Aha, Toby,' repeats Hugo, and without lifting the baby from the holdall he plugs him with the milk.

Blessed silence reigns all the way to Tiverton during which Duncan hatches a plan to shake off the parasite, who is stretched along the van floor, snoring. In Tiverton, Duncan stops at a Tesco Express, but leaves the engine running in the hope that Hugo and Toby will stay asleep. Hugo's rucksack is in the footwell so Duncan surreptitiously checks each compartment. He withdraws a wad of twenty-pound notes and pops this into the driver's-door pocket. He finds a pair of green plastic binoculars, several notebooks and some pens, all of which he replaces. The main body of the bag contains clothes. Duncan pushes his hand into them, examining the space, feeling for evidence of what? Weapons maybe. Knives? A gun?

'Not good,' tuts Hugo, appearing over the back of the seat. 'Anyone would think you had a search warrant.'

'I was wondering if you'd bought any food with you.' Duncan manages to sound calm enough.

'Food? Really? Convinced. Not.'

'Here, run along and get us both some chocolate. A sandwich. Whatever you like.' Duncan hands Hugo a couple of coins.

'I will, if you come with me. D'you think I'm that stupid I'd leave you to drive off without me?'

'Fine. We'll go together then.' Duncan takes the keys and nips round the back to let a dishevelled Hugo crawl out. 'You've been out for the count for over an hour. Didn't you get enough sleep last night?' Duncan asks, attempting what he hopes sounds like friendly nonchalance.

'Oh plenty, plenty. Thing is, I know to snatch forty winks whenever I can, because I never know what's going to happen next. That's the beauty of hitching.'

Duncan locks the van and the two men wander into the store, each trying to manipulate their position as the nearest to the entrance. A female customer follows them in. She hesitates in the doorway and Duncan takes his chance. He rushes out, spinning the woman so she shrieks. He leaps into his van and straightaway locks it. He accelerates onto the street, leaving Hugo for dust, forlorn on the forecourt.

'Hey, hey, Toby baby!' whoops Duncan, 'we shook off the weirdo! Let's head for the beach for a couple of hours, get you cleaned up, get me some coffee, then find you your new mummy!' Duncan realises Hugo's rucksack is still in the footwell. Without hesitation, he pulls over, leans across the passenger seat, opens the door and tosses the bag onto the pavement, with the wheels rolling. A quick check of his mirrors and far back down the road is Hugo, not running but walking with his hands on his hips.

Duncan flashes Hugo farewell with the warning lights. 'Run, run, as fast as you can, you can't catch me I'm the gingerbread man! Yah-hoo! What a lark. What a buzz. A bit close for comfort, son, but you can chill out now. Daddy Dunky is gonna take us both to paradise!' With Zeppelin's 'Whole Lotta Love' rocking away the cobwebs and a clear road ahead, Duncan is free. His hair blows in the air-con breeze, as outside the autumn leaves swirl over the rushing red soil of the ploughed fields. Life is good.

'I can see the sea! I can see the sea! Daddy, Daddy, I saw it first!' He laughs out loud, mimicking Sophie and Meg as if they are with him. He tips over the brow of the hill and is confronted by a broad, lilac sky with long, lazy clouds that stretch over a bed of grey-green choppy waters. He pulls into a layby to absorb the enormity of the view, to feel the buzz of adventure and, across the bay, huge waves crash impressively against massive rocks and white foam bursts and flashes skywards. Even in November, a gang of seal-like surfers hover over the waves like cormorants, their black wings outstretched. They swoop and fall and emerge to fly again.

The year before Steve died the lads had a week in Newquay. Me and the guys surfing the giants! An adrenalin rush of memories washes over Duncan. *When did I ever stop all the fun? Why did I grow so old? I've become an aimless Joe, bored as hell, thirty-five next birthday. I wonder why Jules's not tried to phone? It's not like her not to check up on me. Probably poor reception.*

Toby stirs and Duncan moves into the back to change the boy's nappy.

The first few bars of an appalling, tinny rendition of Beethoven's Fifth Symphony sound out and repeat. Dot dot dot daaash. Dot dot dot daaash. It is meaningless to Duncan so he doesn't register or respond. Instead, he scrambles out of the van to stretch his legs, clutching Toby over his shoulder. The tin symphony replays. Duncan cocks his head. It seems to be coming from the passenger seat of the car. He opens the door and discovers a phone in the glove compartment. 'What?' But he answers it. 'Yes?'

'I thought you'd never pick up!'

'You . . .'

'Don't worry, I'll find you soon enough. Then we can swap back again. Merely a little prank on my part to lighten the day.'

'What do you mean, swap back?'

'Easy. I'll give you your phone back so I can pick up mine. Now where've you got to? I'm on a bus heading for Bude, so I shouldn't be all that long.'

Duncan is already searching for his own phone, which he always stores beneath the dash, under his wallet. His wallet is there. He pats down his pockets and checks Toby's bag.

'No point looking sunshine 'cos I've got it here. Needed insurance, see, or should that be *assurance*? I never could work out the difference. In case you legged it. Which you did, so I was right. Good of you to leave my bag on the pavement. For that act of kindness, I be grateful.' Hugo affects a Cornish accent. 'The actions of a man of conscience. You can't be all bad. That's why I didn't tell Julia about the baby. I thought—'

Duncan splutters, 'Julia? You talked to Julia?'

'As I just explained, I didn't tell her your little secret, whatever that is. I do wonder, is Toby your love child? Why are you running? Can't imagine what your game is, but I never judge a fella before hearing both sides of the story.'

'What story?'

'You tell me. Maybe it's time you spilled the beans. Tell you what, in Bude there's a large car park near the beach, with a visitor centre, most likely closed at this time of year but I know of a quaint little caff around the corner. You can buy me lunch and tell me all about it. No doubt I can be of service to you.'

'But you spoke to my wife. Why did you have to do that? What did you tell her?'

To amuse himself, Hugo had called a few of Duncan's contacts, but if anyone had replied Hugo had either hung up or said he'd accidentally called a wrong number. But when Julia had answered with the single word, "Darling!" he'd scored a bullseye.

'She phoned *you*,' he lied. 'And since you weren't around, obviously I had to answer. Said I found your phone but not to worry, I'd get it back to you. I said it wasn't strictly your fault. She was checking, checking, checking like she didn't believe me. Is he alone? Is anyone with him? She meant a woman, of course. Suspicious type. Wonder why? Hey-ho. See you soon.'

Hugo hangs up, leaving Duncan shaking. He lifts Hugo's phone to smash it, but stops himself because he needs it. 'I can't contact the Nowiks without my phone and I can't trust Hugo with it . . .' Fury and panic threaten to overwhelm him. 'Hold yourself together. You can salvage this mess.'

Duncan battles to clarify his thoughts. He locates the car park at the foot of the hill and parks well away from a row of camper vans and other vehicles belonging to the surfers.

He rests his head on the wheel and waits for Hugo.

Julia 3
Where There is Darkness

Her phone rings. Duncan's name is on the screen and Julia, who has been on tenterhooks at work and feigned sickness to go home early, snatches at it. 'Darling!' Silence. 'Hi! Hello? Duncan?' Julia checks the phone isn't on mute. She hears the voice of a man who is not her husband.

'That Julia?'

'What? Who's speaking please? Who is this?'

'The name's Hugo. Hugo Quin. And how may I be of service?'

'What do you mean, *service*? You rang *me*. Where's Duncan? Who is this? Why have you got his phone?'

In panic, Julia hangs up. Her heart is racing and she is trembling. *Who is this creep? Take control of yourself, Jules. You didn't give whoever it was a chance to explain . . .*

She scrolls through her contacts, locates 'Duncan' and decides to risk it, to make a silent call and force the man to speak first. She doesn't have long to wait.

'You want Duncan.' The voice is matter-of-fact.

'Of course I do. What have you done with my husband? I mean, what's he up to?' Julia visualises a serial killer, a brothel owner, an aggrieved husband whose wife is, right this second, with Duncan. Or maybe the mystery man is holding a knife to her husband's throat and he is helpless. Julia shudders because her trust in Duncan is so fragile, delicate as ancient parchment, and her belief in him crumbles at the slightest whiff of uncertainty.

'Tut, tut. Already so suspicious. I have his phone quite by accident. Thus, I have made arrangements to return it to the owner.' He sounds to Julia like a patronising teacher explaining to a parent why he'd had to confiscate their child's phone, but that it will be returned at the end of the school day. Julia steels herself to discover more.

'But how could you make arrangements to return it? Where is he?'

'Methinks he be heading for seaside, my lovely.' Hugo's Cornish caricature again.

'You're not listening to me. *How* did you make arrangements to return his phone if he hasn't got a phone and you don't know where on earth he is?'

'Um, well, you see he's got mine. Picked it up by mistake, er, you see, when he booked in at the Premier it was very busy. We both left our phones on the table – picked up the wrong ones. Easily done.' *Not telling porky-pies – acting. I do enjoy a spot of drama.*

'Right. Well.' Julia splutters, unconvinced yet unable to conjure a satisfactory retort.

'Have no fear, my dear. I shall return his ECM – Essential Communication Machine – at our lunchtime business rendezvous. Then you may talk to your husband to your heart's desire.'

'Is . . .'

'Yes?'

'Is he alone?' She couldn't resist.

'Aha. That'd be telling.' Hugo hedges to allow time for a spot of cold reading, after which he will adjust his reply accordingly.

'Telling what? Either he is alone or he isn't.'

'Your son is safe. He is never alone.'

'He's not my son, you idiot! He's my husband. For crying out loud, get that phone back to him by twelve or, or. . . Oh, I don't know. Just do it.' Julia hangs up and paces the kitchen. She turns on the TV and checks the news.

'Ridiculous,' she tells herself. 'Of course he's not in any trouble. Duncan's fine. He'd say I'm over-reacting as usual. No earthquakes in Cornwall. No motorway pile-ups. No helicopters falling from the sky. Nothing.' She checks the clock. 'I'll give him until one and then . . .'

Julia cogitates with no idea what to do. She could try the police: 'My husband lost his phone and a complete stranger is going to return it to him and I feel inexplicably worried. Could you please check he's okay?' But they'd cough into their coffee; 'You're havin' a laugh. He's a grown man. Didn't the man tell you his name and say they had a business meeting? Let your husband sort out his own petty problems.'

Julia busies herself making the beds. Pippa is due to clean tomorrow, which is a good thing because dust-balls are gathering ominously in every corner. Duncan hates paying Pippa because Julia has plenty of time to whip round with a hoover and duster, which surely burns the calories as efficiently as any gym workout. And Julia pays Pippa to iron his shirts straight onto hangers. Duncan refuses to allow Julia to pay a dry-cleaner to press his trousers for work, but Julia can't understand his annoyance. It's only a couple of quid and it makes all the difference for perfect creases.

Julia spots a comb on the carpet between Duncan's locker and their bed and picks it up to place it in his drawer. She closes the drawer. She is almost out of the room when she stops short. For a moment she stands perfectly still, then she cocks her head like a sparrow that is tempted yet fearful of crumbs offered on an outstretched hand. Something is *different*.

Julia returns to the locker drawer and opens it cautiously. She could swear she'd seen some sort of lizard or small snake nestling in a compartment at the back of the drawer divider. She holds her breath for a few moments but nothing moves or springs out at her, so she squeezes open the drawer a few more centimetres.

'What the . . ?' she gasps. She picks up a beautifully carved bronze chameleon clinging to a bronze stick, about the size of her little finger. Julia rolls the prickly object over in the palm of her hand, marvelling at its beauty, the way its surface changes from green to red in the light, the exquisite curling tail and long toes, and those oversized eyes, jewel-encrusted with emerald, turquoise and crystal, blended and polished to perfection.

'Where did you spring from, little fellow?' she whispers. She plants the chameleon onto the locker so it stands upright on its knobbly walnut-wood base. Julia perches on the edge of the bed considering why Duncan might have hidden this wonderful object from her. 'Obviously it's not my birthday present because that was last month. And it isn't for his mother because she hates creepy crawlies. Not likely for Christmas. And not – oh yes, oh my word, of course, Christmas is only six weeks away. You gorgeous, gorgeous man! You're a daft thing, Duncan. It's not very well hidden, is it?'

She shakes her head and smiles, kissing the chameleon and whispering, 'So sorry to doubt you my lovely Duncan. I love you too.'

Julia returns to her cleaning with renewed vigour. *Some thoughts are positively uplifting.* The radio fills her lonely space. Julia has reason enough to believe that her man really will phone as soon as he possibly can and she can face the day ahead.

The chameleon lies curled at the back of the drawer and where there is darkness there is

no

colour.

Hugo 1
To Be Investigated

Hugo stretches his legs along the back seat of the single-decker coach, wrapped in his coat and with his deerstalker hat warming his ears. The bus driver assesses Hugo in the mirror. You get some right weirdos, but this is one of a kind. The driver decides against challenging Hugo about the boots-on-the-seat thing – it's not as if he's doing any harm apart from a bit of mud.

Hugo records information the way he always does, in a ring-bound notebook. He loves to file facts and theories. In the few hours since he met Duncan Wilde forward-slash Chris Simons, he has plenty to write about. And all is not what it seems. Hugo scribbles vigorously.

Wed. 5th Nov: Keys found outside Premier Inn. Matched to white Berlingo car-derived-van. Sliding door – passenger side. Ignition ignited. Diesel – half tank. Clock – 64,623 m. Empty crisp packet – salt and vinegar. Bag of sandwiches; flask – black coffee, apples, chocolate (fruit and nut). I ate one apple. Drank coffee. No sugar. Terribly strong. Licked fingers clean. Lucky I had a torch. Found baby clothes, nappies and six cartons of formula milk, two large plastic bottles of water (I think water but didn't test), five towels, two blankets. No need to unravel my own sleeping bag as discovered one in the van, plus pillow. No time to use them as the ungrateful van owner turned up 11.23pm, threatened me. I controlled him with skill. He kindly paid for a room for me so I overlooked his rudeness. Name: Mr Wilde? Chris Simons? Or Christopher Simon

Wilde? TBI.

To Be Investigated. I know from the phone call the man's real name is most likely Duncan. So Duncan Wilde plus his son. But what's that Simon thing about?

DW goes to son. Baby or toddler I don't know yet? Me – 5.45am rise. 6.15am van check. All quiet. 8.37am after boring wait, DW tries to get away without me. I force him to offer me a lift. Defo a baby boy – Toby Wilde. 9am (rough ETA) destination Tiverton (?) Tiverton maybe a lie. He'll try to shake me off like the rest of my lifts do. He almost had me with his garage/chocolate ploy. Good thing I left my phone and borrowed DW's phone for ~~assur~~ insurance. DW dropped my stuff nearby, so he's basically honest (my theory). 10.02am I wait at bus stop to head in Bude direction, as advised by passing postman. 10.05am phone call. Female on DW mobile – name Julia. No surname but defo DW wife. She was v shocked to hear me instead. ~~Resured~~ – reassured her. I said DW is not with any woman so, no affair. I said 3 things to her. 1) He's very caring 2) Toby's fine 3) I will return Duncan's phone to him asap.

Julia is v fussy woman. On and on with questions so I hung up. She hasn't phoned since. 10.16am bus arrives. Comfy seat. Presently transcribing all contact numbers from DW mobile. Total contacts – 37. Most suspicious is D-DIT HQ. What is that? Sounds like fertiliser? Fertiliser for a bomb? Further clues required. Devon delightful – earth red, sky blue, weather calm after light shower. 11.45am slow journey. Many bus stops. All records up to date and complete. Dismount.

Hugo's feet crunch heavily across the gravel towards the white vehicle. 'Aha! There's a fact I should've recorded earlier. How remiss of me.' He copies Duncan's number plate onto his hand with biro, to be transferred later to the notebook. 'You never know,' he scissors his fingers at the gulls overhead, 'when you'll need a particular snippet of information.' The flock of white birds whirls higher, raucously screaming, cutting the sky with their sharp beaks.

Hugo raps on the van window. Duncan sits up sharpish, realises it is Hugo, then rolls his eyes and sets his teeth, ready for a confrontation. He opens the door and slams it behind him as he jumps out. He clenches his fist as he rises to tower over Hugo, who raises his hands in mock submission.

'Easy boy,' Hugo says. It is time to take a best guess, cold-read, stab-in-the-dark move, to observe how Duncan reacts when the muck is stirred. 'Relax, Mr Simons! Julia says she loves you and trusts you and wants you home as soon as possible, so you can chill out and return her little Toby safe and sound.'

'Give me my phone you lying, thieving –' Duncan's top lip tightens. His facial muscles twitch in an effort to keep control.

'Touchy, touchy! I'm no thief. Merely a specialist investigator at your service.'

'You? A specialist? Ha!' snorts Duncan, breathing heavily but lowering his hand.

'Lunch is on me,' says Hugo, faking magnanimity. 'We must take our time to decide where we go from here.'

'There is no *we* and nothing to decide. My mobile and you're out of here.'

'Fair exchange – mine first,' says Hugo as Duncan's phone rings in Hugo's pocket.

Hugo answers immediately. 'Yes?' He steps back away from Duncan. Duncan strains to hear the female voice as Hugo says, 'Ah, so *you* are Monika. And Novik is spelt with a double-u. No Wick. Yes, yes I will most certainly relay your concerns to Mr Simons. No, no, I'm his assistant. Yes, he is extremely involved on your case and will return your call as soon as he's available.'

Duncan approaches Hugo, softly, softly as a petulant child wheedling yet threatening to throw a tantrum. 'Give it me. Give.

Now, or I'll do you for perjury.'

Hugo claps his hand over the mouthpiece of the mobile, his bushy eyebrows warning Duncan, *Don't interfere – this is a serious call. We don't want to sound unprofessional, do we?* After some seconds staring at Duncan, eyeball to eyeball, Hugo removes his hand from the mouthpiece and turns on the charm.

'My sincere apologies for the distracting background noise, Mrs Nowik. Very well, I am sure we'll see you later. Polly!' He hangs up.

'Polly?' blurts Duncan.

'Put the kettle on. You will want a brew there, won't you? Mrs N asked me if I was your research assistant and I thought it easiest to say yes. She's expecting us mid-afternoon. Right, where does she live, this Monika?'

'None of your business. Give me . . .'

'Okay, I'll ring her again, shall I? Tell her you're up to no good. She's expecting a Mr Chris Simons? Let's see how she reacts to your name change, Mr Wilde. And if violence is on your mind, you may like to know I left a little note on the seat of the bus with your name and number, should I suddenly disappear unexpectedly.'

'You what? Who the heck do you think you are? And don't give me that private investigator codswallop.'

'Swift of tongue and man of peace, I travel here to bring release.'

'What's with the poetry? Release of what? You think you're some sort of prophet?'

'Lunch?' says Hugo, hugely entertained by the idea of being a prophet. 'And bring Toby along. He'll be getting cold.'

'Get in,' says Duncan, thinking only of how to retrieve his phone without a physical fight. 'We'll drive across there, see, where that row of shops is, and we'll find some place open. I don't believe you left any note on any bus. What did you imagine I might to do to you? Push you over a cliff? Come to think of it . . .'

Fifteen minutes later two men, one dressed for a fake conference in a smart jacket and shiny black shoes and the other in khaki trousers and worn-at-heel walking boots, sit opposite each other enjoying egg and chips like they are best mates. Hugo chatters and laughs at his own jokes, while Duncan sits silent, sullen and furious.

Cradled in the crook of Duncan's arm, Toby sleeps through it all.

Duncan 7 and Hugo 2
Jagged Rocks to the Left

'Seriously man, you need to let me be. I appreciate you found my keys and returned my phone, but there comes a time . . .' Duncan cradles Toby, jiggling him more through nerves than tenderness. What had Hugo said to Julia? Had he mentioned Toby? Duncan is about to launch into a furious speech, when Hugo interrupts.

'You're right. There does come a time for the parting of the ways. I hear you,' Hugo says, wiping his mouth on his sleeve. Duncan visibly relaxes – the man understands. He is going to leave after all. Best not tempt fate by mentioning Julia again.

'I'll pay for lunch, even though you offered, then off you trot and investigate stuff or whatever it is you do.' Duncan forces a hasty, lopsided smile. Softly, softly does it. He asks the waitress to please fill his thermos with boiling water 'for making coffee.' When it is cool he'll use it for mixing Toby's milk.

The waitress adores babies and she is totally besotted with Toby. She smiles and coos, 'What's his name?' Duncan nearly answers, 'Tommy', because he doesn't want to leave a trail, but he daren't concoct a new name with Hugo listening, so he pretends not to hear the girl. He wishes she would hurry up with the hot water.

'Adam,' Hugo blurts. 'And I'm Adam's uncle.'

'That's my favourite name! How old is the little darling?' The waitress leans in.

'Two months,' guesses Hugo. Duncan's tongue is sticking to the roof of his mouth so he can't speak even if he knew how to intervene.

'Oh, but he looks so tiny. Was he prem?' chatters the girl.

Hugo bows. 'Yes, *pre*-mature, but if it's all the same to you, we need that hot water pronto. It's to make up Adam's milk, don't you know. I know my brother here said it's for his coffee but he intended to say it's for the baby. He gets unbelievably tongue-tied since his dear wife died. So sad. He is coping admirably.'

'Oh, I am so, so incredibly sorry!' The girl flushes and rushes off to fill the thermos, while Hugo swings back on his chair, grinning.

'She's far more likely to do something for a baby than a grown man. Poor little Adam's lost his mummy,' he announces in a triumphant stage whisper.

Duncan shifts Toby into a better position as he stands up to leave. He hisses at Hugo, 'What d'you have to say that for?'

'Say which bit for what?'

'The sob story. Me having a dead wife,' he spits.

'Oh, I thought you'd be more bothered about me inventing the name Adam. Thought it up on the spot. Figured you hesitated for a reason – which no doubt you'll divulge in your own good time. And the dead wife? Girls are a soft touch for the emotionally wrecked husband left all alone to care for their poor little baby son. See how quickly she's fetching your water now.'

Hugo orders apple pie with custard and signals to the waitress to make that two portions. When it arrives, Duncan glares at Hugo to hurry up. Stop messing.

'Delicious,' Hugo says, wiping his sleeve across his mouth. He pushes back his chair and shuffles outside into the sand-swept street.

'Tastes of cardboard,' mutters Duncan, scraping the last crumbs of pastry together and licking them off the spoon. As he pays the bill, he is irritated by the pity in the eyes of the waitress. He pushes the door open with his thigh because both hands are full with Toby and the thermos, then he stumbles outside to where Hugo waits, tapping his outsized watch.

'Mrs Nowik'll wonder where on earth we've got to if we don't get a move on,' says Hugo. 'And have you considered what you'll do with Toby when you want that "private" chat with her? And don't you think you'd sound more impressive if you could speak her lingo?'

'She's fine talking English.'

'*Por favor nao introduza na sanita objetos que possam danificar esta sistema.*'

'You speak Polish? Whatever you just said, there's no way you get to do any negotiating with the Nowiks.'

'Polish? No way. That, my friend, was the whole entire sum of my Portuguese repertoire.'

'Meaning?'

'Please do not drop objects in the toilet that might damage the system.'

'It's you that's damaging my system with your every word. Listen, Hugh . . .'

'Hugo.'

'Whatever. Back in there, you agreed to a parting of the ways.'

'No. You don't listen, do you? I agreed that there comes a *time* for the parting of the ways. Obviously that time is not yet.'

'Toby is none of your business and in my business we call that *confidentiality*, as in keep your fat nose out of it.'

'But Mrs Nowik expects you to have an assistant,' insists Hugo.

'So I'll tell her you fell down a mineshaft. I doubt she'll be remotely interested.' Duncan opens the passenger door, slams it shut and locks it. He reverses into the road and jets off down the street. Hugo is once again left standing, a solitary cowboy in some spaghetti western, open-palmed in a whirlpool of winter sand.

Duncan negotiates the narrow lanes out of the town, where vanilla walls of tall houses hit the lowering sky and every window is streaked with yesterday's salty tears. He crosses a neat canal way, a breakwater cutting down to the sea, and he wonders what it must be like to live in Bude when the weather is foul, to be isolated, cut off from the protective buzz of the big city. But today is not foul; it is crisp and cool.

Ten minutes later Duncan rolls into a layby, a space for tourists to face the sea, a time to admire the view and reflect; where his thoughts drift unchecked.

Fuming with Steve. He must have turned deliberately. He would have expected me to follow. To try to save him. I could have died with him! Did he kill himself? No, not Steve. He wasn't the sort. I don't think he was the sort. Maybe he was depressed. He should have told me. I fly from the half-pipe and skim the surface of the wind, scanning the snow for a suitable landing spot. My skis waver because Steve, being way over to the left, distracts me. What's he playing at? I fight for balance, every sinew in my body battling to control the lift with the forward thrust of my torso and the downward force of gravity. Jagged rocks to the left of me, a fallen branch with spears of split wood to the right and for one terrifying moment I think I'm going to smash and die.

Duncan's mind is on the mountain, even so he phones Monika. She answers immediately with a breathless, 'Yes?'

Duncan shakes himself into the present. 'Chris Simons here. I can be with you in sixty minutes if that suits you.' Duncan assumes his business tone: adoption researcher par excellence, caring professional, qualified to make emotional assessments, fighting on behalf of clients and of course, all those helpless little children who've been mistakenly denied adoptive care.

'Naturally we are home. Waiting. Keeping the kettle boiling, as you English say. Our electronic gates are open ready. Drive right on up to the front door and I'll meet you. You'll see how marvellous the view. Then you must look round the . . .'

'We'll talk later, over that brew.' Duncan grits his teeth. Hangs up. Toby is restless so Duncan hauls him onto his lap, changes his nappy and provides another bottle. The engine is running for warmth. Duncan selects a CD and shuts his eyes.

When he wakes, he's surprised that the sea is so close, stretching and sighing, shifting restlessly to the horizon, and he can hardly fathom why he's here, with a baby hanging over his lap, chewing druggedly at the dregs of milk in the teat. Voices disturb him. Three cars have pulled up and a crowd of teenagers are spilling out and scrambling onto a low stone wall right in front of him. They lark about, posing, pulling faces, taking selfies on their phones and iPads. *This is me in front of the sea. Here we are. This is us. Me. Him. Her. Having a laugh.* Suddenly, one of them knocks on Duncan's window and he instinctively moves his shoulder to shield the baby's face from prying eyes.

'Hi! Can you do us a favour?'

Duncan lowers the window. He tries to appear easy going, untroubled. *I'm a tourist, stopping for a brew, admiring the view. Anything to help but unfortunately I've got a bad leg and can't get out of the car, is what he thinks*, but he says, 'What is it?'

'Could you please, please, please take a pic of all of us together?'

She's gorgeous; a wispy blonde, all smiles and oversized, over-eager eyes.

Duncan is charmed. 'One tick!' He checks his watch. Monika can wait. He closes the window and moves Toby into the back, tucking him into the holdall with an extra towel.

Once out of the van, Duncan locks it, because he doesn't trust Hugo not to parachute in like some SAS guy on military manoeuvers. Duncan takes the girl's iPad and holds it, steady, steady. Ten faces peer down from the stone wall, arms akimbo, clinging to each other like seaweed, as behind them the sky turns navy.

'Ten green bottles, hanging on a wall . . .' Duncan sings and suddenly they all join in. *'And if one green bottle, should accidentally fall . . .'*

At this, all ten youngsters leap off the wall towards Duncan, flinging out their arms and kicking back their feet. Duncan clicks away, capturing the moment.

'Star,' says the girl, hugging Duncan, who suddenly feels very, very old although he is only thirty-five.

'No problemo,' he flirts. 'Where are you lot staying?' but the girl is already in her car and all the kids are slamming doors and tearing off for their next photoshoot at Widemouth Bay. *That lot would never give me a second look. Not in a million years.* Duncan checks his face in the mirror and tugs at a couple of grey hairs. *I need a haircut.*

Duncan revs the engine and heads off to find Monika's place. The rainbow's end.

The house blows Duncan away. Not literally, of course, but even by his standards it has a magnificent, impressive façade. He regrets not taking the van through the car wash before rolling up the long drive or, better still, hiring something classier. But then again, adoption researchers are probably overworked and underpaid.

Too late for hesitation. Looking at this mansion, they must have won more than they let on. Or maybe they aren't quite as stupid as they seem.

Duncan positions his vehicle in 'get-away' position, facing down and away from the house. He reckons Toby is due a decent sleep but even with the windows shut, he can't risk him crying and being heard from inside the house. He rolls the van forward as far as he dares without appearing rude. He leans over the seat and touches Toby's cheek with the back of his fingers and the baby is warm. His tiny eyelashes flutter slightly at Duncan's contact. *I trust you, Daddy.* Toby's mouth twitches and he opens it wide to yawn, then he reaches his skinny arm out of his nest. The tiny fingers grip Duncan's forefinger.

'Why hello, Mr Simons, do come in from the cold!' Monika is calling from beneath the covered porch, framed by four ornate white pedestals. Duncan releases Toby, locks the van and strides forward with one arm stretched forward to bridge the chasm between himself and the short, chubby woman. She is talking before their hands shake.

'What on earth were you doing in there? I saw you arrive but you took absolutely ages to knock on our door, so I *had* to call out to you. I cannot tell you how anxious I've been to put my case to you, Mr Simons. Come in. No, no, your shoes are fine. A little wipe. There you are. Excuse the mess, you know how it is. Take us as you find us, warts and all, as the English say. What would you like? A little drink? Or shall I show you around? You'll see

119

we have everything that is required for a little one and more.'

Duncan coughs. What do adoption researchers do? 'That won't be necessary, I'm sure everything is in order. May we sit and talk somewhere?'

'Oh, of course, how silly of me. You will want to make notes and records.' She bustles into the reception room and waves Duncan towards an imposing lilac armchair. He sinks into it, immediately regretting this low, subordinate position. The woman is talking but it doesn't matter what she rattles on about, as long as she can access half a million in cash. *This one's nutty enough to stash money under the mattress*, Duncan smiles.

'Do you need to interview Erik *with* me, or do you prefer separately?'

'Interview? No, no, let's not worry about Erik for today. I only need to hear your side of the story,' says Duncan.

When Monika sits down, her short legs don't reach the carpet and her tiny slippered feet kick back and forth. Duncan glances at them and Monika quickly crosses her ankles. It doesn't do to show nerves. What if he writes in his casebook: *Too nervy for parenthood? Adoption refused.*

Monika launches forth, unable to restrain her verbosity. Duncan daydreams: *Julia is rifling through the attic for the missing baby clothes. She is rummaging in my wardrobe, wondering why I keep old shoes stacked at the back, in their original boxes. Julia is puzzled by the war medals she's discovered tucked behind the cufflink drawer, the ones I removed two months ago from a semi on the Palatine Estate.*

Monika's voice grates on and on but Duncan's heart is racing like a black run. *When did I start wearing cufflinks? Charity balls and D-DIT Christmas palavers. And tie pins? And bow ties? Useless gifts for the man who's got everything. That girl in the flat had nothing, yet I took her bank card and she had the nerve to give me the wrong*

PIN code – that wreck of a girl outwitted me.

Monika is on her feet, advancing towards Duncan, going on and on about the personal pain she's been through. She says she knows he'll understand. She says he is the first man to listen without interruption so already she adores him. Duncan's shirt is dripping, tacky against his back. His mind flicks a switch.

The girl is on the mattress, hair matted against her forehead. The baby has fed from her. He is sleeping. What's this? Monika Nowik on the window ledge, pressed against the filthy glass, looking in with a face that is round and white, crimson lips aghast. The girl is pushing away her own baby. 'I can't do this!' she is shouting. The woman on the window ledge is outside, also shouting, but no sound can be heard. Erik is in the room, hunched, hyena-like, skulking on all fours in one corner. He cowers, snarls, pants. His long tongue drips from his palsied mouth. 'We'll pay anything to fulfil Monika's dream. Anything!' In the street below, revellers ride the red bus, skeletons and screaming banshees crane their necks to see through the window, mocking Duncan's pathetic attempt to enjoy this act of darkness.

'. . . so they told us, "You are not a suitable match. You are the wrong ethnic mix." But you tell me, Mr Simons, you are the expert, what *is* the right ethnic mix? Must the British be so politically correct that they only give opportunity to single, brown, one-legged, drug-free Northerners?'

Duncan thinks he might be about to cry. *I never cry. I must not.* He finds himself worrying about the girl. *The one who lost Toby. He imagines Toby's mother coming after him. This mother can smell her own infant and she is coming! There's a girl in the sunlight, her skin translucent as the wings of a dragonfly. Wingless she darts effortlessly down the motorway, alighting here and there on a bulrush, a fence post, a silver birch. Light and free from responsibility, yet storm clouds are gathering. Lightning strikes at the audacious lone oak in the centre of a barren field, which bursts into a zillion shards. An avalanche of thunder rumbles, the ground groans and unzips to reveal a jagged, livid crevasse through which someone falls from the white, white sky. Steve! The girl flies easily over the chasm that Duncan is trying to create. Light. Sorrowful. Searching for the child that she chose to release. Her innocent eyes plead . . .*

'Are you quite well, Mr Simons?' The woman is too close. Erik drifts towards him, an apparition over the cream carpet.

'Erik, fetch this poor man a glass of water.' Duncan hears Monika. He feels beetles on his neck, tunnelling beneath his collar and tumbling down his back. Their sticky feet tickle him. He leans back to squash them against the chair.

'He is sweating. See how his shirt sticks to his back. Something is not quite right.'

'Ambulance?'

'No. We don't need interference. The authorities, they will come. And I'm not so sure that our Mr Simons is truly what one might call an authority. Mr Simons, drink some water. You must take these.'

Duncan interprets a silhouette. He sees Erik swaying, framed within the picture window against the late afternoon sunset. Duncan takes the water, gulps it with the painkillers.

'Right,' he says, as if he'd been fine all along, 'Where was I? Oh, yes. After all you have said I have formed my assessment. All that remains is to discuss the particulars.'

Monika repositions herself on the sofa. She thinks she may have Mr Simon's approval but then again, she is in the habit of hearing what she wants to and last time, with the social, she was bitterly disappointed. She must take great care.

'Finance,' Duncan says at last.

'Finance?' Monika, bewildered, shakes her head.

'Anything,' says Erik.

'And confidentiality,' adds Duncan.

'Of course. We keep secrets all the time, don't we, Erik?'

'Newborns are a rarity, so the paperwork is more costly. Then there is the cost of transfer, the cost of continued social work care, the cost of . . .' He is being ridiculous but Monika and Erik aren't objecting.

'Yes, yes. We understand there is a cost to everything.' Monika flaps her hands downwards, emphasising that finance is the least of her worries. Yes. He *is* saying yes, isn't he?

Duncan is tempted to suggest half a million but he daren't over-egg the thing.

'Fifty thousand, cash,' he starts. Monika almost falls off the edge of her seat. Her head is bobbing up and down, so Duncan understands the amount is well within their capacity. He can push for more. 'This covers all legal documentation, travel for further assessments and initial meetings, including today. Then a further fifty to finalise the matter. To protect the origins of the baby, you will be given a story about him that you must . . .'

'Him? It's a boy! Oh Erik, we have a son,' says Monika, falling to her knees on the deep carpet.

Erik crosses the room. He perches on the arm of a chair beneath the tasselled shade of the standard lamp. The shade forms a halo over his head. Erik asks a question for clarity. 'Fifty thousand and fifty pounds? Or twice fifty which is one hundred thousand pounds?'

Duncan can't hedge his bets at to the best outcome, so he plays his cards down the middle, answering a question with a question. 'What do you think, Mr Nowik? What is your boy worth to you?'

The phone rings. No one moves. Nothing is more important than this negotiation. The phone insists on starting and stopping.

Then ringing again.

'Get rid,' says Monika to Erik, with a flick of her hand. She is sitting on the floor now, back to the sofa with her legs stuck out in front of her. Duncan recalls seeing Hugo in the van with his legs stuck out, and how he'd considered dragging him out by his ankles.

Erik answers the phone. 'Yes?' Erik listens for a moment. He makes wide eyes at his wife and wider eyes at Duncan. 'Yes, as a matter of fact he is here,' says Erik, offering the phone to Duncan. 'It's for you.'

Duncan takes the receiver, his eyes widening. *Who . . .?*

'Need a hand with the paperwork?' says the too-cheery voice.

'You!'

'Now, now, remember who they think I am. Your research assistant. At all times remain professional. By the way, young Toby here is somewhat upset. What would you like me to do for him?'

'What? Where are you? How do you know he's . . .' Duncan blusters.

'As I said, professional.'

'Stay right where you are. I'll be right with you.' Duncan hangs up. He stands up and brushes off his trousers. 'So sorry, but my assistant urgently needs me to help him on another case. I'll pop by tomorrow and if you have the money ready, in cash of course, then we will arrange for you to meet the infant.'

'We've kept aside a huge amount in cash, haven't we, Erik? After the win, they advised us – don't put all your eggs in one basket, so we spread it around a little. Like fertiliser, Erik said! Spread it. See what grows. We kept back three hundred thou—'

'Darling,' hisses Erik, glaring at his wife.

'Oh, for goodness' sake, stop being so wimpy for one minute in your life, Erik Nowik. Mr Simons is a respectable gentleman, well-trusted by the authorities, so who am I to withhold information? You yourself said it is only money.' Monika struggles to her feet, waving her hand at Erik to pull her up. 'And when will he be finally ours?'

'It depends. There are tests. The first test is to keep quiet. To keep the story out of the press because, of course, the baby must be safe from harm and speculation. That is why you have been chosen, because you live in such a remote situation. If you start talking, the birth parents might put two and two together and find you. You are welcome to tell people you have been accepted as adoptive parents, I think – but no story. No mention of me. Our meetings must remain confidential.'

Duncan feels his spirit about to burst through his ribcage, as if his very heart beats with the sole purpose of scaring it out of him. He inhales. He feels in charge and totally *alive*. Duncan remembers to use his mouth to speak. 'No, no, you stay right there, Mrs Nowik, I can see myself out. I insist. You have had a shock. It is a very happy shock but you must relax. No, Mr Nowik, I don't need you to show me the way. Your wife needs you beside her.'

'But what time tomorrow?' Monika is saying, reluctant to let Duncan out of her sight.

'One o'clock.' Duncan strides from the lounge, rattles the handle on the front door and slams it behind him before anyone can follow. Toby is wailing. His insistent call can be heard, probably for miles, like a wolf cub howling over a rising, westerly breeze.

Hugo is crouched behind the van, hiding from the Nowiks. Duncan is so relieved that Hugo isn't standing on the doorstep, babe in arms, that he can't help smirking. *You can be pretty sensible for a crazy, but I see that I'm going to have to take you a long way away from all this. A very long way.*

Hugo 3
The Breeze Hotel

Hugo repeats his trick of diving headlong from the front seat into the back of the van to deal with Toby.

Tiredness overwhelms Duncan. Earlier, he'd considered sleeping in the back of the van if only for a night of anonymity, but a hot shower and soft bed is calling.

'Admit it,' calls Hugo as he offers Toby a bottle.

'Admit what?'

'I saved your bacon and deep down you're grateful to me.'

'I admit it.' Duncan drives carefully. The narrow roads with the high hedges are a nightmare, but at least an oncoming vehicle can be seen by its headlights.

'So, where should we stay tonight? The kid stinks.'

'Nappies in the side of the bag. Wipes in the plastic box. Clean kit somewhere. Rummage. You'll find it.'

'I'll put him in this little white number, shall I? The one with the embroidered daffs.'

'Daffodils?'

'Yup. The one with the lacy sort of collar thing.'

'For Pete's sake,' mutters Duncan. He slows to check out a B&B and judges it too shabby. In any case, B&Bs tend to be overly personal and friendly. Proprietors ask questions. On the other hand the Breeze Hotel is a huge, blue lump of a monstrosity claiming 'ensuites and sea views'. The men decide to check it out and quickly learn that the second floor is under renovation and the ground floor is full of OAPs on a cheap winter break.

'However, on the third floor room 28 has a king-sized bed and the largest flat screen in the building,' smiles the receptionist. She offers a knowing smile: *I'm no bigot*, but turns a blotchy shade of puce when Duncan insists on 'two singles, preferably on separate floors'.

Hugo requests the use of a laundrette. This further flusters the woman who finds herself saying, 'As a rule we don't offer a laundry service, but because it is the quiet season you may bring your washing down to the basement. You need to do it right away. You are responsible for removing it from the drier before eleven.'

'Eleven tomorrow?'

'Eleven tonight. There is bar food on the menu. Pasties or breaded fish. No chips, but bread and butter if required.'

In the privacy of his room, Duncan scoops the sleeping Toby from the holdall and cradles him. Even sporting a few daffodils, this baby is unmistakeably male with dark eyebrows, soft wavy brown hair and a dimple in his chin. Toby's eyes twitch and his mouth wobbles, tiny squiggles of movement, like an old man dreaming.

Duncan searches his little face in admiration: *Is he about to cry or is it wind? How do tiny people think when they don't know any words or, for that matter, pictures? Do they think at all, or are they merely responsive to patterns, shadows and light? Smells affect them. The milk of a mother. Even stale milk on my collar. Is that instinct or memories? Memories of what?*

A gentle yet persistent knock on the door. Tap. Tap. Tap. Tap.

'Push off,' says Duncan rather too loudly. Toby stiffens his little body in alarm.

Hugo's lips are pressed against the door. 'But we must make a plan,' he insists, while his index finger continues tapping like rain from a leaky gutter. Tap, tap. Tap, tap.

Duncan sighs. He dumps Toby into the holdall and opens the door but he blocks the entrance with his body.

'Hear with both ears, man. You. Are. Not. Wanted. I've tried to be polite, but . . .'

'But nothing,' says Hugo, ducking under Duncan's arm and tossing himself onto the bed. His bare feet stick out, hairy as a hobbit and gnarled from so much walking. Around his waist is a knotted bath-towel embroidered *BH* for Breeze Hotel.

'Where are your clothes?' Duncan is in sleep-shorts and a T-shirt.

'Laundry, I should've asked if you had anything . . .'

'I don't,' says Duncan. '*Some* people travel with a change of shirt.'

'Suit yourself! *Suit* yourself – get it? Oh, be like that, Mr Boring. You should lighten up or you'll have a stroke. Let's get down to business. So – tomorrow you plan to give Toby to Monika. Correct?'

'My client is adopting him.'

'And I'm adopting the Queen's corgi,' says Hugo. 'I must say, these pillows are an improvement on the ones in my room.' Toby snuffles, yawns and stretches. 'I'll be Mum,' says Hugo, rolling over to lift the baby from his dark cradle.

'Leave him be! You'll wake him, you idiot.'

Too late; Hugo is already cradling Toby in the crook of his elbow. For a brief moment Toby's eyes fix on Hugo, before losing focus and wandering in various directions.

'Do you think there's something wrong with his sight?' asks Hugo. 'I don't remember Callie being like this.'

'Callie?'

'My baby girl. All grown up and married now. Three years with mackerel-man and she's still not made me a granddad, but Callie does loves Jason, I suppose. Jason deals in fish.' Hugo gurns and blows raspberries at Toby who, unimpressed, shuts his eyes and drifts off again.

'I've got two daughters,' says Duncan like it's some kind of victory, *my two to your one*. 'And there's nothing wrong with Toby's sight. He can see perfectly well. His focus is still developing but I don't know why I'm explaining that to you. Tell me, what's your real business? Where are you really heading?' Duncan rubs his own chin, hating the roughness of the unkempt stubble.

'Nosey, nosey,' Hugo taps the side of one nostril. 'But seeing as you ask, I used to teach history in a secondary school. They kicked me out for being a few screws short of a flat pack. How rude is that? Of course, they couched it in unnecessary medical tests and legal rhetoric. The last straw was when the little monsters locked me in the stockroom then accidentally on purpose forgot about me. I mean, it wasn't *me* who complained about their behaviour, but the head found out and . . .'

'Why would anyone ever want to be a teacher?' Duncan is leaning against the bathroom door frame, dragging a razor up his neck and over his chin.

'It's a calling and, as such, is very rewarding. Magic, except when the genii (plural for pupils) fly out of the bottle and the genius (that's me by the way) loses control. Those kids got everywhere, standing on their desks, crawling under their desks, sitting on my desk, flicking revolting things at me. It was the Biblical plague of frogs, gnats and flies rolled into one. I, being Moses, one of the most effective leaders in the history of mankind, went direct to Pharaoh, the head honcho. I commanded, *Let these pupils go!* But instead of excluding the nasty little troublemakers, he told *me* to take a running jump.'

'So, you're a genius who lost your job,' smirks Duncan. He exchanges the razor for a toothbrush and continues his ablutions with one eye on Hugo and the baby.

'Yup. With the brain of the great Albert Einstein himself: 1879-1955.' Hugo turns his attention to Toby, patting him lightly on the head. 'It's a pity you won't remember this great moment, young man, but perhaps your subconscious mind will one day recall that you were once in the arms of a brilliant virtuoso, the most astute, most acute, most resolute mind in the history of the universe.'

'The most modest and most mad,' mutters Duncan, speaking through a mouthful of froth, then spitting and rinsing in the sink. 'I'm done. Right, get out – some of us need our beauty sleep.'

'We haven't as yet formed a plan, my friend.'

'Simple. The plan is that you hand me Toby and run along to your room. I phone my wife. We all sleep. And tomorrow I do my job, while you toddle off into the sunset.' Duncan flicks his fingers like a king dismissing his grovelling subject. *You're lucky I let you live.*

'Oh yes, I forgot. Talking about phones, Jules says hi,' Hugo says nonchalantly.

'Jules? You spoke to her again?' Duncan's first thought is to grab the man by the throat and shake him senseless but Toby is sprawled frog-like over Hugo's legs. Duncan storms to the bedside, snatches up Toby and points to the door.

Hugo, clutching his towel, rolls to the opposite side of the bed and stands up. He lowers his head in mock terror, a fake cower as he shuffles backwards to the door. 'Okay, man, keep your hair on,' he says. 'We only chatted friendly-like.'

'And to you, she is not Jules. Her name is Julia. On second thoughts she's not Julia to you either. She's nothing at all. You have no right—'

'Whilst you were *preoccupied* with this little one, I transferred Jules's number from your phone as a little insurance *pour moi*. I only called her to explain that the adoption was going ahead fine and that Monika is a very nice lady, so not to worry.'

'You told her what?' Apoplectic, Duncan lifts Toby in one hand, like a rugby ball poised to throw.

'Aha. Thus are revealed a man's true colours!' Hugo is in the corridor, peering around the door in mock terror. 'Now if you'll excuse me, Mr Adoption-Researcher most high, I have some notes to complete. See you at breakfast.' Hugo pulls closed the door.

Duncan lowers Toby so quickly that his little arms and legs jerk up instinctively then flop back. Toby opens his eyes and wails. Duncan pulls the baby against his chest, jiggling him vigorously. He is furious with himself for losing it in front of Hugo and anxious for Toby to shut up and sleep so he can phone Julia and cover Hugo's tracks without the giveaway of crying in the background.

Still clutching Toby, Duncan forces himself to make two bottles of milk with water from the kettle. One bottle he floats in a sinkful of cold water. Toby appears to calm down so Duncan lies him on the bed and changes his nappy. Duncan plans his phone conversation. It should be easy to persuade Julia that Hugo is a compulsive liar, and to ignore his rants. Earlier in the evening, Julia had phoned, said something about Quin

'The man who found my phone, *Mr Quin – a fantasist. A loony. You can tell he's off his rocker. Don't listen to him, whatever he says. I love you Julia. D-DIT conference boring, but hey. It'll pass. Miss you too. Hug the girls for me.'* Toby grizzles. Duncan sighs. He lifts the little one once more, but this time he rocks gently. Duncan hums a tune, allowing the sound to resonate through his ribcage and as Toby relaxes, the phone call is too easily forgotten.

In the neighbouring room, Hugo wraps himself in a duvet and curls over his notebook, recording every detail of the day on behalf of Einstein.

Julia 4
I Never Forget a Face

Julia hangs up on Hugo. *That ridiculous man keeps phoning, rabbiting with his irritating questions. Doesn't sound a bit like the D-DIT type. My Duncan must be finding it a real drag having to spend time with him.*

Julia considers making fish-fingers as a treat for the girls, because Duncan says he can't stand the smell of them. She can hear him saying, 'At least chicken nuggets contain some sort of meat product. You know I'm happy to be a veggie as long as there's meat in every meal.' Years earlier, Julia had abstained from meat for a whole week, strongly declaring it morally reprehensible to carve up poor, defenceless animals. *How would you like it if someone cooked you? And ate you?*

Her vegetarian phase ended the day she met Duncan and his crew in the après-ski bar opposite the train stop. They'd been comparing stories after a day of thrills, bragging about how they'd spanned some magnificent crevasses on the infinitely more challenging French side of the glacier. Julia's eyes had met Duncan's and she'd smiled. Duncan had pushed aside a couple of chairs, burger in hand.

'Have a bite,' he'd said, shoving the burger into Julia's mouth. As she bit down on the mustard-laden beef, he'd introduced himself. 'I'm Duncan, I'm dangerous and I dare you to join our team. Welcome to the Adrenalin Brothers and look death in the eye.' Julia continued chewing so he'd added somewhat lamely, 'That is if you can ski a bit.' His mates had cheered, but Duncan's eyes never moved from hers.

Hanging out with Duncan had quickly become contagious. He was the sort of guy who'd squeeze the most out of every waking moment. When there was a vertical to ascend, he'd climb it; an edge to traverse, whether garden wall or precipice, he'd walk it; a new height from which to descend and Duncan would be first down. Nothing fazed him. In an effort to impress, he'd conjure up pompous phrases such as, 'Consternation about consequences is for the weak,' or 'Parascend, parachute, paraglide, paramedic, paralegal, who cares so long as excitement reigns.'

Julia had latched onto Duncan and revelled in his reflected glory, the admiration of his jealous friends who, she imagined, never dared push the boundaries of safety as far as her man. Yet it was they and never Duncan, who broke an arm or tore a cruciate ligament. It amazed Julia that, after so long being diffident and uncommitted, pretty soon after Steve's death, Duncan insisted on the whole marriage thing and, once hitched, he seemed to relish each new project: the securing of the impossible job; the buzz of buying the big house; the baby; a miscarriage; the second baby – and his music. Duncan constantly tapped his fingers on the table, his hands on his knees, chopsticks on a tin of beans – anything on anything to create rhythm and release tension.

Before the Big Day Julia's mother had said, 'I hope you know what you're doing, young lady. That Duncan drives me up the wall. He can't sit still for two ticks. What is he *on*? And yes, that is what I'm implying. You have to face it – your fiancé could be on something illegal because if he's not, then he needs some sort of assessment. I'm thinking therapy. You can get tablets for the jiggles, you know, something to calm him down.'

Then *something* had calmed him down but it wasn't therapy. Julia recalls two years ago, Duncan had manufactured a huge row. Whenever he felt like placing blame for his moodiness, he'd talk about his mates who'd left for uni and how they'd stopped communicating with him. He'd always presumed they'd return as graduates to the northwest, if only for the sake of the band. He blamed Julia because since having Sophie and Meg they'd lost touch with the whole skiing fraternity and any kind of social life.

The usual arguments began with Duncan winding Julia up until she reacted, yelling, screaming, chucking plates, giving him an excuse to explode fully, then he'd storm out, slamming doors and thumping walls. Petty disagreements could escalate from bitter sarcasm to life-threatening, white knuckles clenched above Julia's face. Yet Duncan never physically hurt her; he simply took his adrenalin to the very edge of the precipice then, as quickly as it had arisen, it would evaporate. His arms would slump by his side and he'd demand a coffee, black, two sugars, after which he might suggest a walk together along the canal, or even lunch out, but more often than not he would fall asleep on the sofa for hours. He never apologised because he knew for sure that he'd do the anger thing again, given time. It brought him to life.

It dawns on Julia that *that* particular rage, the one about their lack of a social life, was the last real rage. Two whole years have elapsed with only the occasional bicker. Of course, purchasing the Cave helped – but the Cave alone can't explain Duncan's inexplicable change in demeanour, the oddly peaceful way he'd return from a nightshift. Once in a while, he brought home little trinkets, unusual gifts, for no reason except, as he put it, 'that I really do love you.'

'You were wrong, Mum,' Julia whispers into the empty room, as she opens Duncan's locker to caress the bejewelled chameleon. 'My husband does love me. He's become a very contented man.' But Duncan hasn't yet phoned and the evening is drawing in. *By one o'clock in the afternoon* that strange Mr Quin had promised he'd return the phone. Duncan surely has it by now. Julia dials Duncan's number. She waits. The ringing continues. At least the ghastly stranger isn't answering. Julia is about to hang up when a breathless Duncan picks up.

'Darling! Um, I'm so sorry to have been out of touch.'

'Duncan,' Julia says, inhaling mightily and flopping back on the bed to prepare for a long chat. 'Don't explain, petal. I know all about your phone – lucky that dreadful guy got it back to you. It's not like you to be so forgetful. Oh, I've got something funny to tell you - Meg did a drawing of you outside your Cave. Your head is huge and your arms stick out and you're holding a baby, or so she says.'

'That must be how she sees herself then, as a baby. Best be off. Gotta twilight session.'

'A meeting? But it's so late. They'd better pay you double.' She laughs, caressing the spiky ornament against her cheekbone. 'How's your day been? Tell me all about it. The girls are fine. They're staying over at Mum's place. I cleaned a bit. I know I don't need to, but I like it. Went on my runner. Burned eight hundred and thirty calories.'

'That's my girl! My day? Nothing much. A bit of this and that. The usual spreadsheets and number crunching. Catch up tomorrow sometime, hey?'

'Okay, you win. I was hoping to talk some more but never mind. Ring me again before you go to sleep. Pretty please?'

'Of course I will. Love you. Must fly.' And he's gone.

The doorbell rings. Julia leaps up excited, imagining it could be Duncan; *So typical of him to pretend he's miles away when all the while he's standing on the doorstep.* She runs downstairs and flings open the door. Her shoulders drop. It is Rae Hook, minus her dog.

'Hi,' says Rae brightly, 'I hope you don't mind but I thought I'd do the neighbourly thing and pop round for a cuppa. Or you can come to mine if you prefer.'

'Right now?'

'Why not? Is your gorgeous husband in? I notice his van's gone. Mind you, it's often gone at night isn't it?'

'He works nights. Computers. He likes the graveyard shift so he can be home as much as possible for his family. And he hates to let his bigwig clients down.' As usual, Julia over-eggs the explanation. She presses the switch for the outside light. 'My goodness is it that time already? I do hate November. Nothing to look forward to except dark evenings and drizzle.'

Rae is up to her chin in a tight polo-neck sweater, swathed in a delicate, floral scarf that Julia instantly envies. The woman has one foot inside the door. 'Do tell me all about that graveyard shift, it sounds terribly exciting. I never get any chit-chat since I moved here. You were so friendly at the surgery, I knew you wouldn't mind a bit. So . . . can I come in?'

'Oh, of course. How rude of me. Ignore the mess. Come into the kitchen.' Julia flicks the kettle on and decides against showing this woman into the snug. She settles on acting friendly but not so cosy that Rae is confident to call in a second time. *I suppose I can stretch some good will to show sympathy for a neighbour whose husband can't keep his job. Poor woman had to downsize.*

'Tea or coffee? Personally, I rarely drink anything stronger but you're welcome . . .'

'Oh, coffee's fine. Any decaf? Great. I always bring my own sweeteners.' Rae scrapes back a chair and Julia flinches. Sophie and Meg have learnt to *lift* the legs.

'My word, that is absolutely stunning!' Rae exclaims, grabbing at an object on the table.

'My chameleon!' gasps Julia, horrified because she'd brought it downstairs without thinking. She'd dumped it onto the table as she rushed to answer the door – thank goodness it wasn't Duncan after all! But now that dreadful woman is holding her treasure. Rae is turning the thing over and over.

'What was the occasion? Was it a gift? Oh, do tell all.'

'No, not really. Just an ornament I was dusting. It lives upstairs.' Julia reaches out her hand towards it as the steam from the kettle dampens the cupboard above it.

'Somewhere I've seen an exact replica of this,' Rae is saying, ignoring Julia's open hand. She lifts the chameleon near to her face and squints at it, examining every facet. 'Hmm. I'm in the trade you know. Only part time. I'm trying to remember . . . I wish I'd brought my glasses. Didn't expect to see one of these ever again. Amazing. Unless . . . Well, of course! What's your husband's name again?'

'Duncan.'

'Unless Duncan was the one who bought it. But he can't have done. I never forget a face.' Suddenly Rae lights up, 'I remember! It was seeing it out of context that surprised me.'

'You remember what?' Julia steels herself, forcing herself to make the coffee with furious, quivering hands.

'Selling this very thing!'

'When was that?'

'Oh, ages ago. It must be, let's see, at least, what – eighteen months, two years? It's my thing, my profession, which is why I remember. We had it specially designed and sold in our Preston branch. The buyers were an Asian couple. But tell me, exactly how long have you had it?'

Julia passes Rae a porcelain mug of coffee. Her rising anger is inexplicable. She imagines pouring the scorching liquid over the woman's head. 'What do you mean, *Asian couple*? Tell you what, why don't you tell me all about why your husband lost his job? Was it his fault? I suppose you'll say something about the credit crunch. Cutbacks. It happens.' She can hear herself prattling. *You came round uninvited. What do you expect*?

Julia sees alarm in Rae's eyes. The woman is fighting back tears. Not exactly fighting, more brushing them away. She is gulping at her coffee even though it must be too hot. She hasn't added a sweetener.

Even so, Rae finds the courage to continue. 'The people who bought it, they were from Pakistan. I'm sorry if this upsets you, but I do remember because they had it created specially, in memory of their dear little boy who loved reptiles. They asked for a lizard but our designer persuaded them to go for a chameleon. More exotic. More unique.'

'How can you have *more* unique? Either it is unique or it isn't. Maybe they absolutely hated it. Maybe they wished you hadn't bullied them into buying something they hadn't asked for. Maybe they couldn't afford your ridiculous prices. Well, they must have sold it on, mustn't they? Everyone's hit on hard times. Even Asians.' Julia bangs her mug down, splashing coffee onto the table. She brushes the liquid onto the floor with her hand. Rae scrapes back her chair and stands. The dregs in her mug are still steaming. With an unsteady hand, Rae places the chameleon onto the kitchen table so that it is upright beneath the penetrating ceiling spotlight and the colours of its jewelled eyes multiply.

Duncan 8 and Julia 5
Walking on Eggshells

Julia hides the chameleon on the windowsill, behind the winter-flowering cactus, but she can't get the beast out of her mind, so she returns it to the centre of the table where it glares at her, its bulbous eyes glittering. Julia returns its stare, accusingly. *What do you know that I don't?*

'Cham-e-leon,' Julia types into her tablet. '*Definition: a changeable, fickle or inconstant person.* Nope, not that. I need to know about the creature. Ah, here. *Originated in Africa and Madagascar, having long slender legs, a prehensile tail and tongue and the ability to change colour.* Fascinating. Oh, look at this . . .' she chatters to herself, beginning to enjoy flicking through photos of the colourful creatures. 'Here's one from the Yemen called a Veiled Chameleon. Pretty impressive. It sounds sooo sneaky! *When veiled chameleons are stressed, they often display strong colouration, such as bright yellow or sometimes even black.*'

Julia regards the shiny object with suspicion. 'I don't believe a word Rae Hook utters. She's trying to wind me up with so much tosh. That spikey piece of junk is the last thing any loving parent would buy in memory of a dead child.'

Julia carries the thing upstairs to Duncan's locker. 'You are absolutely hideous,' she tells it, 'and I don't love you anymore. Duncan can take you back to the shop and change you for something more attractive. Something with wings. A dragonfly maybe, or a butterfly. Better still, a kingfisher!' She slams the ornament back into its dark space.

The phone rings. It is Duncan. 'Hi, darling! You all right? How's my girls?'

'Fine,' Julia snaps, but Duncan doesn't read her mood.

'Where are you, Jules? At home or having a wild night out without me?'

'Honest truth? Lying back on our bed thinking of you.' Julia looks at the bed then perches on the edge of it, clutching the phone to one ear with both hands. She is shaking. 'You phoned earlier than I expected.'

'You sound a bit . . .'

'Yes, I am. I mean, I did feel edgy. But I've calmed down a bit now. You know me, if I'm on my own for too long my head goes all over the place. You wouldn't believe what I started imagining, and it was all the fault of that new woman, Rae. Yes, I know you know her. Hey, it is soooo good you got your phone back.' Julia forces herself to relax. After all, none of this is Duncan's fault.

'Yes, my, er, *colleague* was being facetious because I was driving. Ignore him in future. Hopefully you won't hear another word from him.'

'He sounds like a right—'

'I know. He is a bit. Unfortunately he lives in Lancaster, so don't let him con you into giving you our address. He's a bit like Rae – they're both too nosey for their own good. If he knows where we live, he'll think it is fine to call in whenever it suits him.'

'I was wondering . . .' Julia starts.

'What?'

'It's about something I may have done wrong.'

'You did something wrong?'

'Well, I didn't mean to but . . . Listen, I'm so sorry, darling, but when I put your comb in your locker it caught my eye. So gorgeous and irresistible. I know I shouldn't have but . . .'

'Oh, you mean that ornament? Forget it. Why should finding it be something you did wrong?'

'Well, I thought maybe you had bought it for me as a present and wanted to keep it a secret.'

'Present? I'd never buy you a piece of junk like that. No, it's totally my fault. I should've handed it in as soon as I found it,' says Duncan, nice and steady. A useful story he'd come up with in the last fifteen seconds. Duncan needs to get a hold of Hugo's mobile and delete all those contacts and call records, or else he'll never hear the end of him.

'You *found* it?' repeats Julia, audibly relieved.

'Why, what did you think?'

'At first I thought you'd bought it for me as a present, what with Christmas coming and all that. It seemed really pretty and I loved it. But then I heard it might be, well, stolen. Yes, Rae Hook told me. That woman. Honestly.'

'She might well be right; someone could have stolen it and dropped it. A while back, as I said, I found it lying on the pavement among some leaves. Although how Rae would know anything about that, I have no idea.' Duncan forces himself to pace each word evenly, relieved that Julia can't read the shock on his face.

'Rae works for a jeweller. She claims she met the clients who had it designed.' Julia feels mortified for suspecting her husband; she can't explain why she allows herself to ride this rollercoaster of suspicion and relief but right now she chooses to stick with Duncan and to defy her mother's unreasonable warnings.

'Rae Hook was in our bedroom?' Duncan imagines the woman

rifling through his locker.

'No, silly. I had it in my hand when she called round and I accidentally took it downstairs with me. She saw it in the kitchen.'

'I, er, found the thing a couple of weeks ago,' repeats Duncan blathering on, unable to drop the subject. He racks his brains. *When on earth did I do that break-in? It was a challenge. I thought they'd put anti-theft paint on the guttering but it was just a sticky residue. Snails, maybe. The bathroom window was hidden, because the house wrapped round on itself with a crumbling, red-brick chimney sticking out at a weird angle. I flicked myself over the edge of the small window and hung down inside to unhook the bigger one. My stomach bruised on the sharp edge of the catch as I leant in to gather the shampoos and a razor, to drop them into the sink, so they didn't crash when I climbed in.*

People rarely, if ever, put CCTV into their bathroom but from habit he'd donned a ski-mask, then covered his feet with blue plastic bags, elastic bands gripping his ankles. He'd crept through the house, hesitating in the doorway of a room with open curtains, streetlight flooding in. The room contained a bed covered by a dinosaur quilt and posters on the walls of lizards and a ferocious komodo dragon. Stupid parents. Sophie would be scared stiff if she woke in the night with those monsters staring out at her.

Duncan had crept along the corridor. Whenever the floorboards creaked, he cursed himself for failing his imaginary rice-paper test. As a child he'd been inspired by Kwai Chang Caine in *Kung Fu* crossing the flimsiest of rice paper without wrecking it. Duncan and his little friends walked barefoot over newspaper without creasing it. Like true Shaolin monks, they had also tried to walk through walls whilst repeating 'Ah,

Glasshopper', and crashed their foreheads painfully, with much hilarity and no success.

Maybe I should practise walking on egg shells because I still can't master this silent, floating thing.

Snores had emanated from the bedroom to the right. Duncan crept downstairs to sniff about. He'd seen an alarm system by the front door but couldn't tell if it had been set. He'd have to smash a window for a swift getaway if it did go off. A small, red light blinked in the corner of the corridor. A sensor. He tensed. Nothing. Not set.

He padded through to the front room and turned on the light. Two cerise sofas dominated the room, draped in gold-embroidered throws and scattered with oversized sequinned cushions. Claret velvet curtains shimmered from on high, falling voluptuously onto a deep, cream carpet. Julia hated any display of exuberance and lack of subtlety but Duncan found himself admiring the audacity of it all, the lack of obedience to British rules of colour and texture, how *blue and green should never be seen*, yet creation itself juxtaposed sky and earth in every impossibly stunning hue.

What caught Duncan's eye was a weird chameleon ornament perched upon the mantelpiece beside a gold-filigree-framed photo of a dark-eyed boy of about Sophie's age. Considering how much gold decorated the room, there'd been nothing worth taking. A grey Panasonic TV dominated one corner and beside it an overly ornate lamp, decorated with shimmering elephants. A gilt mirror adorned one wall and hanging from the other wall was some heavy embroidery depicting a Hindu temple. Duncan pocketed the chameleon. It would have to do.

He crossed to the kitchen, checking surfaces and cupboards for anything of interest. Footsteps creaked slowly down the stairs. Whispers. The soft pips of a mobile phone set low. Duncan tiptoed to the back door where, to his relief, a key filled the lock. He turned it, and the click was so loud, like the massive tick of a grandfather clock that he rushed outside, slamming the door and running, running . . .

I ski down a sharp arête, at breakneck speed. To my right is a sheer drop to the valley. I love this. I love it! I love it! I love it! Steve? You're chickening out of the best thrill of your life, swerving over there, to the broader place. I choose the narrow way. Look out, mate. I'll meet you at the foot of the mountain. I am number one.

'Hey!' a man shouted, but Duncan vaulted the two-metre stone wall into a neighbour's garden, tripped over some garden toys and flung himself over a low, prickly hedge. Still wearing the plastic foot covers, he raced along a back alley towards his waiting van. He jumped in and, without turning on the headlights, released the handbrake so it rolled noiselessly downhill. Across the city a blue light flashed between the houses, responding to a call – potentially heading in this direction.

Duncan allowed his van to glide into an empty driveway then parked and slumped behind the wheel, his heart in his throat, until the danger had passed. He removed the blue bags from his feet and shoved them into a carrier bag ready to dump in the nearest wheelie bin, then he tucked his gloves under the driver's seat and headed home to bed. It hadn't been worth stashing his loot in the Cave because the pocket-sized chameleon was the only spoil, so he'd eased himself into bed beside the sleeping Julia and tossed it into his locker drawer.

'. . . and so she got a certificate for coming top in spelling.' Julia is drawing breath and Duncan has no idea whether she means Meg or Sophie.

'That's our girl!' he says.

'Have you been listening to a word I've said? I'm talking about Sandra, my niece. She's struggled in school and now she's doing well.'

'Oh, right. I thought . . .'

'Oh forget it. When *are* you coming home?' Julia is winding down, Duncan's story about finding the chameleon in the leaves seemingly accepted. He could drive north tomorrow, straight after the transaction, but an extra day or two would be a treat. He wouldn't mind bumping into those youngsters again, if they're still hanging about in Widemouth Bay or somewhere nearby. Monika will be more than capable of caring for any baby. *I know she'll never change her mind and reject Toby. After all, I am an adoption researcher and in my professional assessment, Monika is articulate, wealthy, willing and desperate. And Erik is compliant. The perfect parents.*

The conversation with Duncan dries up so Julia blows him a couple of kisses and hangs up. As is her habit, she hits the treadmill to burn the tension, trying to loosen the muscles in her neck that had been tightened by that dreadful Rae Hook.

Duncan 9 and Hugo 4
A Far Cry from a Wallet

Toby wakes repeatedly throughout the night until Duncan gives in and props himself up with pillows to cradle the tiny boy against the soothing drumbeat of his own heart. *I wonder why I never enjoyed these quiet moments with the girls. I was too busy working silly hours, then sleeping all morning. And Julia did it all. Don't think she trusted me with her girls. Our babies. After last night's call, I'm sure she suspects nothing of Toby. She said some bitchy stuff about that Rae Hook person, but that's my Julia – sharp in attack, mean in defence.*

Duncan smiles. Julia's quick-witted sarcasm still attracts him. She is sharp as a blade, at once furious then giggling, spiteful, then generous. Her vivacious, reactive nature has kept him on his toes but now . . .

Her dark mischievous eyes – I miss what we had before . . . Hugo said he'd phoned her, but he must have lied because Julia hardly mentioned him and she made no reference to adoption or anything unnerving. Hugo lied, or else he was winding me up for his own amusement. Or both.

Duncan sleeps fitfully, but Toby is comfortable and doesn't wake until . . .

Hugo knocks at the door. *Why does he have to be so loud?*

'Breakfast and a complimentary copy of the Express for your Lordship!' Hugo chirps for the whole corridor to hear.

Duncan reacts as if to a fire alarm, leaps up and opens the door. Toby tumbles onto the edge of the bed. Hugo strides in, drops the newspaper and, seeing Toby in a precarious position, dives across the space to save him. Duncan rolls his eyes.

'Feed Toby so he doesn't cry.' Duncan thrusts a bottle into Hugo's hands. 'And keep the bottle upright so he doesn't suck in air.' He disappears for a shower. When he emerges he is dressed in a pair of pressed chinos, checked shirt and crew-necked pullover.

'Whoo, whoo! Take a look at Mr Smarty Pants!' Hugo addresses Toby, shifting him over to his left arm. Toby messes with the teat, eyes shut.

Duncan pours two coffees, then devours the squashed cinnamon swirl Hugo procured from the dining room.

'I had a full English,' Hugo says, patting his stomach. 'Black pudding, two eggs, the works. Talking of food, here's a little joke to wake you up. What does a clock do when it is hungry? Goes back four seconds. And I might do exactly that if you don't get a move on.'

'Eat what you like but we need to understand each other,' says Duncan, unsmiling. 'Because I have a job to do and you are . . .'

'Indispensable? Incorrigible? Getting up your nose? Pick a, b or c.'

'Why do you insist on hanging about? I've done nothing to deserve you and it's costing me a packet to pay for your rooms. Buzz off for the day. Go see the sights or whatever it is you do on your travels. Ever been to St Michael's Mount? What about Land's End? This is your lucky day.'

'Get your facts straight, Mr Posh Daddy. It's *me* who's paying for *you*, since *you* are using *my* cash at every turn – or have you conveniently forgotten what you removed from my rucksack?'

Hugo tosses the empty bottle onto the floor and hoists Toby over his shoulder to pat his back. 'Parenthood is like riding a bike. You never forget how.' He grins as Toby burps. 'And talking of finances, I'd say you suffer from addictive kleptomania and you can *take* something for that! Do you get it? It's a pun.'

Duncan thinks about the rolls of twenties, the first impromptu theft since the day he left D-DIT. It had been pointless to take Hugo's money. Inexcusable. Disappointing. Low. The whole sorry event had lacked the nervous anticipation of breaking and entering, the stealth, the impulse, the sense of triumph. It shocked Duncan that he'd been reduced to stealing on impulse, with no battle of conscience and no emotional satisfaction. Duncan had never before stolen from anyone he knew personally. How strange that Hugo hadn't mentioned it before. If the shoe had been on the other foot, Duncan would have . . .

'I said, do you get my little joke?'

'Yes, yes, kleptomania. Take something. Ha, ha. Not funny.'

'But extremely clever, if I do say so myself. It doesn't amuse me that you took my hard-earned cash but I'm not one to make a fuss. So long as you continue to spend my money, I figure the least you owe me is a couple of hot meals and a few nights in this beauty spot, culminating nicely in a lift back to Lancaster.'

'Watch your step. Don't push me too far. If it wasn't for Toby, you'd have been mincemeat the minute I met you, but I have a family conference to attend. Bigger fish to fry than you. So here's the deal – I'll pay you whatever you ask, drive you to wherever you choose within a fifty-mile radius. In return you let me check your phone contacts so I can eliminate those you stole from me. Then we'll shake hands and go our separate ways.'

'No can do.' Hugo glances at his chunky fisherman's watch and waves his wrist at Duncan. 'See this gear here; it's synchronised to the tides of the River Lune in Lancaster. This masterpiece of engineering enables me to safely fish the Lune for two hours before high tide and for one hour after, without fear of drowning. I understand the habits of fish, see. In estuary and salt-marsh fishing, when there's a high outgoing tide the fish concentrate on the tidal outflow areas and head for the deeper holes in the creeks. Catching the biggest fish is all about being in the right place at the right time.'

'What in thunder are you prattling on about?' Duncan folds his few possessions into the base of the holdall, covering the lot with a folded plastic bag in case Toby leaks. He picks up the baby's bottle to rinse it out in the ensuite.

'Hmm. How to explain to the simple-minded?' Hugo lies back on the bed beside Toby, his feet dangling over the side. 'Here goes. If you don't know the tides and you wander too far from the shore, you'll get stranded on a sandbar and need rescuing. Imagine the embarrassment for a man such as you, with such high status, all alone on sinking sand, freezing water lapping against your chest, just because you overestimated your own ability to beat the speed of the sea. Without me, you will drown. And I'll tell you another thing, this little beauty also records atmospheric pressure, and this morning, I'd say . . .' Hugo glances at the multi-dialled watch '. . . there is a sudden drop in the said pressure.'

'So?'

'So a storm is brewing out on the Atlantic. And a storm is brewing right here, in the life of young Toby. And whilst we're on the subject of Toby, where is his mother?'

'She's – it's confidential.'

'Sure it is. Keep confidence, if you insist, but I'm thinking of the poor old Nowiks. They'll be on tenterhooks this morning, so let's be considerate and be on time for them. I'll pop into my room to pack and then we'd best be off. Have you secured the, er, vital paperwork?' Hugo heaves himself to a standing position, cocks his head, winks, then zips off to do whatever strange people do when they are alone.

Duncan racks his brains. *What to do? Could I dispose of him? He doesn't seem to belong to anyone. No one would miss him – except maybe his daughter, wherever she is. Perhaps I could chuck him down a mineshaft onto a pile of rotting sheep.*

Toby lolls contented in the middle of the bed, his dark eyes drifting towards the light that sifts through the net curtains. Duncan nods in his direction, 'What do you think I should do, kiddywink?'

A knock at the door. Duncan grits his teeth. 'Go away, man. Give me at least five minutes.'

Outside, Hugo cups his hands against the wood, pressing his mouth against his hands. 'Did you mean what you said back there?'

'What did I say?' Duncan presses the side of his foot against the door.

'About money. And driving fifty miles?'

'Every word,' nods Duncan. *The fool bites the shiny bait.* Monika and Erik will soon hand over the cash, sufficient to pack Hugo off to Timbuktu or better still, the moon.

Twenty minutes later, Duncan and Hugo arrive in the town centre. Duncan parks down a side road. 'Name your price,' he says. 'And 'specially for you, I'll phone Mrs Nowik to make a later appointment so I can drop you wherever you like, within limits. Let's say anywhere within an hour's drive. Your choice. How's that?'

'Oh, but I'm going nowhere yet. I'm still making *arrangements*, so to speak, so until then . . .'

Duncan flinches. 'Don't you ever do anything in a straight line?'

'Why should I? When I was a toddler I loved colouring in, but I scribbled all over the place. I didn't stay within the lines. And it was fun. At what point in my life did I learn that it was only socially acceptable to behave so neatly? To live within the lines? I dunno. But the adult me can't breathe for long in such a straitjacket, so like Houdini I must from time to time, escape.'

'But if you did what you're supposed to do, you might surprise yourself and actually enjoy it. Listen, if you want my offer to stand, I get to check all your phone contacts and delete the necessary.'

Hugo smiles. 'All in good time. First, I vote we get going. Knock this business on the head.' Hugo leans in to Duncan. He places a hand on the steering wheel. 'May I make a suggestion, Mr Simons?' Hugo's face is close enough for Duncan to smell the unisex hotel shampoo on his stubble. 'That you don't deliver young Toby in a holdall? Invest in a decent basket or a car seat. The social services might be cutting back but a holdall is a dead giveaway. You may as well deliver him in a sack of potatoes.'

'I was thinking I'd get a blanket and carry him in,' splutters Duncan. 'That's our, um, usual method of transaction. In my experience, the parents always want to provide everything brand new. However, we'll call in at a chemist for a complimentary pack of nappies. If you're sticking around, you're welcome to do that job since you're so keen to be involved. First, your phone.'

'Tut tut, patience, my friend,' says Hugo, holding out his hand to receive two of his own twenties from Duncan for the shopping. 'The info in my phone is my insurance that you won't abandon an old man by the wayside ever again.'

Hugo jumps out of the car, asks directions to the chemist and disappears around a corner. The signal is low on Duncan's mobile but he phones Julia to keep her sweet.

'Hi! We're on a break. Gotta be quick. Yes, yes, the conference is better than expected. How're the girls? Give them a hug for me! Try the fuse box or ring Harry – he'll sort it for you. I should be home in a day or two. All depends how much work we cover this evening. Okay, I'll ring again tonight. Love you!' He hangs up. Julia seemed quiet but at least she hadn't asked awkward questions.

The baby is grizzling but Hugo has returned.

'Great. Chuck the stuff in the back. Toby needs a feed and a change. Let's head down to the beach car park to do it.' *Time to move in for the kill.*

While Duncan feeds Toby in the van, Hugo removes his boots and socks and rolls up his trousers. Wearing his hat and camouflage jacket, he pads barefoot down some granite steps then gingerly traverses a raft of pebbles until he can walk comfortably on the damp sand. He flings his arms wide as he swings round to face Duncan, with unadulterated joy stretched across his face. He shouts at the top of his voice for all Cornwall to hear; 'The motion of the ocean is a lotion to my soul! Do you hear that, Mr Simons? It's the first line of my Ode to Bude!'

Duncan can't help smiling as he changes Toby's nappy then freshens him with wet wipes. He zips him into a cosy blue one-piece that Hugo has purchased. He stuffs the 'daffodil' outfit into an overflowing bin, where black-backed gulls squabble over the off-season thin pickings. Duncan checks his watch. *Not too eager. Not too early. Twenty minutes then . . .*

'Let's go see the sea,' Duncan whispers against Toby's cheek. He runs his little finger along the rim of Toby's white woollen hat, over the curve of his forehead. 'This is for your own good, son. She's a mess, your mum. A disaster. If it weren't for me you'd have ended up in the system, or worse, died of neglect in that flat. She couldn't even give you your first feed without my help. So it's you and me, kiddo. And that barmpot out there on the sand, but he doesn't count. Sorry, kid, but we can't shake the old guy off just yet. He has his uses.'

Duncan wraps Toby inside his coat. He wanders quietly to the water's edge where waves roll the length of the sands, roaring to a crescendo then fading into the distance like a passing train. 'You'll be surfing those rollers before you know it,' Duncan whispers.

Hugo is approaching, talking loudly, ear to his mobile.

What now?

'Right, fine, lovely. See you soon. What time again? I'll jot that down. Perfect. A white van. With a black stripe. Yes. Yes. My friend Duncan. Very kind of him. Brilliant. I'll book you in. Fairly cold here but not raining. Bring a coat. Love you too.' Hugo hangs up. He smiles at Duncan broadly and his eyes have a smug 'sorted' look.

'My girl's coming Sunday, that's if her hubbie Jason can get the time off fishmongering. He's always working. Reeks of fish. I've booked the best hotel in Bude – a belated birthday treat for my daughter. Can't believe she accepted because, well, she knows what I'm like. She can't trust me not to mess up but when I said the train tickets and three nights are all paid for she was *soooo* excited. You'll owe her that money when you meet her because she's had to pay for everything up that end. All we have to do is pick them up from the station on Sunday.'

'Sunday? You'd better explain yourself. What are you playing at? I owe you nothing. Nada. Zilch. Zero.'

'What was it? Oh yes, you will give me *any* amount of money and drive me to within fifty miles of here to get rid of me. You're lucky I'm merely asking for a thousand, give or take. And it's less than *ten* miles to the station to pick up Callie and Jason, so you're on to a winner. Why the long face? All's fair in love and war.'

'I don't love you.'

'Maybe not. But neither do you hate me. You drag me into your dodgy racket and repay me with false promises and bribery. What kind of adoption researcher does that? A measly grand is all I'm asking. I'm guessing two returns from Lancaster are about seven hundred, plus whatever it costs for three nights in a hotel in November. Come to think of it, a grand may not be quite enough. Better make it two. And, take note, I've asked nothing for myself.'

'All right, all right. Come with me to the Nowiks if you must, but first change out of that gear and give yourself a shave. And when I do business, whatever I say, keep your big mouth shut. When I call you, your only job will be to carry Toby into the house, then hand him to me. I will pass him to Mrs Nowik. It is my job to ensure he is safe with her. I will be arranging some further meetings to assess . . .'

'I think we can cut the bull, don't you, Duncan Christopher Simons *who would have called the police on me if he wasn't up to something fishy himself Wilde.* You are no more going to assess this adoption as surf to the moon on a Cornish pasty. So cut it. Call a spade a spade and let's go dig a trench and watch the tide wash up it.'

Friday Afternoon

The gates are wide open at the foot of the Nowik's drive. From the slate-framed upstairs windows, the silhouette of Monika can be seen scanning the countryside to catch the very first sight of her baby.

As it is, it seems almost sensible to allow Hugo to come along with him. It means that he, Duncan, can concoct some paperwork with Monika and Erik while Hugo hangs about in the van caring for Toby.

Hugo has changed into a purple cable-knit sweater and grey cords; his only other footwear – checked carpet slippers – is marginally less unsightly than his walking boots. The two men agreed that if the Nowiks comment on them, they'll say Hugo was merely respecting Monika's carpets and his leather brogues are in the van.

'Do you feel *nothing*?' asks Hugo as they approach the house.

Duncan purses his lips. While working for D-DIT it had dawned on him that most people are only bothered about their own little lives. No one at work really cared what went on in his household; bereavement, an accident, or financial concerns –and why should they? He was nothing to them. What difference does it make whether anyone ever bothers with anyone else? *I am on the verge of losing my only son and no one, except maybe Hugo Quin, cares.*

The silence warns Hugo and for once he holds his tongue. This is a serious business and for the life of him, Hugo can't fathom the root of the problem. No lists, diagrams, mind-maps, thought clouds, equations, could possibly unravel this enigma. For Hugo, there are no clues because there is no truth; nothing to evaluate, neither facts nor tools with which to solve the Toby puzzle. However, the ride is fun and for reasons too wonderful to comprehend, Duncan is allowing Hugo to work with him.

Duncan jerks the van to a halt and grinds the brakes. His nerves jangle. He wipes his palms on his trousers but they refuse to dry. He is hit by the desire to smoke, the distant memory of how a couple of drags had calmed him before facing an exam or a particularly intimidating mountain. The shock of redundancy had been an embarrassment, a shame he'd been unable to vocalise. Some of D-DIT had been sacked by text then phoned the press to stir muck. But Duncan had been summoned to the CEO. He had guessed at a positive review, promotion at last.

I'm safe from the cuts because I take pride in D-DIT. I hit every deadline. I'm a smooth operator. A team player. A natural leader. I match every CV cliché ever composed. We're letting you go. You're what? Not everyone's offered such a generous severance package. We value you, but we're letting you go. I find myself on the wrong side of the door and there is no going back. To beg, to crawl, to grovel for the dignity of work is to be debased; humiliated. My boss drops me overboard into a sea of unemployment and I am drowning. I think to phone Julia. No answer. I need her but she's out, which makes me fume. I clear my desk. I leave the office, seething. No one looks up from their screens. Not one nod of farewell. At home I wait for Sophie and Meg to sleep, so I can tell Julia the news, but suddenly she is running on her machine, then her mother phones. They talk for ages. Then it is morning and I have told no one.

Duncan's silence is a habit impossible to break. For years his secrets have festered in the stagnant pool at the back of his mind, but recently they've been spilling into reality, stealthy as carbon monoxide.

I never wanted a nine-to-five. Night shifts had offered a satisfying challenge as I crossed different time zones to support international requests. I'd been confident at D-DIT, hungering for recognition, climbing each ladder rung by rung until the ninetieth square was in sight. So how did I land on square eighty-nine, to be touched by the forked tongue of some vicious serpent? The downward drop was so fast I was almost through the door before something stopped me in my tracks. Which fool left their wallet and phone lying around? I hadn't nicked so much as a sweet or a pencil since school. So let them catch me! I slip the objects beneath my jacket and sidle into the cloakroom where I remove seventy quid from the wallet then toss it, with the phone, into an open locker. No one grabbed my arm to pull me back. No one challenged me. No one cared.

But a baby is a far cry from a wallet.

Duncan signals for Hugo to stay put until it is time to introduce Toby. The front door opens, framing a coiffed and freshly manicured Monika standing on tiptoes, craning her neck to see inside the van. From the passenger seat, Hugo nods at her, offering a nauseating wave of his fingertips.

Duncan forgets to shake Monika's hand but she doesn't notice. He mutters something about bringing the baby inside only after the mundane matter of paperwork and expenses has been dealt with. Duncan towers over the woman, blocking her view, forcing her to step back inside her own home. The chasm of the hallway engulfs them and the door slams shut.

To pass time, Hugo scribbles in his notebook. It soothes his anxious mind.

Morning: walked on beach. Wrote 'Toby' in the sand with my big toe. Duncan moody.   What's he playing at? Where did he find Toby?

#1 Fact – he is not DW's son.

#2 Proof – DW doesn't strap T in safely.

2b Fact – DW dressed Toby in female outfit – daffodils and lace.

2c Observation: DW held Toby in a threatening way towards me – no father would do that.

#3 Fact– DW's wife's name is Julia.

3b Julia does not know about Toby.

3c Toby is not from an adoption agency.

#4 Fact – DW does not know Moni—

Duncan raps on the van window. Hugo slaps his hand over his notes.

'What are you playing at? I've called you from the door twice already. Hurry up. Bring Toby.'

Hugo drops his book and pen onto the floor. 'What about the nappies? Shall I bring them with me?' but Duncan has already dissolved back into the house.

Monika and Erik stand in front of their very modern fireplace like royalty posing for an official photograph, terrified of rocking the precarious boat and losing their precious cargo overboard. Monika's heart beats so hard she thinks she might faint. Her hand reaches out to grasp Erik's and this unexpected gesture of dependency causes a lump in Erik's throat. It makes him dare to hope that, when this is all over, they might move abroad together, maybe to Poland or America, someplace familiar, where he understands the culture. Erik knows they'll never fit into Cornwall, but Monika is determined to live what she calls 'the dream'. She refuses to acknowledge the distain of the locals. *Go away, emmet. Foreigner, you're not one of us.*

Hugo dithers in the doorway of the lounge, clutching the tiny bundle in a white shawl. Monika had long imagined this moment, how she would rush towards her baby, grasp it to her bosom and fall instantly in love; instead she is rooted to the spot, staring at an unfathomable hole in the toe of one of Hugo's slippers. Duncan is concocting random details, faking officialdom, but nothing matters because Monika comprehends nothing. She hears Duncan with all the clarity of a drowning woman.

The baby is registered as Toby Nowik. Date of birth: October 31st 2014. Born: Lancashire. Father: none. Mother: deceased. The child is awarded to Monika and Erik Nowik with the full approval of the authorities.

Without warning, Hugo holds Toby out towards Duncan to remind him to stop pontificating, to hurry up and hand the baby over. Duncan is procrastinating, waving a large brown envelope to emphasise some point or other, so Hugo decides to walk towards Monika.

The sudden forward movement of Hugo's slippers triggers the release of tension and Monika drops Erik's hand. She cries out, 'My baby!' and Toby is in her arms. The woman walks backwards with her prize, step by step until she sinks with the baby into the sofa. Her chubby little legs dangle helplessly above the carpet. Her eyes fix onto the child and she is entranced.

The scene reminds Erik of a soapstone carving he'd once seen in a window in Frankfurt depicting the Madonna and Child, pale, soft and glowing. In this moment his wife has never looked more serene.

'Right,' blinks Duncan.

Erik advances to shake his hand. 'I expect we'll be hearing from you again, then.' Erik is speaking so Duncan nods. *Why will they be hearing from me? Did I promise to follow up the case?*

'The money?' says Hugo, thinking of his daughter's expenses.

'Right,' Duncan repeats, dazed. Erik points to two plastic boxes with substantial clip-on lids that are stacked by the door. Duncan, reluctant to accept that his son has so passively transferred into the arms of that woman, registers the boxes with a nod but he cannot speak.

Hugo lifts one box, puffing out his cheeks because it is surprisingly heavy. He is dying to ask if Duncan has counted the contents but Duncan has managed to lift the second box and is nudging Hugo on.

'Something is not right,' says Hugo, unhappy at being pushed about.

Monika and Erik shoot him a look. Some things are better not said. Especially the truth. Especially when no one can change the facts. *This child is the most rightful Toby Nowik. Hasn't Mr Chris Simons pronounced this only seconds ago?* On the sideboard is a certificate to prove the truth of it, signed earlier in the ornate European script of the new parents. (After some creative manipulation, Duncan had printed an adoption certificate from Google Images. He then applied what he considered to be a satisfyingly realistic gold-embossed snowflake and two pieces of red ribbon.)

Duncan clears his throat. 'Myself and Mr Quin here are leaving. You both need time to adjust. Any problems, phone either of us at any time. Our agency never abandons new parents to flounder unsupported.' He is shoving Hugo out into the hallway.

'I must insist that something is not right,' insists Hugo.

'Don't talk so loud about things you don't understand,' Duncan hisses. He grips Hugo's arm, pinching down hard as he turns to face Erik with a gritted smile.

Erik reads through the fakery; he knows a charlatan when he sees one. In a previous life Erik had been a doorstep salesman, flogging cleaning products at inflated prices and convincing sentimental women to pay over the odds for a bottle of something and a rag. *Yes, Mr Quin, something is wrong. I am not stupid. But for now, whatever is wrong, this is better than before. Something was wrong when we were rejected. Maybe in life, something is always wrong.*

Erik watches as the van rolls down the drive, vanishing into the oncoming sea fret. It is only two o'clock in the afternoon but already dark, even for November.

'Why're you giving me that weird look? You're putting me off my driving.' As if to prove a point, they round a bend and Duncan has to brake hard for a herd of cows jostling each other as they cross the lane between fields. Several beasts stumble against the high Cornish hedges; others confront Duncan through the windscreen, with their large doe eyes and dribbling mouths.

'You never said goodbye to Toby,' says Hugo, who had hoped at least to give their baby a kiss on his forehead.

'It's known as professionalism. Separating one's emotions from the job.' Duncan cuts the engine. 'If I got teary-eyed over every child I handed over, I wouldn't be able to do my work effectively.' The windscreen wipers flick away the mizzerly dampness and the cows jump back in alarm.

'Can they put a nappy on a baby?'

'You can, so they can.'

'But we had Callie. I've had experience. What about feeding him? Do they know how much and how hot and how . . .?'

'Look,' Duncan says firmly, 'remember I spent a bit of time alone with them before you came in. I was *preparing* them. They have completed training, undertaken adoption classes. They're adults. They know what they're doing.'

Hugo notes the tremor in his voice. The farmer tips his hat in thanks and the way ahead is clear. Townie that he is, Duncan accelerates too quickly, spinning the wheels in the watery green muck, spattering it up the sides of his vehicle.

The men stop at a small roadside café. Inside, Hugo orders two pasties, one of which he stuffs into his coat pocket. 'You never know when the munchies will strike,' he laughs, 'These beasts are designed to withstand being chucked down mineshafts;

behold the utilitarian beauty of the pastry edged with twisted-granite.'

Duncan rolls his eyes but humours Hugo by nodding approval. Paying lip service to this charade might aid his defence if ever the matter blows up in his face. Hugo may be short of a few planks, an unknown quantity, the x or y of an unbalanced equation, but with Hugo anything is possible – he could wake up one morning and call the police. Surely the police would never believe the accusation of an outcast, an insane loner whose mind plays all manner of tricks upon him?

'I used to be a vegetarian but I went cold turkey.' Flakes of pastry spray from Hugo's mouth as he guffaws at his own joke.

'But you're eating beef!'

'Joke. Cold turkey. Gave up being a veggie. Cold beef's not so funny. So where are we staying tonight, buddy?'

'Decide for yourself. I'll let you have the money, along with a small bonus, then drop you in Liskeard so you can meet your daughter on Sunday. Get a taxi or bus or whatever you like to pick her up. You'll be a free man. And so will I.'

'Aren't you worried I'll spill the beans?'

'That never crossed my mind.' Duncan brushes crumbs off his jacket. He walks out of the café and into a newsagent's.

Hugo rushes after him. 'Get me a Lion Bar or anything with nuts and raisins!'

Duncan pays for an *Express* and a Deighton novel, two purchases he'd never make back home.

'Listen, Duncan, I've been wanting to tell you. Callie's not coming to Liskeard after all. I got a text. The train only takes them as far as Exeter then—'

'Great,' mutters Duncan sarcastically. 'Nothing's ever straightforward with you.'

'No, but you didn't let me finish. What's happening is much simpler because now they can take a coach all the way to Bude. Callie will confirm their ETA when she can.'

'And you're telling me this is good news?'

'Of course it is. You'll love her. She's so . . . together.'

'With you for a dad?'

'What are you implying? I was a first-class father.'

'Get in the van. I'll dump you in Bude. Take your share of the money and lord it up for a few days.'

The men cover a mile or two before Hugo starts rummaging in his pockets. 'Telephone! How interesting – she's chosen to dial *my* number, not yours.' He grins, phone to his ear. 'Hello, my dear! How can I help you? Yes, he's here but he's driving. No, not at a conference today. He is massively busy with a vital transaction.'

'What're you saying?' hisses Duncan, tugging Hugo's arm.

Hugo moves the phone to his left hand and shushes Duncan by flapping his free hand in his face. 'A message did you say? And you want to talk to him immediately. May I enquire what it concerns?'

Duncan grimaces, furiously scanning the narrow lane for a place to stop. He discerns the cutting edge of Julia's voice. She rarely calls during the day and Hugo is rabbiting on to her with all manner of rubbish. 'Yes, I do believe his phone is off. Or maybe his battery is low. He forgets to charge it. Typical, is it? Don't worry, I'll remind him tonight.' Hugo covers the mouthpiece with his hand and whispers, 'She's not giving any clue about what she wants.'

Duncan's forehead is glistening. Perspiration in November. A bead of sweat crawls over his cheekbone. A revelation of panic. Hugo watches a bead of sweat dropping like a tear onto Duncan's collar but he says nothing.

Lisa 4
What's She Hiding?

Lisa wakes with stomach ache. The area around her navel feels deeply bruised, as if she's been thumped. Lisa presses it, trying to ease the tenderness. Her mother comes into her mind.

Mother is sober. She has a key because I trust her and she takes the stairs two at a time, so sprightly. She brings me an armful of roses, and chocolates and perfume. Congratulations, darling! My grandson is beautiful. Your father would be so proud, if only he were here now. If only. Here, let me take the baby. There we go; I'm a natural. It all comes back you know, motherhood. Like riding a bike. You support his little head like this.

Lisa focuses on one of the cracks in the ceiling and decides it is wider than yesterday. The place is falling apart. Her mother refuses to leave her head: *You lazy cow. Why aren't you dressed properly? It's broad daylight. When I was seventeen I had real responsibilities as a nurse, caring for the sick and dying, but look at you, twenty-four, slobbing out, wasting your sorry little life.*

Lisa scrapes the sleep from her eyes and realises her cheeks are wet. A little salt hits the corner of her mouth and she licks it. She forces herself to stand and stretch. Today's the day of Sam Martin's lunch party but she'll only go if she can get her act together.

She runs the bath cold, while boiling the kettle several times to warm up the water. By the time the electricity people chase the owner for payment she'll have long since scarpered. No one's checked the property since Lisa moved in. A great place like this, abandoned. It shouldn't be allowed.

Lisa closes her eyes, holds her breath and slides beneath the water until the tip of her nose is submerged. She moves her head from side to side and her hair fans out like eels. For the first time in a fortnight she washes it, hauling herself up, and the water cascades over her shoulders. She likes her minty tea-tree shampoo, but never before has it smelt so powerful and intoxicating. She massages her head, scratching her fingernails into her scalp, scraping away her mother's criticisms. She leans forward, pushing her hair down beneath the cold tap and rinsing it. At last, she tosses her head back and her eyes open wide. 'I'm alive!' Lisa shocks herself with the sound of her own voice.

She stands up too quickly and the room spins. She dries herself with a thin scrap of towel, the one she's used since she arrived so by the time she is dressed, she is shivering. She pulls on her hoodie and her boots. Her stomach aches as she bends to tie the laces with chilly difficulty. She packs her rucksack with everything she owns, but she divides the money between her socks, pushing it well down against her ankles. She daren't risk someone entering the property while she's away – she might never be able to return for her stuff.

Without a phone or laptop there is no way to tell the time but Lisa guesses it is well after nine. She closes the door, setting the latch in such a way that it won't inadvertently lock her out. Outside she pauses, checking left and right for signs of life, but all the blinds are shut.

She nips round the side of the post-office and out onto the main road that heads into town. The bakery is open. Lisa pops in to buy a cheese roll which she puts in her coat pocket and, as she walks, she breaks off tiny pieces and pops them into her mouth. *Don't eat in the street; it's unbecoming. Just because you look like a tramp doesn't mean you have to behave like one. Shut up, mother.* The crumbs hit the grumbles in Lisa's stomach, giving her strength.

Lisa finds herself in the town centre. Everywhere is open except for the charity shops, so Lisa goes into McDonalds on Penny Street and orders a milky coffee with three sugars, watching the cobbled world expand until Oxfam opens at ten.

Back at the flat, Lisa changes into her charity clothes. A bronze and gold ethnic top originally from Wallis, some skinny black jeans, multi-coloured chunky beads, and some high-topped grey Converses, a size too large but fine over thick socks. After all that effort she longs to crash out on the mattress, but she's determined to go to the party. Once again, she gathers her possessions, flattens the money into her socks and ventures out.

Every door of the terrace is a new colour: racing green, cardinal red, navy blue, numbered 21, 23, 25 . . . and real people, real life. Lisa has always been drawn to kindness. Sam Martin must be a generous kind of guy to invite a bunch of total strangers for lunch.

On the doorstep of number 29, several crumbling chimney pots overflow with variegated ivy, and a makeshift sign reads, *Doorbell broken – please knock.* Inside there is laughter and all at once there are too many people. Lisa is terrified of being mocked, of smelling of dustbins and looking disgusting.

She hesitates in the cold breeze but someone has seen her from the bay window and is opening the door to her. 'Come in, come in quickly, or you'll let all the warm air out!' The middle-aged woman removes Lisa's coat. Lisa would prefer to hold onto it, but the woman hands it to a girl who runs upstairs to throw it on a bed.

'So glad you could make it. Better late than never, hey?'

Some people have kicked off their shoes by the front door and are standing around in their socks, picking at sausages on sticks and squares of cheese, tomatoes and crispy bacon on fingers of bread. Lisa hopes her boots are not too dirty, but she won't remove them for anyone. She accepts a glass of hot fruit punch, each sip a comfort. The party reminds Lisa of fresher's week at uni, when everyone assesses everyone else, makes hasty value judgements based on superficial glances, each one hiding their communal fear of rejection.

Lisa instinctively likes the dark-haired girl who ran upstairs with her coat. She's about Lisa's age, relaxed and cheerful and at home in her surroundings. She cheerfully offers cups of tea to an elderly couple who say no to food and refuse to sit on the settee because it is too low: 'If we sit down we'll never get up again.'

'So which number are you?' A buxom woman in baggy T-shirt and jeans addresses Lisa. She laughs. 'I should say, "What's your name and where do you come from?" but that sounds like a dated game show, doesn't it? I'm showing my age!'

'I'm Lisa,' she says and dives in with a question so she won't have to reveal the house number. 'Do you live here?'

'Yes. As I said on the invitation, I bought the house only last year. It was in a terrible state. Everything needed doing. You know what these old places are like but I couldn't resist the low price, even with the busy road into the city. You get used to it, don't you? I mean, the traffic.'

The woman chats while Lisa tries to work out which person is Sam: she's hoping he's the geeky, gorgeous guy over by the TV, showing photos on his iPhone to anyone remotely interested. Lisa assesses him as single, open-faced, intelligent, kind and . . .

'By the way, I'm Sam,' continues the middle-aged woman. 'And the sweet girl pouring the tea is my tenant, Callie. She and Jason moved in here five months ago. They virtually pay my mortgage and they're a dream to have around the house, so helpful and easy-going. I completely landed on my feet with them.'

Callie's ears are burning. She looks straight at Lisa and their eyes meet. An understanding of friendship passes between them. Neither smiles, but Callie walks over and says, 'I just had a premonition.'

Lisa raises her eyes, resisting the impulse to roll them because she doesn't believe in that sort of thing, yet she doesn't want to appear rude. Callie tips her head to one side and continues. 'When Jason left for work this morning he told me I should make some new friends. "Get a life," he said. "You know. Have some fun."'

'Jason?'

'My hubby of three years already and I've no regrets. He works for a fishmonger on the market. Early mornings, long hours, stinks of fish. Everyone notices. He can't hide it! He loves the customers, the city and the, um, um . . .'

'The camaraderie!'

'Wow, big word!'

'Begins with a cee, which is where you were heading.'

'Right on. Cuppa coffee?'

'No thanks, I've still got this fruit punch.'

'Is it really revolting? I made it yesterday for the party; chucked in all sorts of bits and bobs to infuse the flavour. Cinnamon sticks, orange slices bobbing about like a—'

'Shipwreck in Sri Lanka,' suggests Lisa and smiles. She rubs her stomach.

'Why Sri Lanka?'

'I think maybe you get cinnamon from Sri Lanka, but it was the first thing that . . .'

'Then that'll do nicely,' laughs Callie, scanning the face of her new friend. *What's she hiding? Who is she really?* The two girls sit on the floor with their backs against the wall and are still chattering long after all the guests have gone.

Lisa curls on the mattress, facing the flowery wall. She allows herself to think about the infant. The loss of him is unreal. Separation had not yet succumbed to grief or anger. The bubble that envelops her is emptiness. Emotion-less.

Less.

What is less? *I have a son. I had a son. He is real. He was real. He was here and then he was not. Someone took him away. Who took him? The social? My father? Paul?*

Lisa's hands rest on her stomach, spongy and flat. Feathery cracks distress the cream ceiling. A bluebottle slowly tracks across it. *How can a fly walk upside-down with its back to the earth, free from gravity? My mother is folding the bed sheets. Her mouth moves, forming words. I strain to hear but the words shatter into individual, black characters that tumble and scatter across the white linen. I can decipher them: 'It's all very well being brainy, but what's the point of A-grades if you lack integrity?'*

Integrity; now there's something a parent should model before demanding it of the next generation. My mother claims to be on the wagon but evidence to the contrary is in the glaze of her eyes and the odour that lingers long after she has left a room. 'I'll show you integrity,' I tell her, eye to eye. She is shaking the pillowcases, flattening them against her ribcage to save on the ironing. 'Integrity is wholesome honesty. Let me be honest for once. That's right, Mum; I know how to speak truth, no messing. That's integrity. The truth is that Paul loves me and I love him and there's nothing you can do to stop us. You married Dad but someone should've stopped you because you never loved him.'

Mum flaps her hands in my face like I'm an irritating bluebottle. She says, 'What about Gareth?' again and again. My mother had quite fancied Gareth for herself.

'He dumped me,' I tell her, for the umpteenth time. 'I told you he dumped me, didn't I? Gareth dumped me, like Dad dumped you. I never blamed Dad for pissing off to France. If I'd been in his shoes, I'd have left you years before so I'm going to go now, leaving you with your stinking bottle and your bad breath and your fake caring. No child of mine will ever be ignored for the price of a bottle of vodka.'

Was my baby a figment of my imagination? A phantom child conceived in my mind to love me unconditionally?

Lisa rolls over to where her boy should be. She pats and pats the mattress, sits up, thrashing here and there, crazy for her little one. She stumbles to her feet and rushes to the window because there's a gangly figure sliding down the drainpipe taking her bank card; a piper playing his flute, enchanting her baby – *follow my tune.*

Forgetting about possible onlookers, Lisa clambers onto the inside sill and clings with her fingertips to the latch on the wooden sash halfway up the window.

'Lisa, what's up?' Callie is in the doorway at the top of the stairs, staring wide-eyed into the room. Lisa jumps back off the sill, thudding to the floor, landing on her feet. It's pointless trying to hide, pretending to be fine, because the mess is blatantly obvious, within her, overflowing from her. She sways as the blood drains from her head, trying to remember if this is the girl from the party.

Callie grips the door jamb, regretting coming upstairs unannounced.

After Lisa left Sam's house, Callie realised that she hadn't said which house she lived in and Callie had intended to invite Lisa out sometime next week. They could head into town for a coffee or walk along the banks of the River Lune, maybe spot a heron or, with luck, a kingfisher.

After she'd helped Sam with the dishes and swept the wooden floors, Callie nipped out to knock on every door along the terrace but no one had heard of any Lisa. Now the two girls face each other, as if for the first time.

'It was open. You had to live here. It's the last house on the terrace. I thought maybe I had to come upstairs to knock,' Callie stutters. 'I'm so sorry if it's a bad time.'

Lisa shuffles forward until her hand finds the back of the armchair and she steadies herself. She cannot feign confidence as she did earlier because her party clothes are strewn across the floor; she is in her tatty jeans and filthy hoodie.

I think I had a baby. He is missing. I don't know what happened to him. I think I gave him away. Maybe he never was? Lisa cannot find her voice.

'Lisa.' Callie attempts a level of authority. 'Do you really live here?' Both girls survey the space as if they have accidentally stumbled into some kind of alter-Narnia.

'Don't tell anyone,' Lisa whispers hoarsely. 'I need to stay in this place for a little longer. I promise I'll go soon. I know the flat doesn't belong to me.' She curls around the back of the chair and twists herself over one of its arms, collapsing into its sagging embrace, then she draws her knees up under her sweatshirt, pulling them to her chest and her tired eyes peer over the top.

'So you don't live here,' Callie says. Lisa slowly shakes her head. 'Where are your family?' Callie steps into the room, absorbing the peeling wallpaper, the mouldy walls, the dripping tap.

Lisa shrugs.

'How long alone?' Callie begins to cry with quiet, unchecked tears. Neither girl dare move towards the other because they only met at lunchtime.

'I lost something,' gulps Lisa, dry-eyed. 'Can you help me find him?'

'Him?'

'Did I say him? I meant . . .'

'Your boyfriend?'

'Paul? No. I know where he is, and my mum was right all along. Paul doesn't love me. The one before was called Gareth but my mum flirted with him so he dumped me. And Dad left.'

'Your dad left you? Have you lost your dad? I lost mine, in a way but not because he left. Over the years he kind of lost his mind but I still love him. I'll tell you something funny about him if you like.' Callie inches nearer to Lisa. She decides to brave the edge of the mattress and lowers herself down onto it then, like Lisa, she hugs her knees to her chin.

Callie looks up. Again, their eyes meet, longing to communicate yet hardly daring to trust. Outside the whole world drives by, or walks or cycles, stopping and starting, obeying the traffic lights but here, inside the squat, the small world is still.

When Callie speaks her voice is clear; something about her is so ordinary and calm. 'Dad's name is Hugo Quin and he used to teach history in a secondary school but he had more brains than sense. The kids ran rings round him. I dreaded his lessons because I was his daughter. He used to wink at me and everyone laughed.'

'That's sweet,' says Lisa softly, smiling the weakest of smiles. 'I bet he was so proud to be your dad.'

'Maybe he was, but it was beyond terrible for me in Year Ten,' Callie says. 'Anyway, Dad has this *thing*. An "ability", he calls it. Sometimes, but not all the time, thank goodness – sometimes when he thinks of a number, like when you say the time, it turns into a date in his head.'

'Like twelve-thirty?'

'Exactly like twelve-thirty. For Dad, twelve-thirty becomes the year 1230. Then it sparks something off. He genuinely can't help himself from turning into someone from history, or maybe literature, and he carries on like normal but with a funny voice.'

'I don't know anyone from 1230. 1066 is all I know.'

'Nor me. It's random. So it might be, oh, I don't know, 1945 which reminds him of Winston Churchill. Or six minutes past four, which in Dad's mind is 1606, the year Shakespeare wrote *Macbeth* and off he'll go on one of his *Macbeth* rants.'

'He sounds very clever.'

'He is. But he drove my mum crazy with it. And the kids at school mocked him. Can you imagine – his own pupils bullied him? In the end, he lost his job and then my mum had to kick him out because she couldn't stand him messing about all day, so I kind of lost him. Although when he remembers to take his tablets, he stays pretty level. I haven't seen him in ages because he lives with my Uncle Iain, who is his half-brother. Uncle Iain owns a rubbish hotel north of here and he lets my dad work for him as a janitor. Dad mostly likes it there. He gets his own room for free.'

'So he's lost, but not really,' suggests Lisa. 'At least you know

174

where he is.'

'Yes, when he's not off trekking all over Britain on one of his bonkers' missions. I don't know where he goes and Mum pretends not to worry about him but really she frets all the time. She misses him – she misses the Hugo she married, but she can't possibly have him back to live with her. Uncle Iain keeps her informed when he can be bothered.'

The bluebottle buzzes round Lisa's head. She swipes at it, surprised when she bats it to the floor. The girls watch it recover as it crawls, stunned, over the carpet.

'So who have you lost, Lisa?'

Lisa inhales deeply and, as her breath is released, she feels the warmth of it over the backs of her clasped hands. Finally she says, 'I lost my baby but if they find him they'll take him away again.'

'You've got a baby? Was it the social? Did they take it?' says Callie. Like a little owl, Lisa has lowered her head further behind her knees until only the top of her hood is showing. Callie wants so much to believe her but Lisa is not the same girl from the party. She's some confused kid inhabiting a freezing flat, who clings to windows and spouts rubbish. Nevertheless, Callie reaches out to her. 'If you lost your baby, maybe I can help you find it.'

Callie offers impossible salvation. It is in her nature to give hope, to be gentle. Callie heaves herself up. She places both her hands on Lisa's head, pushing back the hood and stroking Lisa's hair.

Lisa sighs deeply. She'll trust anyone who shows a shred of kindness, from the immature Gareth to the manipulative Paul. And right now she trusts Callie, the newest person in her life.

Into her hands I place my spirit.

Lisa 5 and Callie 1
Fixing a Smile

Callie returns some hours later, laden with shopping. From the mattress, Lisa observes dully, like a patient watching a nurse or carer go about their usual routine. Callie hums nervously as she stocks a couple of shelves with baked beans and tomato soup, bread rolls and pasta, apples and bananas; the fridge she fills with milk and orange juice, eggs and cheese. She makes cups of tea and the girls hug their mugs in front of a rickety electric fan heater.

'One day I'll pay you back,' whispers Lisa, shielding a silent scream. She is tumbling through the universe. A part of her has been sucked into a black-hole – but which one? There are so many dark places . . .

'There *is* something you can do for me.' Callie is bright, her eyes shining. 'Lisa? Are you all right, Lisa?'

Lisa blinks: scanning black-holes must wait. 'Yes, yes of course. But I doubt . . .'

'A very strange thing's happened, but it's really, really amazing. Please hear me out because I think it will do us both good.'

Lisa sips her tea. She stares at Callie. When she speaks her voice is flat and slow. 'Good? Something good happened?'

'Yes. When I left you earlier, I was out shopping and can you believe it? Dad phoned. My actual dad for crying out loud! He's called twice in two days!'

'I thought you'd lost him.'

'Yes, but not literally as in a police case. I lost him as a father. He forgot how to be a real dad. Anyway, I didn't tell you before because, well, it didn't concern you, but yesterday Dad phoned me out of the blue, said he'd come into some money and he wanted to pay for me and Jason to go by train to Cornwall to stay in a posh hotel. I had to sort out the tickets myself but he absolutely promised he'd pay me back in cash, because he doesn't trust banks or computers. Dad lives totally in the "now", so, and here's the thing – the tickets are for *tomorrow*, because apparently he's in Cornwall right this minute. And even more amazing – he'd love to spend some time with me.

'I had to decide really fast and I couldn't resist, because he's my father after all. I've booked two returns which cost an absolute packet but Dad swears blind he has the money to pay for it all. He's got a job so I'm pretty sure he can afford it. I did check the internet to make sure the hotel is for real, because you never know with Dad – and it's true. I phoned them, and Dad's booked me and Jason in under his surname, Quin. Typical! Then I phoned Jason to ask him to come with me but his work isn't flexible and even though he's owed loads of holiday, he can't drop everything just like that. I was dead upset because this is my actual dad after all, and I haven't seen him in absolutely ages. Anyway, I had this idea. I phoned Jason again and said, "As you can't get the time off, would you mind if I went with a girl I met at Sam's do? She's so lovely. You'd like her." That's you, obviously. And he was totally happy because he goes on and on at me to make new friends.'

Lisa hugs the blanket tighter. 'I don't think I could go that far away. You see, I feel . . .'

'I know. It's a big deal. But maybe if you had a break – think of all the food, the comfy beds. Oh, you've got to get out of this dump, Lisa. You haven't told me everything and I'm not asking you to, and I know I can't really do anything to help – like I can't find your baby – but I need to see my dad. Make sure he's okay. And if you come with me, you can relax a bit. Then, when we get back, I promise I'll do everything possible to get you the help you need.'

'I don't know . . .'

'Whatever you decide – it's up to you, but I absolutely have to go. Sam might come with me if you don't, but honestly I'd rather it was you. Imagine all that sea, walks on the beach . . .'

'I haven't got a swimming costume.'

'You can borrow one of mine. We won't be sunning ourselves on any beaches, but the hotel pool looks amazing and the whole place is totally gorgeous. Palm trees and everything. Please say you'll come.'

'I haven't got a proper bag.'

'You haven't got a lot of things but I can sort all that out. Sam will drop us at the station really early tomorrow morning. We'll be there mid-afternoon. We do the last bit by coach, so we'll be able to talk and sleep and see the views and…'

'All right,' Lisa sighs. *What difference does it make, to be here or there, near or far, with or without a person?*

'I know it's miles away, but Dad's never done anything like this before. For the first time I think he's seeing his little girl as a grown-up. He may have lost it *upstairs*, if you know what I mean, but at least he lost it in a really, really good way. And I'd love for you to meet him.'

'Okay. But please don't tell Sam about me. I mean, don't mention all this. Don't say anything about the baby. Promise me, please.'

Callie jumps up and hugs Lisa. 'It's going to be so great! Give me your washing – whatever needs doing. I'll put it through Sam's washer and bung it in the drier. You can bring some of the food I got you. Make sandwiches maybe? And I'll bring the rest. Wear warm stuff. I bet it's pretty cold by the seaside at this time of year.' Callie fusses round the room tidying and collecting and chattering, while Lisa rocks and hugs herself.

Sunday morning, and the carriage is half full, even at this early hour. The fields fly by in strings of muted colours, punctuated by trees and pylons that loom up through a foamy mist. Lisa leans her forehead against the grubby window and allows the chill of the glass to calm her. She's left a few bits and pieces in the flat, and all that food. What if the owner suddenly checks in and finds them? Callie, who hardly slept a wink last night, is out for the count, curled tight as a dormouse, opposite Lisa.

Jason had driven the girls to the station. Yesterday, Callie had expressed such tangible love for her husband that when Lisa met him, she'd felt vaguely disappointed. She'd imagined someone less ordinary somehow, more Brad Pitt and less Declan Donnelly but, then again, he did have an incredible, melting smile, a strong handshake and cheery hello, even before the crack of dawn.

Terraced houses stream by, their windows mostly netted or closed-curtained, but every so often a light is on and Lisa catches a brief outline of someone moving behind a pane of glass. *Are they getting up for work or screaming at their kids? Eating muesli or dragging on a cigarette? Is life worth dressing for behind any of those walls?* Then there are streets and cars and buses and bridges and a wide river and more fields, and the watery sun is rising on a world that is not Lisa's.

'You want to know what it is? A boy. What is your PIN? The code for the bank? Shut up or they'll hear you.'

'They?'

'Tell the truth or I'll be back.' The shadows of the man wobble against the white tiles. How easily he lifts me and places me onto the mattress. He covers me with the sleeping bag and places the baby against me. My eyes are shut. I hear a tap running, the kettle boiling. The man is cleaning and washing. He washes my feet and my legs and then he dries them. So kind. So gentle.

The train stops at Bristol Temple Meads. Callie pours coffee from a flask into tiny plastic cups. 'I don't know if you take milk and sugar but I put it in anyway. You should build up your strength.'

Lisa sips the coffee and it is good. Callie hands her a Belgian bun. The girls look directly into each other's eyes and quietly find a smile within the other. *We can do this thing.*

They disembark at Exeter St. David's. Someone points out the Country Services' bus stop, where they hang about for half an hour. Callie laughs: 'We must look like a couple of hippies with our canvas bags and scruffy, long hair,' although she's never seen a real hippy.

Lisa adds, 'All we need now are some coloured beads and flowers in our ponytails.'

Callie pays the driver and he tells her not to worry, he'll shout when it's their stop. The girls sit up front, to the left of the driver. As the coach twists through the ever-narrowing lanes the two girls chat like long-lost sisters, covering every subject from school dinners to ex-boyfriends, spiritual beliefs to embarrassing parents.

'Oh my goodness, there's the sea!' gasps Callie, as they tip over the brow of a steep hill.

Lisa cranes her neck. She wonders if she'll ever build a sandcastle in the sunshine surrounded by her own real family.

'Your destination, young ladies,' calls the driver.

They are the first of the passengers to jump down. Callie immediately scans the street for signs of her father. As they'd approached Bude she'd sent Hugo several texts but without a reply. She didn't want to alarm Lisa with the possibility that Hugo might have had one of his funny turns and taken it upon himself to hitch-hike to Land's End or the Outer Hebrides. And if he hasn't paid in advance for their hotel, they could well be stranded.

'Oh look, there's a Nat West,' says Lisa, although her card has been stolen and she has with her an abundance of cash that Callie is ignorant about.

'We may need a bank if Dad doesn't materialise,' mutters Callie, turning on a spot where four quiet roads meet in a broad, grey area of tarmac, a roundabout of sorts. She presses her mobile against her ear. 'If he doesn't answer soon we'll have to find somewhere for a brew. It's going to rain.'

Steel clouds cloak the town. Lisa wants to believe in Callie's dad even more than Callie does. The warmth of a friendly benefactor, a parental hug, an unconditional smile . . . She hangs over a low rail that runs along a wall the length of the street, and stares into the slow, green water of the Bude Canal. Once more she clasps a hand over her stomach thinking how flat it used to be and how wobbly it has become. *What's the point of a perfect figure if there is no life within it?*

'There he is!' yells Callie, and she drops her bag onto the pavement and runs down the street towards Hugo. Some metres away, Lisa sees a greying man in a shapeless jacket and baggy cords shuffling towards them. On his head is a fleece-edged deer-stalker hat with flaps over his ears. The street is almost deserted, but when Hugo hears Callie he raises both hands high, as if hoping to be spotted in a crowd. Callie runs at her father, flinging her arms around him and he lifts her so that her feet flick backwards.

Lisa's hand flies to her mouth. *What about my daddy? Where's my baby?* She busies herself, fishing in her shoulder bag searching for something and nothing. Eventually she finds a tissue with which she wipes her eyes and blows her nose, then she fixes a smile for the sake of her new friend.

Lisa 6, Hugo 5, Callie 2
The Starcliff Hotel

True to Hugo's word, the Starcliff Hotel is luxurious without being unbearably posh. A guest could relax in jeans and T-shirt, or pad over to the hydrotherapy centre enveloped in the white towelling dressing-gown and slippers provided. Hugo may be a man of confusion but one thing Callie's mother often repeated, 'Your dad is, and always will be, a man of utmost integrity and us girls must always respect him for that.' Even so, Callie is anxious to ask Hugo about the expenses, but not right this minute while he is basking in his own magnanimity.

'I'll see you to your room which, when you told me Jason couldn't come, I got them to change from a double to a twin. Top floor. You have the very best view.'

Behind Hugo's back, Callie and Lisa exchange surprised glances. They take the lift. Hugo continues talking as if he runs the place, which is infinitely superior to Iain's northern establishment. Iain had promised their late father that he'd keep an eye out for Hugo but there's no love lost between them and Iain is relieved when Hugo disappears on his random travels from time to time.

'I suggest a cup of tea and a shower and maybe a nap if madam so desires.' Hugo winks at Callie. 'Then you must feel free to enjoy the facilities, all food included, but please resist the extortionate mini-bar. Purchase your junk food at the Spar down the bottom of the hill on the left.' Hugo demonstrates how to swipe the key-cards. He oversees Callie as she tries hers out. The door opens so he bows, sweeping his arm majestically low as both girls enter the room, giggling.

'So glad you could come, Lisa, my dear,' Hugo says. 'Any friend of Callie's is a friend of mine. Now, you'll need an hour to recover before checking out the splendid facilities.'

Callie hesitates. Hugo is standing to attention in the doorway. She longs to hug him again. Instead she says, 'Which room number is yours?'

'Fiddle! Didn't I tell you? I'm not staying here. I'm already booked into a most marvellous B&B down the way. Don't look so disappointed. My choice. You know me – *je préfère*. Anyway, I have already tasted the delights of the sauna herein and eaten a sumptuous meal downstairs with my colleague, Duncan.'

'You've got a colleague?' Callie raises her eyebrows, one higher than the other, in disbelief.

'There are so many, many things you don't yet know about your dear old dad, but enough of me. We waste precious time. I'll be off. Keep that thing charged – it won't do to lose touch.' Hugo offers a mock salute. Then he clicks his tongue. 'Idea! I'll return to eat here tonight with you and we can gossip away – that is, if Lisa doesn't mind associating with a rheumatic geriatric from the Adriatic. Strike that last bit. Enjoyed the rhyme.'

'Dad, you're not old!' Callie laughs, pushing him gently on his arm. Hugo backs out of the room and as the door closes Callie places the palm of her hand against it and smiles.

'You're so lucky,' says Lisa, kicking her trainers under the bed. 'He's a real sweetie!'

'I am and he is. But he's up to something.'

'Well, how was the hydrotherapy?' asks Hugo as they order a meal in the restaurant.

'I could hardly prise Lisa out of the Jacuzzi. She didn't want a sauna but I had one. Jason would have loved it. I phoned him and he sends his love and says thanks. We can't afford a holiday so he feels a bit guilty he can't treat me because we're saving like crazy for our own place. It is virtually impossible to get a deposit together, but hopefully next year . . .'

'Thanks very much for all this, Mr Quin.' Lisa charms Hugo with her polite acceptance of him.

'Go on, spill the beans, Dad,' Callie smiles. 'What's your game? How did you put all this together?'

'Beans, beans, they're good for your . . . Oh, you mean tell you all about my adventures? You'd never believe me if I told you the truth. But here goes. You see, I hadn't had a break since I hitched to Scotland ages ago, so I got this incredible urge to head in the opposite direction. I'd been north, now I've gone south.'

Lisa nods politely but she's thinking how full she feels and she's hardly touched her food.

'I was hitching, like I do, but this driver got sick of me and chucked me out in the car park of a Premier Inn. The one on the M5 near Bristol, you know.'

'No, I don't know it,' says Callie.

'That was when I found some car keys on the gravel. You know what I'm like, Callie; I had a little *thunk*. Methought, "There's no point handing these in without first doing a little research," so I pressed the remote and hey presto!'

'You vanished in a puff of smoke!' Lisa laughs, surprising herself with her own happiness.

'Not exactly, but I did let my genie out of a bottle, so to speak.' Hugo winks at Lisa. Minus his hat he appears younger, more presentable. A haircut would help, possibly. Lisa stares at the ragged holes in the elbows of his green pullover. Hugo isn't the least bit self-conscious about holes or messy hair, or anything else for that matter.

He gesticulates dramatically as he relates how he found the keys and how they'd unlocked a van, and how he'd waited for the owner to appear. He describes Duncan as 'a charming young man, very appreciative of Hugo's thoughtfulness', and how

Duncan had insisted on rewarding him by paying for a room. The girls are wide-eyed, obviously enjoying every embellishment, hanging on every word, so Hugo continues with his version of events, minus the baby because, as a man of integrity, Hugo couldn't possibly let Duncan down on that matter.
'Can't you sleep, Lisa?'

'I don't think I want to. The bed is too comfortable. If I sleep I'll miss out on the feeling of all this luxury.'

'When we get home, let's try to find you a brand new bed. There's a charity furniture store somewhere – that's if you want. I know it's late, but do you mind if I open the curtains for a few minutes? I'm wondering if we can see the sea by moonlight.' Callie moves to the large sash window and stands on tiptoes, not because the window is high but for the joy of it all. 'Come on over here!' she whispers. 'The moon is huge and white. He's smiling down on us. Look at his eyes and his cheesy grin.'

Lisa wraps herself in the duvet and shuffles across the carpet. The girls stand side by side, in awe of the moonlight sparkling on the sea, rippling up and down the beach, elongated elfin fingers tinkling on piano keys.

'Where do seagulls go at night?' says Callie.

'That sounds like the start of a joke, like why do birds fly south?'

'It must be tough for a bird to be out in all that vastness at night when it is stormy or freezing.'

'A few weeks ago, I was out all night in a storm,' says Lisa. 'At first it was scary, with lightning flashing across the hills. It was so hot I took my hoodie off and stood in my T-shirt. At first there wasn't any rain. The thunder rolled. Dogs began to bark, one nearby, then one far away. Soon I could hear loads of dogs. Animals hate storms.'

'Maybe they thought the great pit bull in the sky was out to get them! Were you all right?'

'I climbed over a fence into someone's garden to see if their shed was open, but I found something better. A side door to their garage was unlocked, so I sneaked in and found a load of blankets they'd used for protecting the floor from paint. I made an amazing bed and fell asleep. The hard floor wakes you very early, which is a good thing because you have to sneak out before anyone finds you. I went back there loads of times and never got caught. The trick is to tidy up really, really well so no one suspects.'

'I'll remember that when Jason kicks me out onto the streets!'

'He'll never do that.'

'How do you know? You only met him for a few minutes this morning.'

'I just know. His voice is soft. Even though he must have been dead tired, he wasn't grumpy. I can't imagine him ever losing it and if he did, I bet he'd say sorry and make up quickly. And I bet he never gets drunk.'

'You're right. His only downside is he comes home stinking

of fish!'

'Callie, look – down there! Can you see someone on the beach? A man just hanging about. What can he be up to at two in the morning?'

'Hard to see in the shadows. He's throwing something into the sea.'

'I think it's pebbles. Look he's picked up another. Maybe he's homeless. Or maybe he's an insomniac.'

'There's no law against being on the beach in the dark, but— Oh Lisa, it's Dad! I told you he was unusual – half the time he lives on another planet. He's probably playing at being King Neptune or something.'

'Do you think we should go and get him?'

'Don't be daft. He can look after himself. Come on, Lisa, let's get back into bed and let's leave the curtains open so we can see the clouds racing. They make the moon look like it's moving somewhere yet getting nowhere.'

'Please won't you phone your dad first? I'll never sleep for worrying about him.' Lisa watches Hugo throw another pebble.

Callie rolls her eyes. 'All right, just for you – but he'd never worry about me like that. However nice he's been to us today, it is virtually impossible for him to worry about other people. Mum says he can't empathise.' She picks up her mobile. Far below, the tiny figure of Hugo is patting himself down, feeling each pocket until he locates his mobile in his jacket.

'Callie, are you all right? Is something wrong? What is it?'

'We're fine, Dad. Turn round. Look up at the hotel.'

Lisa says, 'Quick, turn on the light.' Framed in the shining window, they wave. Hugo waves his arms high and then affects a sweeping bow. The girls giggle.

'What are you doing down there, Dad?'

'Living!' shouts Hugo, almost loud enough for them to hear without the mobile.

'Well, that's fine then. Good night. God bless.'

'God bless, my darling Callie!' Hugo stretches out his hands and whirls around and around, a child on a roundabout, until a cloud shrouds the moon and Hugo vanishes.

Callie sleeps easily. Lisa clutches her pillow. She senses the scent of her newborn. *He had hair, dark hair, and cold feet.* 'I never saw your face,' she whispers under her breath. 'Let me see your face. Where are you in the world?'

Duncan 10
The Sands Inn

Duncan books into the unremarkable Sands Inn, after two days of general relaxation, sight-seeing, loitering on beaches, reading in cafés and putting off his return 'up North' to his family, his irritating neighbours, his drums without a band and continued redundancy. He hasn't the foggiest how to move forward, what he wants out of life, where to go, or how to achieve anything worthwhile. After all, what can be done when so many extraordinary youngsters can compete for the top jobs in IT, and with middle management an increasingly precarious position?

'Pick a room. No other guests allowed in with you,' the landlord speaks sharply. 'The shower in room 6 is bust. Otherwise they're much of a muchness.'

Duncan turns in early and, following an unremarkable conversation with his wife, he falls asleep. Two hours later Toby wakes for a feed. Duncan sits upright. He plants both feet on the floor, yet he can hear no crying. In panic, Duncan checks the holdall.

'Toby? Where are you?' He rummages through his clothes like a madman, flinging them across the carpet until his mind wakes with a terrifying rush to remind him that Toby has gone. The holdall is empty except for a tiny soiled vest, folded into a side pocket. Duncan stares at the grubby garment with a confused expression. *How did I lose my boy?* He presses the vest against his cheek and closes his eyes. It had had to be done. It was a double mercy: for the young mother who couldn't cope and the older woman desperate for a child. Duncan has to move. To do something physical. He splashes cold water over his face, pulls on a pair of jeans and a sweatshirt and heads downstairs to find the bar which he presumes will be empty at this late hour.

'Come in, mate!' beckons a jovial man with dark, curly sideburns bubbling over his flushed cheeks. 'Can't sleep? What will it be? Sit with us. Introductions! This is Mike the Pike. This here is Lanks – don't mind him! He's tipsy. I said, "You're tiddly, Lanky!" And here you 'ave Pete Pascoe, genius creator of genuine pasties, which he flogs across the border.'

'France?' Duncan asks and all the men laugh.

'Devon. The Cornish border is the Tamar. Spot the emmet,' says Mike the Pike and for some unfathomable reason this is hilarious to all the men. 'Where you from then?'

'North.'

'North?'

'That's what I said.'

'What's your business in Bude?'

'House-hunting. Thinking of moving my family here. Leaving the rat race.'

'Fat chance. There's no jobs in Cornwall.'

'Right.' Duncan can't think of an excuse to leave, so he perches on a wobbly stool beside the inglenook fire-place. He accepts a half pint of lager from Pink Cheeks and sips it, with all eyes upon him. He sips again and wishes they'd stop staring at him.

'Yours the white van, is it?' Pete Pascoe, one eyebrow raised like Elvis, a friendly sort.

'Er, yes.'

'If you're looking to sell it, I've been looking for a set of wheels like that.'

'Not at this time.' Duncan fakes a relaxed pose. Another sip of his drink.

'What's your line of work?'

'IT.' He'll make them pull teeth. They'll soon get fed up and shut up.

'He means computers, Lanks,' explains Pink Cheeks.

Lanks raises his eyebrows.

'You been seen about,' says Mike the Pike.

Duncan raises his chin. Sips his drink.

'My boy says he saw a man of your description up Widemouth Bay. "New guy hanging about laybys," he tells me. "Shifty type," he says.' All the men guffaw like it is one big joke.

Duncan smiles, uncertain how seriously to take this. *Don't defend yourself.*

Pink Cheeks raises his glass as if to toast his mate's speech. Mike the Pike continues, 'My lad Philip, the one what saw you, he swore you was feedin' a baby, so I says to him, "A bloke by himself in a van, feeding a baby? In November?" So my lad tells me, "This old geezer got out of his van and took a photo of me with my gang." What's that all about then?'

Duncan clutches his glass with both hands. The story has morphed in the telling but it is true enough. The dim amber light partially conceals the shock on his face.

'So you don't trust outsiders because they're outsiders. That's a strange kind of welcome. Don't you lot depend on tourism? Sounds to me like you're biting the hand that feeds you.'

'Don't mind Mike,' laughs Pink Cheeks. 'He's always got too much to say after a few. You should ask him why *he's* here, at this time of night, gabbing on with no home to go to.'

'Why?' starts Duncan, any excuse to divert the attention from himself.

'His wife got herself a toy boy!' More raucous laughter.

Duncan stands, exaggerates a yawn and says the first thing that comes into his head. 'I'll be heading on up now. Nice meeting you.'

He makes it to the door before Mike calls after him, 'I'm not called The Pike for nothing. Very long nose. Sharp teeth. You don't fool me. You want to know what my boy really told me? He said, "That bloke is bent."'

Duncan checks out of the Sands Inn before breakfast. He settles up with the landlady, who lights a cigarette while apologising in case her boozing husband and his cronies disturbed his sleep last night. Duncan wonders which of the four men belongs to this weather-beaten woman. Most likely Lanks, judging by his age and appearance, but then again, Pink Cheeks had been the one acting more like a landlord, inviting him to join in and offering a drink. Outside, Duncan notices the rusting sign hanging heavy above him. 'Sands Inn' it reads; a flaking blue inscription beneath a painted hour-glass, through which the sands of time run.

Duncan heads to the beach café where he and Hugo had eaten. A gangling kid wrinkles his forehead at Duncan in silent question: *What d' you want?*

'Sandwich,' Duncan interprets. 'Bacon.' He chooses a corner table, away from the window. It is far too early to phone Monika and there's nothing to do except hang around. The temptation to chase up some of those Cornish youths for a share in their zest and soul has dissipated. After years of living in Lancaster, where hardly anyone knew his business, he is already recognisable within some unwelcome spotlight in Bude.

Those drinking guys had unnerved him. On the plus side, there are no missing babies on the news, no Monika screaming down the phone rejecting Toby, and no flashing blue lights or shameful handcuffs. Matters could be far worse. *That reminds me, after today, the SIM card Monika uses to contact me must be destroyed.*

Eight twenty. Duncan's Blackberry rings so it can't be Monika. It certainly won't be Julia at this time of the morning; she'll be sorting the girls for school. Hopefully it isn't Hugo. Nope. Hugo is behaving because his daughter is with him. He'll have moved on.

The phone screen confirms it is his wife. *What now?*

'Daddy, Daddy, Mummy said we could talk to you before school because we got absolutely ready extra fast.' Sophie sounds so mature. 'Can we Skype you, Daddy? Please can we? Only for one teensy minute.'

'Hello, sweetheart,' he says, stuffing bacon down his throat.

'You sound like a funny bunny,' she giggles.

'Eating breffatht,' he says, hamming it up, playing for time. He swigs his coffee and pulls a face. *Skype?* He scrapes back his chair. *Gotta look like I'm in a swanky conference centre. The Starcliff Hotel is less than a minute away.*

'Skype Daddy,' chants Meg. 'Skype Daddy! Skype Daddy!'

'Okay, okay. Tell you what – put me on to Mummy and we'll sort it out for you in a couple of ticks.'

'Hi, darling!' Julia yells. She is flying about in the background, jangling her car keys, checking her hair.

'Time to Skype?' bluffs Duncan, hoping Julia will be too flustered to agree.

'Of course. We decided it would be a lovely treat, didn't we, girls? Before you head off for any seminars or whatever your timetable is. Missing you loads, darling.'

'Give me two ticks to find a better signal and I'll call you. Ciao!' Duncan hangs up, rushes out to his van and, grinding the gears, he accelerates up the hill to the Starcliff Hotel. In the forecourt he slams on the brakes then jumps into the back of his vehicle, where he wriggles into his white shirt, grabs a tie and jacket and races into the hotel foyer, eyes darting this way and that searching for a large room, suitable for conferences.

He dashes into the men's toilet to tie his tie and flatten his hair, then rushes out past the receptionist who glares at him. He stops in his tracks, charm and calm personified, nodding and smiling disarmingly. 'Sorry, won't be long. Important business call. Can I take it in there? Thanks. I'll be booking in with you in a jiffy. You're a star, love.'

He winks. Instantly he is reminded of his late grandmother quoting: *He that winks with the eye deceives with the heart.* Duncan brushes aside the memory and opens his iPad. He manoeuvres himself in front of an impressive, outsized artwork in an ornate gilt frame; oily lumps of wild sea crashing over jagged cliffs, sliced through with sharp-winged, red-beaked gulls.

'My three beautiful girls together!' Duncan grins as their heads fill his screen. He holds his iPad at arm's length, so Julia can see his shirt – all set for work – but not his fading jeans or scruffy trainers.

'Never smile like a crocodile!' Meg sings and Duncan gnashes his teeth broadly. Snap, snap! He blows his wife a kiss. He spins around the room. *This is where it's all happening. This is where Daddy is working. As you can see, this is a stunning room with a stunning view. Incredible painting. Huge mirror. Furniture to die for. Sorry got to go. Byeeeee. Byeeee. Love you. See you. Speak later. Kiss*

kiss. And they've gone.

The relief is palpable. The room smells so clean and the sofa so tempting . . . only for a few minutes. Why would anyone care if he sprawls over those cushions? As he drifts off, Duncan is soothed by the guests clattering cutlery and murmuring their good mornings in the adjoining breakfast room.

'Push it open for me!' Callie laughs, anticipating a fun day ahead. She is carrying two coffees from the breakfast room. Lisa leans against the huge oak door which leads into the sumptuous lounge but her muscles are still weak from the birth and it takes effort. Callie heads straight for the huge bow window and deposits the mugs onto a marble-topped table.

'That view is absolutely magnificent,' she says, turning to Lisa. But Lisa is not beside her. She is standing motionless beneath a monstrous chandelier in the centre of the room.

'What's wrong? Lisa, what's wrong? You're white as a sheet. Come here. Hey, come on!' Callie guides Lisa to one of the huge armchairs and helps her sit but Lisa's eyes are staring straight ahead. She sits bolt upright, leaning forward, gripping both arms of the chair.

'Lisa, do you need a doctor? Stay here. I'm going to find the receptionist to get a phone number . . .'

'No! Don't leave me,' Lisa tries to cry out, but her voice rasps weakly.

Callie kneels on the floor beside her. 'At least let me get you a drink of water. Sweet tea —'

'Don't go. Look.' With her eyes, Lisa guides Callie to where a man is snoring, stretched out on one of the sofas.

Callie shrugs – she'd ignored him when they'd come in. 'Lisa, he's just some bloke sleeping. Probably hungover.'

'He's the one,' Lisa shivers.

Callie swivels on her knees until her body blocks the view of the man. 'You know him?'

'No, but . . .'

'So let's get out of here if you don't like the look of him.'

'I can't. I need to talk to him.' The man's eyes flicker. With a snort, he turns over and away, tucking his knees up against the sofa back. The jacket that had covered his shoulders slides onto the carpet.

Callie lowers her voice to a harsh whisper. 'But I don't understand. You've never even been here before. It's a hallucination, some kind of breakdown. I know what that's like 'cos my dad sees things, says things. But it's not real, Lisa, trust me. It can be all in the mind.'

'Those laces,' she says, as if they are vipers about to strike.

'His shoelaces?' Callie stands up. She pulls Lisa to her feet and Lisa responds robotically. 'Forget beauty treatments – let's get you some proper help.'

Without warning Lisa leaps forwards, blazing towards the man, landing on his back like a wild cat, scratching and hitting, shaking and biting. Callie gasps. The man wakes and yells. He shoves Lisa hard onto the carpet. The receptionist flies into the room, followed by several guests, in time to see the man roll off the sofa and onto Lisa, then pinning both her arms to the floor beneath his knees. Lisa arches her back like she's possessed, kicking her feet against the air. She snarls through her teeth as she lashes her head from side to side. Duncan raises one fist as far back as possible, his elbow crooked towards the crystal chandelier.

'Stop it! Stop!' shouts Callie, throwing herself against the man. He looks up, shocked to see a second girl.

'What're you doing to my friend?' Callie screams as Duncan pushes her away with his shoulder.

Lisa writhes but whatever strength she'd summoned is fast fading. The man lowers his fist, but with his other hand he grips one of Lisa's wrists. A crowd is gathering. Two men dither nearby, unsure how best to intervene. Duncan sits back, his knees pressed onto Lisa's arms. Lisa stops fighting. She is sobbing, 'My baby. My baby. My baby!'

'She attacked me.' Duncan attempts to appear calm and sane before a gathering audience. To the receptionist he adds, 'Is she one of your guests?' but the receptionist is busy reassuring the crowd that she's phoning the police this instant.

'Call them if you think it'll help. It's up to you, but your boss might prefer you to consider the Starcliff's reputation and how a visit from the police may have an adverse effect on business.' Duncan reaches out his hand to a male guest who hauls him up. He stands open-palmed, with genuine total surprise written all over his face. A trickle of blood seeps through the shoulder of his shirt, crimson stark against the white cotton. 'I won't press charges if the young lady apologises. Let's all keep our hair on and there'll be no need to upset a beautiful day by unnecessarily involving authorities. Are you all right now, young lady? Has your little rant alleviated all that feminine stress?'

Callie helps Lisa to sit on the floor with her back against the sofa. Lisa is shaking, fixated on a tiny streak of blood on the carpet. Callie explains to the onlookers that Lisa has been extremely unwell recently and asks, 'Could you please give my friend some space?' The crowd nods sympathetically and disperses, leaving the formidable receptionist wagging her finger at the man with the mismatched outfit.

'I witnessed everything,' she exaggerates, 'and I cannot allow you to book into our hotel if you're going to upset our guests, especially the women. That fight was plainly no fault of yours but, with respect, I ask you to leave immediately and no further action will be taken.'

'No problem.' Duncan smiles, all compliance and humility. 'Maybe I'll book into the Sands Inn. It's not quite up to the standards of the Starcliff, but needs must. Anything to help out a lady.' He trails after the chattering guests, who are clogging up the doorway.

Duncan hadn't recognised her but his attacker was beyond doubt the Rimmer girl, mother of Toby Nowik, although it is hard to imagine how this miserable squatter could have trailed him all the way to Cornwall so quickly. Inconceivable that she'd hired a private detective – but how else?

On his way out, Duncan is desperate not to shove anyone for fear of aggravating the knot of people in his way. Some turn to meet his eye, an offer of sympathy. Duncan communicates agreement, pushing his lips together, gently nodding, then shaking his head, tutting as if he can't understand what happened back there. And that much is true.

She must have hired someone. Aggressive or what? Unreasonable force. I had my back to her. I was sleeping. If they check the CCTV they'll see me Skyping my beautiful family, then taking an innocent nap when in walk two complete strangers and – the camera doesn't lie.

'I smell you,' Lisa hisses from across the room. The voice is unmistakeable.

The hairs on the back of Duncan's neck prickle but he stiffens, refusing to be drawn. He must not turn or reveal the slightest sign of recognition, although the crowd are reluctant to disperse and their slowness is suffocating. 'Excuse me,' Duncan coughs, and nudges then pushes to get out.

Again Lisa's voice cuts the room, chillingly low and controlled. 'You stole my baby! What did you do with him? Murderer! You killed my baby!' Callie is stroking Lisa's arm and shushing, calm, calm. She looks at Lisa's mascara-streaked face, war-paint daubed across her blotchy skin, and it occurs to her she fell for this friendship too soon.

Duncan is not wearing his jacket. In the scrum he hadn't noticed Lisa hastily stuffing it behind her, against the sofa. He apologises profusely to the receptionist; 'I trust you'll record the true facts of these events. I'm only sorry that I failed to book on arrival because then you'd have treated me as an innocent guest. As it is, I'll make myself scarce.'

The receptionist is flustered, charmed by Duncan's dishevelled magnanimity. She'd choose him over those dreadful girls any day. Nevertheless, she has to keep the guests sweet and the man is right: the Starcliff can't afford negative reviews.

'I suppose I ought to thank you for your co-operation but we must prioritise our customers. I won't involve the authorities on this occasion because, as you said, we have our reputation to uphold. Overreaction could lead to negative press. We'll see how things go with those girls, but if they continue to be trouble, we'll have no choice but to—' The woman looks up. She stops her spiel because Duncan has already left the building.

The moment the lounge door closes, Lisa grabs Duncan's jacket and jumps up. 'There's another way out of here. Quick, come with me before he realises!' Taken aback by Lisa's energetic recovery, Callie follows her through a door in the far corner that leads directly into the breakfast room. Late risers are ordering coffee and bagels and ignore the girls as they cut a path between tables then go out into a corridor on the other side.

Lisa spots the Ladies' and goes into the room. As soon as they are alone, she rifles through Duncan's jacket pockets, finding a comb and a pound coin.

'That's stealing. Please don't do this, Lisa. We have to return it. The poor man was only . . .'

'He is not a poor man. He stole my baby.' Lisa places his wallet and mobile by the sink. 'And he'll want these any minute.' She tosses a bunch of keys at Callie. 'Hurry up and don't look so worried, I won't keep anything that's not mine.' Lisa extracts a bank card from the wallet. 'Bingo, a name! He's a Mr D. Wilde. Wilde with an e. Come on. Let's find some way round to the front of the building and get his number plate before he scoots off. Then we'll go to reception and hand in this stuff in, saying we found it.'

'But your baby,' starts Callie, thinking *if there ever was a baby*, 'was taken in Lancaster. We're hundreds of miles away. It's not possible.'

But Lisa is on a mission. She marches down the corridor looking for an exit, with Callie scurrying behind. Lisa runs around the side of the building and out onto the front car park. She presses the remote central lock on the key fob but, as other guests are departing, she can't figure out which vehicle is responding.

'My guess is that red Mazda,' Lisa declares. 'Memorise the plate.'

'Excuse me, dear, but was it you that was assaulted in the

hotel? Everyone's talking about it.' An older woman in an immaculate trouser-suit approaches Lisa as her husband heaves luggage into the boot of their Audi. 'Are you all right? You must be so shocked! You should press charges. Get him arrested. If you were my daughter I'd take you straight to the police station to report him.'

Callie points. 'There he is! Coming down the steps! Please be careful, Lisa.'

Lisa reacts without panic, turning to the older woman with her most appealing doe-eyed look. 'He left his jacket. We wanted to return it but I feel a bit scared of him . . . would you?'

The woman isn't too sure. 'Let me,' says her husband as he slams the boot of his car. 'You stay right here with Lilian, young lady.' The husband takes the jacket and marches over to Duncan, appearing to offer it to him but, as Duncan reaches out, the man pushes against him, chest to chest. They are the same height but something about the older man lends him greater stature and he speaks with smooth military authority; 'I don't know who you think you are but I hope for your sake you never meet me when there are no ladies present. I strongly suggest that you leave town, crawl back into your hovel and never show your face here again.'

Snatching his jacket, Duncan pulls away and stumbles to his van. The girls recite the number plate until the woman lends Lisa a biro to scribble the information on the palm of her hand.

'Thanks,' says Lisa mutely, wishing the gentleman hadn't been quite so firm because now her enemy is skidding furiously out of the car park, leaving deep tyre grooves in the gravel.

So her intruder was no angel, nor was he her saviour; he was merely an ordinary being who smells of sweet wax. A man who knows where her son is.

Hugo 6
Sweet Wax?

Hugo stands alone on the edge of a seawater swimming pool, a huge area of enclosed water carved into the rocks at one side of Summerleaze Beach. The tide is high and the steel-grey North Atlantic water washes over the concrete surround, topping up the pool.

What a great place to grow up, Hugo muses. *Sun, surf and sandcastles, but not today.* He buttons up his collar against the chill of the light mist that drifts in from the sea. *What to do? Choices, choices. I could nip into the café for a coffee, if it's open. Or I could ring Monika and hitch over to say goodbye to Toby, then try to find Duncan, or else I could hitch home to Lancaster. But I won't bother Callie. I promised myself I wouldn't hassle her. Can't risk embarrassing my girl in front of her friend. Nice to be able to give her that little holiday though. And wonderful how she agreed to travel all that way at such short notice.*

Hugo smiles to himself as he shuffles off up the rickety-railed path that winds to the cliff top. Thin wisps of greying hair poke out from beneath the lining of his hat and stick to his forehead. Hanging from his neck is his prized pair of lime-green plastic binoculars that had cost him two quid in a charity shop a few years back. Hugo counts twenty steps before pausing to peer through the binoculars, adjusting them to sharpen his image of the bleak, uninteresting view. Any excuse to pause to catch a breath. Another twenty steps; another examination. Repeat.

Hugo relishes the changing scenery, the diminishing pool and the fuzzy horizon. *It's like a sponge painting, all blotchy and delicious. I remember when Callie was little, doing potato printing. Ah, those repeat patterns. I loved how the poster paint reduced in thickness from the first print to the last until we could only produce a mere ghost of the original design. We tried finger-printing too – delightful!*

Hugo presses his outstretched hand against the damp rock, imagining that each print of his fingers is a different colour, red, yellow, green, blue, orange, and each is gifted with a naïve expression: smile, frown, sulk, surprise, boredom. Finally, he gives each one a name so young Callie can remember her vowels: Ann, Eve, Ivy, bOb, Una.

Dot dot dot dassshhh. Dot dot dot dassshhh. Hugo's phone rings and alerts him to the presence of a material world. He unzips his jacket and pats himself down until he finds it.

'Hugo Quin,' he announces. Very few people phone Hugo.

'Dad, it's me! You should look at the number on the screen. It tells you it's me.'

'Not wearing my glasses.'

'Where are you?'

'On a cliff side, overlooking the most wonderful outdoor swimming pool. Shame it's so bitter – I'd be tempted for a swim.'

'Dad, it's November, for crying out loud.'

'I've been reading a notice explaining all about how the locals are fundraising to save the pool. Otherwise the council will close it. Imagine how awful—'

'Dad, shush a minute. Can you get yourself up here, please? I desperately need your help.'

'Your voice is all wibbly-wobbly. Is something my fault?'

'Of course it's not your fault, Dad. Not everything is about you. Listen to me. It's Lisa – she's hallucinating. I think she's cracking up. Earlier on she attacked a complete stranger for no reason. She flew at him. I think I'm going to have to take her straight back home. At first I really did like her, but it's no fun being here if we can't have a laugh and chill down. She doesn't even want to use the spa now. Please Dad, come with us on the train.' Callie begins sobbing.

'But sweetie, that's outside my plans. You understand it is imperative I visit young Toby one last time, to say goodbye.'

'Oh, forget Toby whoever he is. I need you. Me, Callie, your own daughter needs you. I don't know anyone here, and Jason is at work so I can't ring him. And Mum's phone is switched off. Is your swimming pool very far away? I could fetch you a taxi.'

Hugo splutters. *The very idea of a taxi for less than a quarter of a mile – honestly Callie.* 'All right, you win, but I'm walking. I'll be with you in ten or fifteen minutes. Then later today I absolutely must go to Monika and Erik's. They're foreign. Rich toffs. A great couple. You'd love them.'

'Please, Dad, say you'll come quickly.' Hugo rarely skips, but his heart races with joy: *Callie needs me.* Whenever he thinks of his little girl he misses her almost as much as he misses her mother. His 'delightful wife, love-of-my-life' Jane had asked him to leave, but he could tell she still loved him. What was it she'd said? *It's one thing playing the fool but quite another being dangerously foolish. I can't do this anymore, Hugo. You'll have to go. I've spoken to your brother and he's agreed to give you a room, as long as you do a bit of work around the hotel. I'll come whenever Callie wants to see you. It's no use begging. You set fire to our bedding! Yes, I know you thought it was the Great Fire of London in 1666. All I said was that the groceries came to £16.66 and it triggered your condition. I can't be so careful about everything I say the whole time. I've tried my best, but it's impossible to live like this. Fire, Hugo. You are too unpredictable. Someone has to think of Callie's safety.*

By the time Hugo arrives at the foot of the wide steps of Starcliff Hotel, he is soaked to the skin. Mist has become driving rain and a fresh wind is biting through his flapping cargo pants. Hugo removes his hat, using it to dab the drips from his face and neck. As he approaches the receptionist, she feigns a smile through gritted teeth. *We are a superior establishment, don't you know?* Hugo bows, mouth open ready to explain his presence, when Callie rushes in and hugs him.

'You again,' mutters the receptionist, pursing her lips and raising her eyebrows.

'Daddy!' cries Callie. She glances at the receptionist and reads her disapproval. 'I'm taking him up for a brew – *if* that's okay with you,' she adds with sarcasm.

'A brew? What do you mean?' says the receptionist. 'Do you mean a cup of—'

'Tea. Black. Two sugars,' says Hugo, cocking his head like a cheeky sparrow.

The receptionist huffs and pretends to type something vital into the computer while the girl drags her father away.

As they take the lift up three floors, Callie gabbles as much information as she can. 'I can't tell you the whole story right now but you've got to talk to Lisa. She's planning something terrible, I know it. Earlier, she saw this man. As I told you on the phone, he was a total stranger. Lisa nearly scratched his eyes out for no reason at all. If we weren't going home tomorrow, I'd change our train tickets and leave this afternoon but I think we can do one more night if only we can calm her down a bit. Shh, now. Don't say anything. This is our room.' She swipes the key-card and lets

Hugo in.

Lisa is staring out of the window at the desolate weather, scanning the curtain of rain for her son, for that terrible man, for the slightest sign from heaven as to what to do. She is clutching herself, wrapping her arms tight around her own body as if someone else is hugging her.

Callie helps Hugo out of his coat and sopping walking boots and props them by the radiator to dry. She pours tea for Hugo and signals for him to sit in one of the two faux-leather armchairs, where he pulls off his socks and wriggles his damp-wizened toes. Callie hands him a fluffy hotel towel with which he rubs his head and then his feet.

'Lubbly jubbly,' Hugo says, but neither girl is amused by his silly accent. Callie widens her eyes and shrugs her shoulders at her father. *What should I do about Lisa?*

Not so many years ago, as a secondary-school history teacher, Hugo had witnessed every mood a sixteen-year-old girl could muster, but never before had he been asked to psychoanalyse a single one of these incomprehensible creatures. Girls could spit. They could bite. Their language could be bluer than the sky. Then again, they could sulk, or cry, or go hysterical on you, and all within the space of a single lunch break. Nevertheless, for Callie's sake he is prepared to risk the wrath of Lisa by offering advice.

'In my extensive experience,' Hugo starts, 'there is very little point in trying to help someone who turns their back on you.' Lisa is motionless, but her fingers dig further into the backs of her arms. Hugo clears his throat with an air of superiority. 'I have been advised that I am somewhat of a fantasist.'

Callie shakes her head. 'Dad!' she whispers, as if he is getting it all wrong.

'I have started so I'll finish.' Hugo addresses Callie, knowing Lisa is listening. 'When my medication is topsy-turvy, then my brain takes a merry dance and I, Hugo Quin, transform myself into someone more wonderful – Quasimodo or Sir Isaac Newton, or even Einstein. So right now, Lisa – that is your real name, isn't it? Lisa? – right now, *who are you really?*'

Lisa twirls to face him, furiously. 'Yes, my name is Lisa and I am nothing like you! I'm no fantasist. *You* can be Einstein or Churchill, or anyone you choose, but if you genuinely want to help me you can find out who owns this number plate.' She thrusts her palm into Hugo's hand. The biro marks are smudged with perspiration.

'Steady on, girl,' Hugo says, taking her hand in both of his and examining it as intently as a gypsy might. He breathes heavily through his nose until he is satisfied that he has deciphered the hieroglyphics. He drops Lisa's hand. 'I should record this in my notebook but it's in my rucksack and my rucksack is in my room and my room is above the café down the hill.'

'I wish you were staying here in this hotel,' Callie says.

'Don't fret your little head about it. This isn't my sort of place. I simply wanted the very best for my wonderful daughter,' grins Hugo. 'Anyway, my attic room is comfy and quaint and suits me fine. Just like your room here, it was paid for by a benefactor.'

'What benefactor?'

'I have a friend whose name is Duncan. I met him recently, quite by accident, and fortunately I was able to do him a very good turn which he has since repaid in the form of a substantial financial reward.'

'It must have been a pretty phenomenal good turn, Dad.'

'Yes. You see, I found the keys to his van and he very kindly. . .'

'Are you going to help me, or are you going keep chatting like

I don't exist?' Lisa interrupts. She is pulling on her coat.

'What's the hurry? Needs must make plans. Lists. Put our mission in order.'

'Hurry? Somewhere out there is the man who killed my baby and the more we hang around playing happy holidays, the further away he gets. In fact—' Lisa collapses onto a chair. After a minute she summons the strength to pull a jumper over her head and again, wraps her arms around herself. 'In fact, I've lost him. I lost my baby and it's all my fault. I can't tell the police because I agreed to it. They'll say I'm an accessory. What if the police tell the social and my baby is alive after all? I know he can't possibly be but if he is, they'll take him off me forever.'

Callie attempts to clarify this to Hugo, anxious not to reveal her own doubts about the actual existence of this baby. 'She believes a man stole her baby in Lancaster, which apparently happened before we even met. Personally, I've never seen any baby. She lives in a pretty rough flat. I only wanted to help her. That's why, when Jason couldn't come with me, I thought this would be a treat for her.'

'He *did* take my baby!' Lisa stamps her foot. 'And it was the same man. He had the same laces.'

'Laces,' repeats Callie, widening her eyes to Hugo to signal, *She's crazy.*

'And he smelt the same. Of a kind of sweet wax. Sickly. I can't quite place it but the smell is so unusual, I'll never forget it.' Lisa wrinkles her nose and inhales.

Hugo raises one hand, serious as an American swearing allegiance to the flag. 'Stop right there. Sweet wax, you say? Funny, only yesterday, I was thinking about that very subject. We were driving along in the van and there was this most unusual odour. I thought it was soap, or aftershave. Then it came to me: scented candles or maybe *wax*. Did you say you lost a *baby*?'

Lisa nods miserably. Callie shakes her head in frustration at Hugo's apparent slowness. 'It's okay, Dad. I shouldn't have involved you. I should have known it would all be too much for you.'

Hugo slurps his tea. 'Be a dear and hand me that piece of Starcliff writing paper, will you, Callie?' Hugo records the number plate. He also lists *Candles. Sweet wax. Baby. Van. Laces.*

'Now I have some questions for you, my dear,' Hugo smiles. Lisa, relieved to be taken seriously at last, relaxes somewhat and moves to perch on the edge of the bed. Callie lies back on her own bed, sighing. 'He thinks he's CID, Lisa. Please don't let him get your hopes up just because he thinks . . .'

'Describe the baby,' Hugo begins.

'A boy. Tiny. Perfect.'

'Hair?'

'Yes, he had hair.'

'Callie was bald as a coot when she arrived,' Hugo chuckles, 'but now everyone admires her glorious locks. No wonder Jason fell for her. If you ask me, he's a lucky so-and-so. What colour hair?'

'Black. I mean brown. I think. It was very dark. I only held him for a . . .' Lisa cradles her right arm in her left, like a baby and wraps herself over it. 'His feet were cold. And then I fell asleep.'

'Describe the man for me.'

'Tall and kind. He never hit me. He never shouted at me.'

'He doesn't sound like your average murderer,' says Callie.

'I was scared because I'd given him the wrong PIN for my bank card.'

'You're alleging he took your bank card. Did you cancel it?'

asks Callie.

'Callie, don't interrupt. Let me do these questions in logical order.'

'No, I didn't cancel it but he can't use it because I lied. He doesn't know the PIN. And in any case, there's hardly any money in my bank.' Lisa keeps quiet about the cash she has stashed in her luggage. She daren't tell even Callie. *Never trust anyone you met less than a week ago.* And here she is miles away, stressed out in Cornwall with a girl she only met two days earlier. Her mother's voice mocks: *You take after me. A bad judge of character. I got your dad, more fool me. And you got Paul. If you don't buck your ideas up you'll end up like me and your best mate will be a bottle.*

'I don't drink,' Lisa says aloud to her mother.

'No one is accusing you of anything like that,' says Hugo, adding the word *teetotal* to his list. 'The make of the van?'

'White,' Lisa says. 'Aren't all vans white?'

'It has a black stripe down the side,' says Callie.

Hugo jots this down. 'I asked for the make. Is it perchance a three-seater Berlingo?'

'What do you mean? I don't know stuff like that! This is such a flaming waste of time.' Lisa jumps up and dashes into the bathroom, slamming the door and locking it. She flushes the toilet and crashes around, turning taps on, splashing her face, making strange sounds, garbled words, sighs and wails. Minutes later she emerges, standing tall, chin up, mouth pursed, determined and decisive.

'Right,' Lisa says, scanning the room for what she might need. Callie sits up, responding to Lisa's sudden change of demeanour. Hugo is sketching Lisa and labelling his drawing with seemingly random symbols and words. An arrow to the hair. *Brown.* Circle round the hand. *Unmarried.* Large teardrop

211

in the margin. *Distressed.* He is decorating a page heading that reads: *Enigma is an anagram of Imagine missing I.* Beneath this he scrawls, *'I use imagination to solve enigma.'*

Lisa glances down at Hugo's artwork then glares at Callie. 'And you think I'm the crazy one. Don't wait for me if I'm not back in time for the train tomorrow. Leave my stuff at reception if you like.' She slings her bag over her shoulder and whips a red-and-white spotted scarf twice around her neck as she pushes out of the room.

Hugo holds his hand up to Callie. 'Don't chase after her dear. Try not to worry so much. She's had a big shock. She'll be back soon enough when she calms down.'

'Do you actually believe her about the baby?' asks Callie. Her dad had always been so literal. He could easily be persuaded that Henry the Eighth had seven wives, as long as someone showed him what he called *'incontrovertible written proof'.*

'More than just believe. I am a hundred and ten percent positive she's telling the truth and that I am the only person on earth who can help her. You wait here in case she returns sooner rather than later. Book yourself in for a massage. A sauna maybe. Chillax as they say! And trust your old dad to know what to do. To quote a certain muscle man, *'I'll be back!'*'

With that, Hugo gathers his belongings and saunters out of the hotel to make some urgent phone calls.

Lisa 7
Hope Rises like a Crazy Thing

Grey, pebble-dashed social housing is clustered round some rusting swings and a couple of benches. Lisa is knocking on doors, searching for her son. She works her way round the estate, knocking, begging, knocking. 'Excuse me, but is there anyone here with a newborn baby boy?' Most reply with a hasty, 'No, sorry love,' but others slam the door in her face. One elderly gentleman invites Lisa in for *a cup of coffee to get out of the rain*, but she shakes her head and runs off up the next garden path. In any case, it is no longer raining.

A door opens and there's a young woman with a crying baby on each hip and a couple of toddlers clinging to her knees. 'No extra babies here – but you can have one of these,' she mocks. Lisa looks from one to the other as if she is trying to decide. 'I'm not serious, love!' says the woman, as it dawns on her that the girl on the doorstep isn't joking.

'But where did you get them from?' Lisa says.

'A seagull dropped them here, what do you think?'

'I don't know what he looks like. I can't decide. How old are they?'

'Four months. Thirteen months. Both mine and that's my lot!' She shuffles back and closes the door.

Lisa pivots on the doorstep. She can hear a baby crying but she doesn't know where it is. *Have I already called at that house across the way? I think I missed that one out.* The distant sound of children calling in a playground, laughter and shouting, the teacher's whistle, and overhead, the seagulls wail. A huge yellow helicopter rattles along the coastline, cutting through the low cloud. Forgetting about food or water, Lisa walks all afternoon, her senses alert to every possibility.

A man and a woman approach, wearing matching mauve cagoules zipped up to the chin. 'Excuse me,' the woman says. Lisa's hair whips her flushed cheeks and her wild eyes flick left and right checking everything that moves. The mouth of the woman is moving and Lisa tries to catch the words on the wind. 'I hope you don't mind me saying but we've noticed you going from door to door. People say you're looking for a baby.'

'Yes, yes I am! Have you seen him?' Hope rises like some crazy thing. Lisa's whole focus is on the woman's lips.

'Have you lost a baby recently?'

'Yes, yes I have.' Lisa half expects the woman to say, *pick a hand, any hand,* and there would be her little boy reaching for his mummy.

'You should go to your GP. Make an appointment. He'll get you a really good bereavement counsellor. I know how you feel, because I . . .'

Lisa's eyes widen. A scream is stuck in the back of her throat. 'My baby is not dead!' but the sound lodges at the back of her brain. She sets off running, running, away from the closed doors and the failing kindness of strangers. The light, too, is failing. All of a sudden, Lisa stops and stands very, very still. The world stops. It is quiet.

Too quiet.

Lisa is standing by a wide gate at the entrance to a field that stretches away, away. Somewhere beyond is an impossible cliff, below which the sand shifts and the interminable waves fold back beyond the invisible horizon and the dark night approaches. Here are no lights, no cars, no houses. Somehow Lisa has left town, but she doesn't care. She drifts on further, up a winding lane hedged high on both sides with brambles. *I'm on the road to nowhere*, she thinks, hearing the music in her head, until she argues with the song and says aloud, 'All roads lead somewhere, so somewhere is where I will go.'

A car pulls up alongside her. The window lowers. 'Hey! Wanna a lift?' Lisa is not alarmed because she has nothing to lose. She shrugs.

'It's a couple of miles to the next town and that dreadful mist is back. You'll get knocked down walking in the middle of the road like that. Come on, I'll take you.'

Lisa opens the passenger door without registering the person or the vehicle. She says, 'Thanks,' and the man drives on, reminding her to fasten her seatbelt as they go. She is so exhausted she hardly notices where they travel. He asks her name but she is silent.

Several hours later Lisa awakes disorientated, in a strange house. Where am I? Not in the flat over the post-office. Not at Callie's place. Not in any hotel. *And where is my baby? I've been looking everywhere for him. He is here. I can feel his presence.* Lisa tries to sit up, but it is awkward because she's on a beanbag, legs askew, in front of a spattering fire. The only light emanates from the TV, where the end credits are rolling to mark the end of a show, and there is light from the kitchen, where two collies whimper for attention from behind a baby-gate that divides the rooms. A grandfather clock ticks mercilessly in the corner of the lounge. *Is the ceiling very low, or is the clock too tall?* Lisa's socks hang over the radiator, one longer than the other.

A woman, about sixty-five, overweight with wispy grey hair, snores softly in the only armchair, head back and mouth gaping. She'd fallen asleep right after her middle-aged son had dragged in the waif and stray. The house is his so he does what he chooses. The man had suggested Lisa remove her boots and damp socks. He'd shown her the bathroom and given her a fresh flannel and a towel. He'd made a mug of hot chocolate and left it on the hearth for her. She vaguely remembered him telling his mother about a casserole in the oven. 'I'll eat later, after work. Give some to the girl,' he'd ordered, then he'd spoken to Lisa, 'Get some rest. If you're no better when I return then I'll phone the police. See if they can help you.' The son has been gone a long while and the woman hasn't shifted from the armchair. The casserole will be cooked dry.

Lisa eases herself to her feet. She lifts the mug of drinking chocolate. It is cold but she drinks the lot because the sugary milk is delicious. She retrieves her warm socks and tiptoes to the front door where she finds her boots and coat. The dogs watch through the bars, wide-eyed, inquisitive. She raises a hand to them. *Stay! Don't get all excited. I'm not taking you for a walk.* The handle clicks as she opens the door.

Lisa slips outside. She pads barefoot down a steep garden path and past some over-stuffed wheelie bins then steps out onto the lane. Beneath a streetlight she drops the boots and supports herself with the lamppost as she pulls on one sock at a time. With a concerted effort she tugs on her boots and ties the laces.

A light flicks on in the front room. Lisa raises her eyes. She sees a human shadow rippling towards her over the lumpy lawn and, in the window, the elderly woman is drawing the curtains against her. With no sense of direction, Lisa trudges off into the night.

Duncan 11

There is a Situation

Duncan only realises he is speeding in the wrong direction when a Gatso flashes. The shock of the light makes him slam on his brakes and stall the van. He checks his mirror, half expecting to be jumped on by a couple of policemen, but there is no one else on the road. He removes the key from the ignition, takes a deep breath and starts again. *Slow down.* He realises he'd driven right through a village without registering the existence of a single house or pedestrian. *Which way am I driving? North or south? Is the coast behind me or ahead?*

The interminable sea-fret rolls, curling and stretching, passing ghosts through the high hedgerows. Visibility ranges from clear to twenty metres and back to clear again with unnerving irregularity. The Gatso doesn't unduly concern Duncan because the number plate is the false one so it can be destroyed later, but the thrill of living on the edge of a precipice is fast diminishing. What was it Will Hoyle had taught him back in Verbier? *A prolonged shot of adrenalin eventually loses its appeal, becoming painful, even agonising. Fear is pleasurable only when the outcome guarantees a safe landing.* Now the increasing paranoia of being arrested, of trouble beyond control coupled with the potential loss of Julia if she discovers his lies is making him sick to his stomach.

He approaches a row of houses followed by a mercifully

open petrol station. Not knowing where the next fuel might be, Duncan pulls in and fills up. He pays cash for diesel and a packet of crisps, keeping his head down, wary of CCTV. Afterwards Duncan turns down a side road and parks outside a semi-detached house painted lilac, juxtaposed with another in custard yellow. Duncan stuffs crisps into his mouth, wishing he could block all thoughts of Toby.

Two wrongs don't make a right but in Toby's case surely they add up to something justifiable. Taking Toby from his mother was probably wrong, and lying to my wife about D-DIT was out of order, but handing an unwanted baby to desperate parents was good. I did good. The cash was a bonus. Is a bonus. Without it, I'd have to break in to more homes. To the Nowiks, all that money is meaningless. I need it to keep Julia happy. Then there's the girl. She rejected Toby, her own flesh and blood, outright. She practically begged me to take her baby. Obviously she couldn't cope. And Monika was desperate, so Toby is well-placed. No need to panic. If Hugo Quin hadn't intervened I'd be home and dry by now.

The phone rings. 'Julia?' he guesses without checking. But it is Monika.

'Hello. Mr Simons?'

'You've beaten me to it, Mrs Nowik. You're on my follow-up list for today. How's the little one doing?' *Chin up. Keep it smooth and creamy. Professional.*

'Toby? He is so beautiful. Lovely. I am in love. But there is a situation.' Monika certainly hasn't adopted the slightest hint of a Cornish accent, let alone an English one. Duncan resists the temptation to imitate her clipped voice.

'A situation? Ha, that's adoption for you. A few minor bits and bats are common in the early days. Teething problems.'

'No, Toby is too young to be teething. The situation, it is to do with your assistant, Mr Quin.'

'Quin?' Duncan leans forward, his mouth instantly dry.

'He telephoned me twenty minutes ago. Checking I'm in all day. He gave me your message, but can you please not arrive before three because at that time Erik will be at the dentist and I don't think he wants anymore fuss. I know it is early days but he is struggling to adapt, you see. It is far harder for a man, don't you think?'

'What message?' Duncan manages to splutter.

'The one about you and Mr Quin doing a visit. *It is vital*, he says.'

'Vital? I mean, oh yes. My assistant. He is very enthusiastic. What would I do without him to complete all the necessary follow-up? Don't you worry. I absolutely assure you no one will arrive before three. You relax. Enjoy being a mother. I'll get back to you. If you hear nothing, then we won't be coming at all.'

'But it is *vital* he told me.'

'As I said, he's a very enthusiastic trainee. Must fly. Catch you later.' Duncan hangs up. He then sees a missed call from Hugo while he'd been paying for the fuel. 'Interfering idiot,' mutters Duncan. *But Hugo can't have reported Toby. He can't possibly, because he benefited from the proceeds of a crime. So what is he up to?*

Duncan, visibly shaking with fury, returns Hugo's call. 'What the hell are you playing at?' he yells.

'Your baby,' says Hugo calmly, 'is not, strictly speaking, yours to give away.'

'And you are not, strictly speaking, anything to do with anybody. So delete those private numbers and get lost.'

'Tut, tut, Mr Simons. Don't get your knickers in a twist. I tried to ring Julia but she must be busy. Didn't leave a message but . . .'

'Julia? Leave my wife alone. She's nothing to do with my work. You have no right—'

'But *she* phoned me remember? Granted, she thought she was ringing you but, you have to admit you are not always, how shall I put it – *available* to her.' Hugo is enjoying himself too much. Duncan's heart is beating so loudly he can feel the thuds through his jaw and in his ears. Hugo is a loose cannon and likely to do untold damage if he speaks to Julia again.

'Listen to me, Mr Quin.'

'Hugo to you.'

'Whatever,' says Duncan. 'We will meet up one final time but only so I can check your phone, remove my private numbers and then you can forget I ever existed. You promised to delete those contacts and I – I trusted you. After all my generosity how dare you ring my client and my wife? Instead of playing silly games, why don't you get back to that daughter of yours and give her some of your precious attention?'

'Very well,' agrees Hugo. 'I'll hang out at our café. Meet me there asap.' He hangs up before Duncan can arrange a time.

Duncan turns back on himself. When he passes the speed camera he slows right down and snarls at it. He parks outside the café beneath the gloomy sky. Across the car park, the tide is almost in, the remorseless waves rumbling trouble upon trouble, tossing tangled weed and broken shells onto the deserted beach. As he gets out of the van Duncan sees, through the café window, the unmistakeable outline of Hugo, who is chatting to the waitress, gesticulating dramatically. The thought suddenly occurs to Duncan: *Those girls at the hotel – one of them is Hugo's daughter! What if her friend is Toby's mother and that's why she attacked me? To think I paid good money for those kids to stay here. I'm a flaming idiot.*

Hugo looks up, sees Duncan and waves. He lifts a mug of coffee and chinks it against the window. *Cheers to you*!

Duncan 12 and Hugo 7
The Ice Plate Shifts

Duncan sits opposite Hugo at their usual table. Apart from the waitress, the café is empty. Duncan leans forward with an open hand for Hugo to relinquish his phone but Hugo is more intent on leading the conversation.

'We meet again. The emu and the kangaroo.'

'The what?'

'On the Australian cricketers' cap is a coat of arms picturing an emu and a kangaroo. Two creatures that can only move forwards, never backwards. That is you and me. Mr Chris Simons and Mr Hugo Quin, always moving forwards, incapable of backtracking. We have very little time to lose, Mr, er, Simons.'

'You have very little life left, if you don't let me delete. . .'

'You have put your own insignificant issues above young Toby's life. You might be able to ignore a suffering, helpless infant, but I have a conscience.'

'What do you mean, suffering? How do you know he's suffering? Why did you phone Monika? You had no right.'

'Questions, questions. Monika is my friend too, you may recall.'

'Mrs Nowik is a client. Not a friend.'

'But I met her. We have spoken. Therefore she is my friend.'

'If you met the Queen of England, would she suddenly be your friend? Could you suddenly phone Her Majesty at any time of day or night and interfere with her private life?'

'As a matter of fact, I did once meet the Queen. She—'

'For crying out loud! Listen man, you can't go around making random appointments for me. And in case you haven't got it into your thick little skull, you are not my assistant. You are nothing. Nobody. Go live your own pathetic life and butt out of mine.'

'But Monika tells me Erik is planning to strangle Toby,' Hugo whispers, aware of the waitress hovering beside the noisy, frothing machine.

Duncan opens his mouth. He closes it again. *That's not true. He's lying. But what if it is true? Why did I name that kid? But I didn't – Julia did. Why should I care for a baby who is not my flesh and blood?* As he pushes his chair back away from the table, the pressure of indecision messes with his mind.

The mountain is a threatening place. The valley so far below, with its matchstick chalets and triangular trees, where stick people in luminous snow gear queue for the ski-lift. Ice diamonds half blind me. I wish I'd known the real Steve. He was my friend. I left it too late to ask what was bothering him. He wasn't coping but how was I to know? The others withdrew to university. Back then my world was my world, with me at the centre, revolving around myself with my insecure jokes, bluff and boasting. Beneath my skis, beneath the snow, the ice plate shifted. I noticed nothing because I wouldn't accept change.

*Will explained that if we accept that there is a high possibility of an avalanche, we'll be less likely to fall victim to the surprise occurrence of one. We can be made aware of how the path of an avalanche might appear. Most avalanche paths are obvious, appearing as an open slope, bowl or gully shape – other common giveaways are bent or damaged trees. Will taught us that loud noises do not usually cause avalanches. They happen because of the pressure of someone or something that is making the noise.'

Right now, Hugo is the one creating noise. Duncan caresses his own scratchy stubble with the back of his fist. He makes a decision. 'Smarten up.'

'If you say so. Your wish is my command. I'm staying in this very place, did you know? Up three flights. Top floor. Want to see my room?'

'I don't care where you're staying. And no, I do not want to see your room. But while you sort yourself, leave that phone with me. You set me up to pay the Nowiks a visit, so you can do something my way for a change. Hurry up.'

Hugo reacts surprisingly quickly. 'Right. Right. I didn't believe you'd turn up at all, so fine. Have it.' Hugo flicks his phone across the melamine table. *Do your worst, Duncan. I have my notebooks. Duplicated information. I'm not the dummy you assume me to be.* Hugo backs through a door marked 'Private. Residents Only.'

Duncan gulps at the coffee then strides out to his van. In his mind, he is cupping Toby's head within the palm of his hand, so the skinny body lies relaxed along his forearm. Toby's dark eyes meet his and Duncan reads the trust in them. *I'd take you home, son, if only Julia would agree, but she'd never participate in such a ridiculous fantasy. You're no abandoned kitten. Julia could never understand how melted you make me feel. She'd nag on at me: 'Never once in your whole life did you remotely consider owning a kitten or a puppy or even a hamster, so what makes you think you can raise some other bloke's baby?'*

Duncan scrolls through Hugo's contacts, surprised at how few there are, at most a dozen including an Orange contract number and the local police. Duncan selects a landline number randomly tapping on the name 'Rosy'. After a few rings a man answers.

'Hello? Robbie speaking. Can I help you?' Duncan is thrown by the deep, jovial response of a Scottish male.

'May I speak to, er, Rosy?' Duncan says.

'Oh, sorry to break the bad news but Rosy passed away only last month. Quietly in her sleep. She was nearly a century old, would you believe. Who's speaking, please?'

'Do you by any remote chance know a Hugo Quin?' From the other end, there is a loud guffaw. The man Robbie is cracking up, spluttering, speaking some nonsense about Hugo being a blast from the past. Flustered, Duncan apologises for being a bother and hangs up.

Duncan locates the two contacts he recognises in Hugo's phone, *Julia* and *Monika*, and deletes their details. He scrolls through past texts and call information, eliminating all trace of communication history, then, as an insipid sun emerges from the lowering clouds, he closes his eyes and rests, his face bathed soft as a Rembrandt in the low light.

Hugo appears. He yanks at the door of the van and heaves himself into the passenger seat. 'All set for a mercy mission!' he declares, 'with a tidier chin and a clean shirt worthy of the great Mr Christopher Simons. Sir, I give you the adoption researcher's assistant.' He holds out his hand and Duncan returns the phone. The two men travel in silence until Hugo, feigning an air of surprise says, 'What's that peculiar smell?'

'What smell? For crying out loud, we're in the countryside, what do you expect? Most likely it's your musty old coat. Right now, smell is not exactly a burning issue.'

'Oh, but I think you'll find that it is. I'm talking *candles*. Sweet wax. I doubt it's your aftershave because if it is, your wife's got a very strange sense of what's attractive.'

'Oh, you mean the Mother's Carnauba Wax?'

'The what?'

'Drum cleaner. I get it off the internet. Smells amazing but it gets under my skin – it could be under my nails, I don't know. It's very protective. Tough, like me. The very thought of it takes me back to the good old days.'

'Like playing drums do you?'

'Addicted.'

'Yet you haven't done it for days. I don't think you're as *into* music as you make out.'

'You've not seen my CD collection? But maybe you've got a point. I've not listened half as much as I planned to because, believe it or not, these past couple of days I've been landed with some very unwelcome company. Way back, I used to be in a band, but you know how it is, we all got busy. Grew up. Grew apart. Things got in the way, work, family, stuff. Back then, making music was a total craic. We did it for its own sake. I loathe all this new get-rich-and-famous-overnight mentality. When did creativity suddenly become all about deadlines and competitions? Back then . . . I miss those guys. . . Steve. . .'

Duncan recovers his composure. 'Why are we talking about drums? This should be about Toby. Since you told me that rubbish about Erik, I can't relax 'til I know for sure Toby's fine. You are to blame here. I warned you to leave the Nowiks alone. It wasn't your job to ring them.' He avoids driving over the body of a squashed badger. A magpie that had been pecking at the road kill, flaps nonchalantly into the hedge.

'One for sorrow,' says Hugo, saluting the bird.

Duncan clears his throat. 'Is it true what you said? About Erik?'

'No. I was lying.' Hugo glances at Duncan, who swerves into a layby and slams on the brakes. He unclips his seatbelt and grabs

Hugo by the collar, leans across and pulls Hugo towards him, nose to nose.

'Toby is not a pet. We don't mess with his life, right? If the Nowiks are okay and if Toby is okay, then I am not interfering. If Toby's not fine, then we take him back. Black and white. A clear choice.' Duncan grips Hugo's collar, twisting both fists beneath Hugo's jaw, but suddenly he slumps and his shoulders drop. For the first time, he appears to be smaller than Hugo. Defeated. He inhales deeply. 'But I can't take Toby back. There's nothing I can do for him.'

'But *I* can.' Hugo massages his own neck where Duncan's knuckles had pressed into him. He studies the twitch beneath Duncan's eye, the down curl of his mouth and the flare of his nostrils.

Duncan pushes away from Hugo, throwing himself back in his seat. 'You don't know what you're talking about.'

'I'm talking about my daughter.'

'Your daughter can go to hell. That crazy kid attacked me for no damned reason.'

'That wasn't Callie. It was her friend. There are fifty ways to skin a cat.'

'Meaning?'

'Meaning, there's always more than one solution to any problem. You should listen to me because Callie—'

'How's your daughter anything to do with Toby? Stop going on about her. *You're* the one who got us in this shambles so *you* can help get it sorted, then get lost. Today we pay the Nowiks an official visit. We check on Toby's welfare. We talk to Erik, *if* he's around. When we're satisfied, we sign off. Official. Finished. Done. No more contact. *Finito.*'

'And if we are not satisfied?'

'We will be. You can skin all the cats you like, but in this case there is no alternative.'

Julia 6
Sordid Imaginings and Furious Tears

Julia stands in the middle of Sainsbury's wondering what to have for tea. If Duncan had been home she would have bought a couple of steaks or pork chops, although he prefers his meat from the local butcher: 'Less likely to be stuffed with antibiotics.'

For Sophie and Meg, Julia will throw together a shepherd's pie or sausages and mash, keeping it simple because they refuse anything with 'bitsin', which is everything from leeks hidden in sausage, chopped veg swimming in soup, or fruit sludge in fresh orange juice. The 'bitsin' list continues, to the irritation of Julia's mother. 'It's a texture thing. They'll never learn to appreciate anything if you don't make them try.' But there's enough bickering in Julia's life so she aims for the smooth option and keeps the peace.

Julia has become so used to prioritising her husband, now that he's away she realises she's forgotten what she prefers for herself: chicken salad with lemon dressing, sprinkled with crunchy croutons? Or steamed, spiced fish? Duncan used to love sea-fishing. There was that time when he'd landed a garfish – something long and eel-like that cartwheeled through the waves. Had they cooked and eaten it on the beach? Julia can't remember.

'Penny for your thoughts!' says a woman over her shoulder.

'Rae,' stammers Julia, forcing a weak smile.

'I thought it was you, you daydreamer!' Rae speaks too fast and smiles too broadly. There's an awkward pause as Julia examines the contents of Rae's trolley. A white loaf, a frozen chicken-pie, pre-sliced ham, processed cheese, chocolate biscuits, margarine. Julia's basket contains a bag of rocket, chicken breasts, tomatoes, peppers and tangerines.

'Tangerines,' notes Rae. 'Good choice. They come into their own at this time of year. Out of season they're totally tasteless.'

The two women shuffle aside to allow other shoppers to pass. Julia bites the bullet, 'Um, I think I owe you an apology.'

'What on earth for?'

'The other day. The chameleon. I over-reacted.'

'Chameleon? Oh, that thing! I totally forgot about it.' Rae blushes, hastily repositioning her trolley in front of Julia.

'I mentioned it to my husband and he said you may well be right about it being stolen. He found it on the pavement a while back and he keeps intending to hand it in. He's definitely going to take it round to the police station next week. It's just one of those things, you know . . .'

'Good intentions,' Rae says over-brightly. 'Whatever would we achieve without them?'

Julia examines her own basket. *What else do I want?* Rae is suggesting that Julia should pop round to her place next time. Another coffee maybe. But not this week, while hubby-without-work is mooching about the house depressed but, to be fair, he is applying for simply hundreds of jobs.

Coffee? Really? Not in this lifetime. Julia purses her lips as Rae cranes her neck to read the signs above the aisles: Dairy. Chemist. Fruit and Veg. Frozen Produce.

'Tangerines it is then. Ciao for now!' Rae melts into the aisle of frozen food.

Back home with the radio for company, Julia sits at the kitchen *table staring into the dregs of her mug. If Rae thinks I'm her new best friend, she can think again. I'd never bare my soul to her or anyone – and if ever she told me a secret, I'd tell whoever I jolly well wanted.*

The radio declares trouble in Syria, a mudslide in an American town, a plane crash in Turkey. Death and disaster. War and want. Distant realities for foreigners to cope with. *I refuse to spend any part of my life listening to sob stories from boring neighbours about their petty failures and infidelities. And Rae Hook's husband's lack of a job is not exactly the stimulating conversation of the year.*

Nevertheless, the rollercoaster carriage of emotions chugs tensely up its perilous track; in the pit of Julia's stomach, doubt and suspicion churn. Her breathing quickens and her diaphragm tightens as if someone is stringing a corset and tug, tugging, tying tight. Her heart beats up through her throat and she can hardly breathe.

'Duncan is – must be – with another woman,' she whispers. She digs her manicured nails into the back of her hand but hardly notices the pain. If only he were here he'd reassure her. Mr Sensible. Mr Logical. Duncan's ability to reason, to keep a level head in a crisis, is why D-DIT kept him on after the cutbacks. Julia pulls her phone from her jeans pocket but before she can phone him, it rings. She stands to answer, preparing to pace the room. She doesn't recognise the number so if it's not Duncan she'll keep the conversation snappy.

'Good morning, my dear. Or should I say, afternoon? Did you know that red deer can consciously slow their heartbeat in order to conserve seventeen per cent more energy? We humans would do well to emulate the red deer.' A familiar voice.

'Do I know you?' Julia affects her most supercilious telephone tone.

'Not exactly *know*, but have knowledge *of.*'

'Can I help you?' Julia is walking upstairs. It is merely somewhere to go.

'I believe you can. My name is Hugo Quin. I had the honour of a brief conversation with you only the other day . . .'

'You're the one who answered my husband's phone but you gave it back to him, so how've you got my number? There is no way on God's earth Duncan would have given anyone my private number.'

'Merely a precaution. Turns out that fortune favours the forethinker, because I must report a very serious matter to you.'

'Why are you bothering me? I don't have to listen to you. I don't even know who you are.' Julia sits on Duncan's side of the bed and pulls open his locker drawer.

'Duncan is under the impression that I have phoned you more than once. I consider myself a moral sort; however, I am inclined to offload the odd porky when it benefits.'

Julia reaches into the drawer. With a fingertip, she caresses the chameleon. *He loves me.* 'Get to the point or get out of my life.' Her other hand grips Duncan's pillow. The day darkens. Raindrops snake fiercely across the window pane, and in the garden, naked branches appear to twist and squirm uncomfortably in the wind. Julia hears Hugo clear his throat in the manner of a politician embarking on the first speech of a campaign.

'Duncan believes I've relayed to you sensitive information concerning a sweet lady named Monika.'

'Monika?' Julia mouths. The four walls close in. The phone falls from her hand onto the deep-pile carpet as Hugo chatters on. The rollercoaster has fallen off its tracks. Far below her, the distant sea crashes mercilessly onto some desolate beach. To reach the phone she must fall after it. Julia slides slowly off the silky bedspread to the shifting floor. She lifts the phone to her ear. The man is mid-sentence, talking about 'Lisa' and 'Callie' and it makes perfect sense to Julia that an attractive man like Duncan would have more than one lover.

'. . . so what I'm saying is that Duncan's going to have to sort things out with Monika and steal Toby back somehow because . . .'

'Is Tobi another girl?' Julia hears the quiver of her own voice, remembering the only other Tobi she's ever known, a classmate with straight-As, slim, sporty and popular with boys and teachers alike. Everyone described Tobi as 'sweet.' *Monika is a very sweet lady . . . Lisa . . . Callie . . . Tobi . . .*

'He is obviously a beautiful baby boy,' continues Hugo.

'Duncan's got a son?' Julia says through a haze of unsteadiness. 'How?'

'Yes, but he didn't keep him. Monika adopted him. But we have a problem. I believe Lisa is Toby's real mother and, as Lisa is Callie's friend, obviously I can't let Callie down.'

'Who is Callie?'

'My daughter.'

'Stop! Shut up for one minute!'

'But I haven't even started explaining. . .'

'Shut up! Shut up! Shut up!' Julia hangs up. Holding her hands over her ears, she curls over, rocking, struggling to put her thoughts in order. Hugo makes several attempts to reconnect, but for now, Julia is lost.

By mid-afternoon, Julia has pulled herself together and settled on a course of action. She phones her mother to explain she has to prepare for an upcoming interview for a proper job – an assistant to a company director, no less. Julia's mother will do anything to lever her wayward daughter out from Duncan's shadow.

'Naturally, I'll have the children any time. They can stay the night if it helps.'

'Two?'

'Of course, darling.'

'And you'll handle the school run?'

'I may be getting long in the tooth, but I'm perfectly capable of looking after my own grandchildren. You prepare that presentation. I always said you're far too good to be only a secretary, even if it is in a surgery. Sock it to them. Of course you'll land the job. They'd be fools to turn you down!'

Julia packs clothes for the girls: PE kits, wellies and Moop. On autopilot, she collects them from school and drops them with Granny. Her mother comments on how pale she looks and suggests an over-the-counter tonic. 'By all means, watch your figure but don't forget to eat!' she reminds her adult daughter, but Julia bites her lip and refuses to be baited into another health discussion. The girls love Granny. They skip into the lounge forgetting to say goodbye to their mother.

Back home, Julia prints Google map directions to Bude, a belt-and-braces back-up in case the Sat Nav plays silly beggars. She applies eyeliner, mascara, concealer and foundation and her plum lippy, without which there is no facing the public. In any case, the plum is Duncan's favourite. She packs her suitcase, remembers her phone-charger, locks the house, sets the kitchen light and radio onto automatic timer, then hides the spare front-door key inside the keystone behind the Kilmarnock willow.

At the garage, Julia fuels up the Kuga and checks the tyre pressures, oil and water. The traffic will be rush-hour thick but Julia is fired up to take on the world. Or at least, Bude. Six or seven hours' drive, including a couple of pit-stops. She ought to arrive by midnight.

With everything in order, lined up and under control Julia feels emotionally strong enough to call Duncan so, immediately before the motorway slip-road, she pulls into a layby and kills the engine.

Don't lose it. Don't sound suspicious. Don't, don't, don't. Find out where he is. What if he's halfway home already? I'll catch him red-handed with this so-called Monika – or possibly Lisa. Whichever girl it is, it doesn't matter as long as I witness it and he can't worm his way out.

Julia cups her hands around the phone to minimise the sound of traffic. She fakes a smile to improve the intonation of her voice. 'Hello, darling!'

'Strange time to call. Everything okay?' His voice is silky as pâté de foie gras.

'Oh, you know me – always thinking about my gorgeous husband.'

'I should abandon you more often. Absence makes the heart grow fonder and all that.'

'What're you doing right this minute?'

'Let me see. I've just concluded a very important meeting that's left me whacked, so I'll set off home in the morning. Not worth risking falling asleep on the motorway. Can't wait to see you. I never expected this thing to be so time-consuming.'

'What was the name of the hotel again?'

'The Sands Inn – oh, you mean the *conference* hotel,' Duncan splutters, grappling around in his brain for the right answer. *Not the Breeze Hotel – that was the other night.* 'Oh, right! You're talking about the Starcliff,' he blurts. 'Yes, I thought it best to stay tonight. Don't want to drive home exhausted. You know what they say: tiredness causes death and all that. Most likely I'll be up at the crack of dawn for breakfast, then . . .'

'Starcliff. That's such an, er, unusual name.'

'Starcliff? I'm thinking maybe starfish blended with clifftop. I bet they paid some fancy designer good money to come up with that name. How are my girls?'

'Fine. They've been at after-school club today. Anyway, I'd best be going. Lots to do. Enjoy your last evening.'

'That's not like my Jules, rushing to hang up!'

'Tell me, Duncan, what *am* I like?' She can't help it, the furious spit rising with the bitter gall.

'Hey, cool it sweetheart, chill out. Sorry I've been away but that's how it is sometimes. *Someone* has to bring home the bacon and keep you in the manner to which you have become accustomed. Only the best is good enough for my Jules.' Duncan's prattle allows Julia time to regain control of her emotions.

'I'm sorry too. For being snappy. I've got a lot on my mind and I appreciate how busy you are. See you tomorrow then. What would you like for supper when you get back? I thought a steak celebration maybe.'

'Steak it is, then. I'll text you tomorrow with my ETA. Love you muchly.' Duncan sends a couple of noisy kisses.

Julia grimaces and presses the red button. 'This is it. Let the truth be known.' She tightens her hand round the chameleon, which digs its sharp claws into the palm of her hand. She drops it into the pocket of the car door and, as she does so, her hand brushes against something. She picks it up and it is the denim purse she'd found on the gravel that she'd not bothered to chuck in the bin.

Julia undoes its popper. Inside is a bank card which Julia holds to the light, squinting at the name. *Ms E. Rimmer.* Well, that doesn't ring any bells. *If I'd known there was a bank card in that purse I'd have handed it to the police. It's bound to have been cancelled by now, so it can wait 'til I get back from Bude. Can't think of anyone called Rimmer. Emma? Eve? Elizabeth? Lisa? Is Lisa short for Elizabeth? Lisa Rimmer – I knew it! He's had that snotty little tart round here while I've been at work. I bet she even travelled to Bude with him.*

Julia's journey to Bude passes in a blur of sordid imaginings, unbridled fears and furious tears. Some minutes before midnight, emotionally and physically exhausted, she drags her vehicle up the steep incline leading to the Starcliff Hotel. Half a dozen vehicles are parked out front in a row but none belong to Duncan. Maybe he's elsewhere, although he'd definitely told her 'Starcliff'. She hadn't planned to stay here overnight, but – *'Goodness, look at the time, what else can I do?'*

The receptionist assures Julia that there are plenty of rooms. November has proved to be unseasonably busy, what with a hen weekend and a couple of conferences.

'I'm quite aware of that because my husband was on the Direction Data IT conference. The D-DIT thingy,' chats Julia, acting nonchalant, yawning.

'Sorry, but I've never heard of that company. So, here's your key. Room 214. Second floor.'

Julia takes the key and tries a different approach. 'I was wondering if you'd mind telling me which room a Mr Duncan Wilde is booked into. I'm his wife. It would be such a wonderful surprise for him to see me.'

'The name doesn't ring any bells. Give me a minute.' She scrolls through the on-screen bookings, shaking her head. 'His wife, you say? Sorry, no Mr Wilde. Are you sure?'

'Yes, positive. He Skyped me from your reception room. A large lounge with a huge mirror? Oil painting . . ?' Julia is overcome with exhaustion, fighting tears.

To the receptionist this is nothing new; jealous wives, suspicious girlfriends, checking up on their man. She leads Julia to the main reception room. 'This one?' she asks, switching on the light as Julia peers around the door. Seagulls over a violent sea, the unmistakeable oil-painting. Julia heaves a sigh of relief.

'Yes, this is the one. And I recognise the wallpaper. Duncan stayed here.'

'Unless,' the receptionist hesitates, 'he was the guy we had to remove – the one that attacked one of our guests. A girl. It wasn't me on duty but there was a bit of an incident. Apparently, an undesirable sort was hanging about in here. We've been warned not to allow him back in. I've got a description on the desk but no photo. Here – look if you like. Six foot something, dark hair, white shirt, dark jacket, scruffy trainers. That's it I'm afraid.'

'Not my Duncan. He pretty much fits your description except he'd never wear scruffy trainers. And he'd never hit a girl. I'll take a room.' A hot shower would be amazing. It would give her space to think.

A breathless, flushed young woman bursts into the foyer. Ignoring Julia, she addresses the receptionist without apology. 'Lisa hasn't reappeared, has she? I've looked everywhere and I don't have a car so it's really hard, I've covered so many streets on foot. She's new to the area. I'm so worried about her. I'll never sleep a wink if she doesn't come back.'

'Lisa?' The name spills from Julia's lips like she accidentally tasted a hot chilli.

'Yes, do you know who I mean? Have you seen her?'

'And has this Lisa person gone off with a man called Duncan?' Julia spits.

'Of course not. She's on holiday here with me. She got upset and went for a walk. Dad said she'd be back, but it's been

238

absolutely ages. I keep thinking I should maybe call the police but I've no idea . . .'

The receptionist swings on her chair behind the desk. She's glad she's on duty tonight; a shift of shenanigans is a welcome distraction in November. 'Isn't Lisa the name of the young lady who got into a fracas with that dreadful man?' she says. All the staff had been gossiping about it. 'He got kicked out of the hotel even though some of the guests swore blind she was the one who attacked *him*. I don't know the full story . . .'

'No, you don't,' says Callie flatly.

'Adding two and two,' the receptionist addresses Callie, 'I'd say that *your friend* and *her husband*' – she nods at Julia – 'have had a minor contretemps. A domestic. *Your* friend hates *her* husband.'

Julia slaps her hand onto the reception desk to steady herself. Her dark eyes search Callie's and for a few seconds they stare silently at each other. 'You'd best come to my room. I don't know who you are, but . . .'

'No, you come to my room. If Lisa shows up, I want to be waiting for her. Give me five minutes to wash. I've been running around Bude for hours.'

Duncan 13 and Hugo 8
Monday Afternoon

The two men stand on the Nowiks' doorstep, listening through the wall to Toby screaming, apparently inconsolably. Hugo squats down, pushes open the letterbox and peers through the gaping rectangle, the hole of which releases a pungent scent of orange and cinnamon pot-pourri.

'Stinks of posh toilets,' Hugo mutters, just as Eric pulls the door open. Hugo trips forward, head-butting Eric in the stomach, stumbles onto his knees then scrabbles across the carpet. Finally, he hauls himself up with the help of a wrought-iron umbrella stand. Eric shakes his head at Duncan. *What's this you've landed us with?*

'You'd best come in,' Erik says, unnecessarily. 'As you can hear, the wife's upstairs dealing with her baby. You can wait in the lounge.'

Hugo's boots leave a trail of dirt as he heads for the staircase and casually ascends. Duncan stands by Eric. Neither moves towards the sitting room.

'Do fathers ever get a say in all this lark?' Erik mumbles. 'I told the social countless times, I clearly said, "I don't want the responsibility. A screaming brat's not my idea of fun, but don't you dare tell my wife or it'll be the end of our marriage." Of course, no baby is a brat, but I wanted to shock them. It was such a relief when they turned us down. Monika was furious.

Refused to accept "no" for an answer. For Monika's sake, I went along with the TV thing. It was her fifteen minutes of fame, as the Brits say. She enjoyed it, letting off steam to the nation. I thought it would be a kind of therapy for her, a public place to spill blame. Before O'Leary, she was all bottled up. I never expected anyone out there to care less what she said. Then out of the blue comes your phone call. It didn't fit. It still doesn't make sense. Not really. Why did the social suddenly change their minds?'

'Well if you don't want to keep Toby. . .'

'I don't.'

'Unfortunately the money. . .'

'Forget the money. Keep it. We got loads more than we admitted. I wish I could burn every last penny and go back to how we used to be.'

'We can't just walk out of here with Toby.' Duncan speaks behind his knuckle, as if someone might read his lips, then he tugs repeatedly at his Adam's apple.

Upstairs, the crying stops. Monika appears on the landing, surveying the men below like some bedraggled angel, her unkempt hair backlit by a window and her pink, quilted dressing-gown tied too tightly at the waist, flaring out like a wilting tulip over her hips. 'Your assistant is miraculous. Such a great man. A natural. He is feeding Toby in the rocker. Erik, why are you standing there? I hope you offered Mr Simons a drink?'

Duncan raises both hands. 'No thanks. You've got sufficient to be getting on with. We're only doing our job. Welfare check – and thankfully Mr Quin was able to help.'

'So you agree for me to keep Toby, one hundred percent, no going back?' Monika is descending.

'Absolutely. No question.' Duncan fakes a smile. *Come on Hugo, hurry along, man.*

'Only, I thought if I wasn't coping, if I admit to needing a little help, you'd have second thoughts.'

'Not at all. Motherhood is completely natural. After a couple of weeks, everything will be second nature, I assure you.' Duncan shifts his weight.

'We employ a cleaner, you know.'

'Very good. Fine.' Duncan glances upstairs. *Come on!*

'And I'm thinking maybe a maid.'

'Fine.'

'A maid? Whatever for?' Erik squeaks, already defeated.

'A *nurse*maid, to undertake my more arduous tasks. Nappies. Feeds.'

'You mean the whole shebang?' Erik nearly stamps. 'What's the point of having a baby, if you don't look after it yourself? I told you . . .'

'But I can't go on like this. Toby cries all the time. Look at me already! I look a mess. I'll end up a total wreck.'

Erik and Duncan exchange knowing glances.

'Aha,' says Duncan. 'Here comes Mr Quin.'

'Have you told your husband about the support worker idea of mine?' Hugo is on the top stair, one step above Monika.

'I have.'

'Good. So tomorrow we will return with a, er, nursemaid, courtesy of the social, of course. Your fees cover it. Naturally.' Hugo winks at everyone but the deception is aimed at Duncan, whose eyes are wide as saucers.

Duncan attempts some damage limitation. 'Tomorrow? But I have appointments. Other parents to interview. Mr Quin, remember your training. We never make these kind of decisions without going to panel.'

'Panel, quote unquote, will decide as a matter of urgency. Right, time to push off.' Hugo shuffles passed them, opens the front door and quick as a shot he is in the van, avoiding Duncan's accusatory glare. As the van rumbles down the drive, Hugo attacks. 'You never checked on Toby. Why not? Feeling guilty?'

'You checked on him. And I don't do guilt.'

'You don't? It's about time you did.'

'No guilt, because Toby is in the best place for him. If you'd seen the room where he was born – oh, I forgot, you never met the wreck of his mother. You never saw the state of her place. You have no idea.' Duncan sprays the windscreen and the wipers whack from side to side, leaving a smear. He flicks the off switch and sighs emphatically. 'I need to replace those wipers. There's always something to cough up for. So you saw Toby. How was he?'

'He had a bruise on his cheek.'

'Now I know you're lying. And you're asking *me* to admit guilt? Only yesterday you said Erik wanted to chuck Toby over a cliff.'

'Nope. What I said was Erik wanted to strangle him.'

'Cliff, strangle, whatever. You cry wolf too often. No one believes you even when you do tell the truth.' Duncan clears his throat. 'Seriously – did you really see a bruise on Toby?'

'I did.'

The two fall silent. The van rounds a corner. Duncan slams on the brakes and it skids a couple of metres on the damp lane. Someone is drifting towards them in the middle of the road.

'Good reactions,' says Hugo, as Duncan drives on. 'I was filing my nails and never even saw him.'

'Her.' Duncan flashes his thanks as a car pulls into a passing place to let him by.

'Her?' Hugo sits up. He checks his wing mirror but it is too dark. 'What colour was her coat?'

'I don't know, do I? What does it matter?'

'Did you see a spotty scarf? Red and white.'

'Now that you mention it, funnily enough there were some spots, yes.'

'That might've been Lisa. What if it was Lisa? Quick – turn round!' Hugo pulls on the steering wheel.

'Get off it, you flaming idiot – you'll kill us both! And if you're talking about the same girl who tried to scratch my eyes out, you can think again.' But Hugo is adamant and doesn't stop pestering. By the time Duncan had found somewhere to turn, and although it was only a matter of minutes since they'd passed the woman in the country lane in the semi-dark and drizzle, however hard the men search they are out of luck – to Duncan's relief. Whoever it was had vanished.

Hugo 9, Julia 7 and Callie 3
Fire after Midnight

Julia dumps her designer overnight bag onto Callie's bed. Without asking permission, she fills the kettle and makes herself a cup of tea. Callie gazes out of the window at the floodlit car park, desperate for a sign of Lisa. Julia perches on the edge of a chair, unable to relax.

'So then, what do you know about my husband?'

'I don't know him at all. At least I don't think I do. Unless – have you got a photo of him on your phone?'

'Of course. Look here – our daughters, Sophie and Meg. And this is my Duncan.'

'Yes, that is him! He looks younger in your photo but I definitely saw him this morning. He was sleeping downstairs on the sofa. Did you say he's called Duncan? It might be a coincidence but I think he may be some kind of friend of my dad's.'

'I very much doubt it, but you'd better tell me who your father is.'

'Oh, you won't know him. Even I hardly know him anymore and I'm his daughter! When he's not wandering up and down the country looking for mischief, he works as a janitor in a rather shabby hotel near Lancaster that's mostly used for social housing. His half-brother owns it.'

'For crying out loud, why would Duncan want to be with a janitor? What's his name?'

'Mr Quin. Hugo. And my dad *does* know a Duncan because he told me and Lisa. He seems to think they are colleagues or something like that.'

Julia reaches over to the bed for a pillow which she pulls into her lap, sinking her fingernails into it. She sits back into the chair. Unused to spilling her true feelings, yet weakened by the long journey and each vile revelation concerning her husband, Julia shrugs. There is a time to be strong, and a time to give up. Duncan no longer deserves loyalty or commitment. When Julia speaks her voice is quiet, resigned, punctuated by sighs. 'Hugo Quin has phoned me several times over the last couple of days. Or maybe once. The other time, I may have accidentally phoned him because he answered Duncan's mobile.'

'Why would my dad phone you?'

'To tell me about Duncan's baby. Duncan has been having an affair with some tart called Lisa and to cover it up, they've had the kid privately adopted by a Cornish woman. Monika, or something. Recently I'd been picking up on all these little signs, silly things that made me question. At home things feel out of sorts – but I love my husband and maybe love is blind. I never wanted to face the truth. But now I see it all too clearly.'

'Signs?'

'Of unfaithfulness. His van parked at an odd angle. He knows perfectly well how I need things to be neat. Everything has its place and everything in its place. It stops you losing things. Less stress. But it was skew-whiff. Also, he sang for no reason whatsoever, like he was happy in his head, inhabiting some other world. He messed up Meg's toy box and when I confronted him, he sat on Slumber-Bear as if I hadn't noticed. He was hiding Meg's comforter. There's no other explanation but he wanted a cuddly toy to give one of his harem – cheapskate! And I found other things that didn't belong. The worst was the chameleon. I so much wanted to believe he'd bought it for me for Christmas, because he loves – loved me – I thought he'd always love me, but now I know it was for his new woman. Is she very pretty?'

'Lisa? Quite. Yes. Well, I only met her at a party two days ago. I liked her. At first she seemed perfectly normal and I really wanted a friend. When she told me she'd had a baby I honestly didn't believe her, but she was so lonely I thought we could be friends. Do you still want to find your husband?'

A fresh burst of anger rises within Julia; 'Husband? Hah! Is that what you'd call him? Duncan can go to hell. Obviously he's bunked off with that bitch, keeping me sweet with his pathetic phone calls. *I'll be home soon. Just another night. Nah, nah, nahdy, nah.* They planned it all along, didn't they? I've been a complete and utter idiot. What am I going to tell the children? That their father is a lying, cheating. . .'

A knock on the door.

'Lisa!' Callie leaps up to answer it but as she crosses the room, she hesitates, turning to Julia. 'Please be patient with my friend. She hasn't been too well. Give her a chance.' Another tap. Callie opens the door and her shoulders drop. It is Hugo.

'Is she back yet?' Hugo prattles as he rushes in, immediately opening cupboards and drawers, peering under the bed with his backside in the air. 'Who are you then?'

'Dad, meet Julia. Duncan's wife. She says you've been phoning her.' Callie has returned to the window, clutching the curtain against her cheek. 'And no, Lisa isn't here. Julia thinks she's gone off with your friend Duncan.'

'But he's been with me all afternoon. Working. We had to make a social call. You know how it is. He goes on about how a man's gotta bring home the bacon. Earlier on this evening, me and him were driving back after making our checks and Duncan spotted a woman with a spotty scarf. Spotted a woman. Spotty scarf. Ha! Oh, you know the one, Callie. I didn't see her myself, but it had to be Lisa. I forced Duncan to turn round, hoping to catch up with her because I've found the perfect job for her – something to cheer her up no end. Lisa is obsessed with babies and I know a woman who desperately needs help with hers, so putting two and two together. . .' Hugo checks behind the curtains for a body.

'If you really *were* with Duncan, where is he at this precise moment?' spits Julia, focussing only on Hugo's phrase, *'Duncan spotted a woman.'*

'After our conference this afternoon, he dropped me off at my B&B, so he'll be back in his room at the Sand's Inn. It's more of a pub than a hotel. Shall I take you to see him?' Hugo smiles eagerly at Julia.

'At this time of night? For goodness' sake, it's half one in the morning. It'll be locked.'

'So phone him, why don't you?' Callie leans into the window. *Come on, Lisa! Where are you? Please be safe.*

'He won't answer. His phone's been off all day. Typical,' sighs Julia. Her body crumples as she sinks her face down into the pillow.

Hugo is fiddling with his mobile. He tweaks Callie's cheek. 'Don't worry, darling. It might never happen.'

'But it *is* happening, Dad. This was meant to be a relaxing break.'

Hugo raises his hand up to silence her. He is listening intently. Seconds pass. 'Nope. Mrs Wilde, you're correct. There's no charge on Duncan's phone. Dead as a dodo. No reply. "Odd as owt", as they say up north. He's switched off. I'll toddle on down and take a look myself, shall I? Perhaps I'll scribble a note for his windscreen saying *urgent*, so the minute he finds it he'll know to get in touch, pronto.'

Julia is on her feet. 'I'm coming with you. Hurry up, man.'

Callie glances down to the car park. 'Where are you, Lisa?' she whispers. She turns to Hugo. 'Dad, I know I'll never sleep for worrying. If I ask the receptionist to phone me when Lisa comes back, can I stay on your floor tonight?'

'Not on your Nellie, my dear. You can certainly sleep in my room but you'll get the bed. I am perfectly used to lying on a stone-cold floor.'

Julia has opened the door and is tapping her foot impatiently. Callie flies about collecting her wash things and dumping a few bits and pieces into her overnight bag, then she leaves the room with Hugo and Julia. She feels hyper-alert, thinking, thinking. *Hopefully, at this exact minute, Lisa is on her way up in the lift. Fancy Lisa and Duncan being a couple. She fooled me so brilliantly. But why on earth did they play it like that? All that drama – it seems so much trouble. Something doesn't add up.*

Hugo happily guides his ladies to the Sands Inn. The shadowed streets are deserted, save for a swarm of moths, milling around a light. Callie is on high alert, hunting Lisa, peering down each side street and over every gate, to no avail.

Julia jumps out of the car. *Where is he? Where's his van?* Hugo trails after her as she dashes around the back of the inn into the unkempt space that passes for a customer car park. Rubbish overflows from a couple of cracked wheelie bins. A rat scrambles down a crack in the drain at the base of a downspout.

'He parks here,' says Hugo. 'I have watched him from behind that wall over there.'

'Well, he's not here now. Have you got any other bright ideas, you silly man?'

'Nope.'

'*Monika's* maybe?' Julia curls her lip in sarcastic exasperation.

'He won't go there. Not at this time of night.'

'Show me. Show me anyway. I want to see where this Monika hangs out.'

Hugo shakes his head. 'Very well, if you have to but I must say, Duncan's behaviour is quite out of character. He is usually highly professional – a man of the utmost integrity. I'm his assistant, you see.'

They slam the doors of the Kuga and buckle up. Callie's head rests against the wings of Meg's car seat. *Considering the Wildes have children, this is immaculate. Not a sweet wrapper or toy in sight.*

Julia snaps, 'His assistant, my foot! Duncan needs no assistant and he has no assistant.'

'But he is an adoption researcher and I assist him. He pays me well.'

'I'm his wife and I say he works for D-DIT. Direction Data Information Technology, if you must know. It's a massive firm. He is an IT specialist. And yes, he earns good money but he'd better not be giving you one single cent. Which way?'

'Left here. Then second right. Then straight on up the long lane. It is only a couple of miles. You won't see anything. It'll be too dark and, anyway, he won't be there. If it hadn't been for me he'd have gone home to Lancaster *tout de suite*. I persuaded him to be completely professional about Toby. He had no intention of checking, you see.'

For a brief moment, Julia seems puzzled. She shuts her eyes. Where had she heard that name recently? Toby. Someone said it. Nope. No bells ringing. The fog of confusion refuses to lift. 'I don't see and I don't want to see, so keep your mouth shut until we get to wherever it is we are going.'

After five minutes of winding through the lanes, Callie sniffs several times in quick succession. Julia assumes she is crying but, for her part and even though she is beyond exhaustion, Julia is determined not to go into complete meltdown. *Duncan deserves all he's got coming to him. I warned him. No second chances. He dared used my pregnancy with Sophie as an excuse for his pathetic, self-serving, self-pitying fling with that dreadful Lesley woman he'd met in a chatroom.* Julia recalls Duncan's doe-eyed, contrite apology: *I don't know what came over me. I was flattered. She was a distraction. I'll find a new interest. Enrol in kick-boxing maybe. In future, I promise to be faithful. 'Til death us do part, I will love you. Hold to our vows. Don't break my heart over one tiny mistake. Forgive me.*

Callie sniffs loudly.

'Oh, for goodness sake get a tissue, girl!' Julia distains self-pity.

'But something's burning? Can you smell burning?' Callie cranes her neck, peering into the darkness but the high Cornish hedges block her view.

'Aha!' says Hugo. 'So that explains it. I had deduced, mistakenly, that Julia must be a smoker. Smoke lingers on one's clothes for days. Methinks nicotine is clinging to your upholstery. My senses are super-sensitive and I'm rarely mistaken, but this time I admit . . .'

Julia gasps, 'Look at that!' Where the hedge stops and a fence begins, the fields and hills suddenly open up. In the distance, an immense fire is raging with flames that roar fearlessly into the velvet sky. Julia slows the Kuga, but Hugo cries, 'That's the Nowik house. Put your foot down. Don't stop. We have to save Toby!'

Callie presses her nose to the window: *You did this, didn't you Lisa?* And tears fall unchecked over her cheeks.

It is two am. Hugo dials triple nine, but he has no idea of the name of the lane or the house. He garbles to the emergency services something about needing fire engines, maybe an ambulance, to attend a huge white house facing the sea, near Bude but not in Bude. As he shouts his rough directions, he jogs up the long drive between the impeccable lawns. He hasn't finished the call when he tosses his phone onto the grass and throws his jacket after it.

'Dad! No!' Callie screams as she leaps out of the Kuga.

From behind the wheel, Julia watches. *I could have had a hot shower, a proper sleep in clean sheets. I could have found Duncan in the morning. What on earth made me follow Hugo Quin?* The Kuga jerks. Julia hits the brakes. She's forgotten to turn off the engine. So tired. So tired. All that driving. All that worry. All that confronting truth, talking to horrible, messed-up strangers. She leans forward, touches her forehead onto the wheel and shuts her eyes.

The extreme heat prevents Callie approaching the house. She is overcome by the powerful stench of melting rubber, of chemicals and metal, the terrifying roar as flames heat every window, the sudden irregular shattering of glass, the slipping of roof tiles and shifting of blackening bricks. Somewhere Hugo is yelling, 'Toby! Toby!' but he is so remote, his voice merging with the bright embers that mingle with the stars and ash flakes drifting on the breeze, away from the cold sea and up over the hill.

Callie stands in the darkness. The heat scorches her cheeks and the backs of her hands. She longs to phone her husband, but she cannot move, but her words hit the night air; 'I'm so sorry, Jason. I trusted Lisa without knowing anything about her. I believed she was good but she conned me. What have I done?'

Someone tugs hard at her arm, dragging her away from the

danger of falling masonry. Even as Callie allows herself to be led down the lawn, her head is turned back. She is scanning the windows for silhouettes of humanity, straining her ears for voices above the crack of bursting glass and hiss of the heat which devours every room and corridor, every fitting and picture and useless ornament. Whoever is pulling her stumbles and together they crumple to the ground.

'I should have taken Toby back when we visited, but I left him in there!' Hugo is beside his daughter, holding his knees, swaying forward and back, forward and back. 'I held him in the rocking chair. I fed him and watched him sleep. He was much younger than Duncan admitted, only a week old. Two at most. A mere scrap. Oh, Toby!' Hugo sobs. Callie wraps her arms around him as he wails loudly; 'I didn't get why Duncan had to leave him with those people. There are plenty of others who would have loved him. I . . . I loved him.'

'Oh, Dad,' soothes Callie. 'That baby wasn't ever yours to love.' A thought occurs to her and she voices the impossible. 'Do you think it's possible that Duncan and Lisa ran off with Toby *before* the fire started? Maybe *they* set fire to the house. Like me, you're always too trusting, Dad. You trusted Duncan, but he is still a stranger to you. But who is he really?'

'Duncan paid me for helping him. I wanted it all for you. And then you came.' Without his jacket, Hugo seems to have shrunk. He shivers uncontrollably on the glimmering lawn.

Callie takes charge. 'The firemen should be here already. They're taking ages! Come on, let's get up off this damp grass. Maybe we should wait in the car with Duncan's wife.' Hugo and Callie heave each other to their feet. In the flickering light they see a bench in the centre of the vast lawn and upon it glows the outline of the back of a man's head and shoulders. He is sitting, facing the sea as the pair walk over to him. The man remains motionless.

'Erik?' Hugo places himself directly before the man's eyes. 'Erik!'

'She took our baby.'

Callie says, 'I knew Lisa did it!'

'Who? Who is *she* that took Toby?' Hugo leans forward, shouting in Erik's face.

'It was that flaming lottery that ruined us,' Erik says.

'Flaming lottery!' Hugo interjects, hearing a pun and pointing at the fire, 'Flaming lottery!' but Erik isn't laughing.

'There is nothing for us here in this English countryside, but she insisted on moving to the middle of nowhere to this monstrosity. I had to stop my job. That money, it stole our life. Before all *this* we had very few friends but they were genuine. After we won, we had many, many friends. Everyone a fake. Spongers. Bleeding leeches. That blasted O'Leary Show made everything worse. Everyone round here started to recognise us. So many strange phone calls. And hate mail. Sacks of it.'

'Hate mail?' Callie repeats.

'Everyone scorned us, saying you can't joke on TV about buying babies. *That's exploitation*, they said. *Scum of the earth*, they wrote. Vileness, *crawl back into your hole. Go home, foreigners.* Monika and me, we argued more and more. She cried and moaned about every slightest little thing. I'd been planning to leave her when this adoption research chappie crawls out of the woodwork. Mr Christopher Simons. It makes me sick how she fell for him. Ooh, Mr Simons wants this and Mr Simons says that. I was surprised when he brought us a real baby so quickly because I thought he was a con job, like the rest of them, only after our winnings. But you know, for a few hours my wife was so happy. Like an idiot, I began to think that maybe Toby will fix our mess.'

Erik scrapes his palms over his knees. 'Don't worry, your precious Toby's probably alive somewhere. Monika took him. She packed the pram. Did you see the size of that thing? Not one of those rubbish buggy scaffolding affairs, but the very best quality, old-fashioned Silver Cross. She loaded it. I told her, "You cannot take one so young outside in the night." She said she had to go very far away in case you brought your nursemaid here tomorrow. Mr Quin, my wife pretended to agree with you but Monika will never share Toby with anyone, not even a nursemaid. Not even me. The pram was piled high. Stuff was all over Toby, smothering him. I came here to sit, to watch them go. I let her walk away with him.'

A crash splits the night. Wood cracks like gunshot from within the raging pile but neither the whirling smoke nor the heat nor any sound shocks Erik into moving. In the distance a blue light flashes. Then another.

'They are coming,' Erik says. His hands are folded one over the other. He is holding something white and grubby.

'What's that?' Hugo asks.

'You mean this stupid paper? Have it. I was going to use it to light the fire but – I don't know – maybe it had meaning. Some kind of hope. So I decided to save it. But of course, it is meaningless. Go on, you keep it.'

Hugo takes the paper and holds it up to the firelight. Shadows lick demonically over two red ribbons sticking out from the seal of a gold-embossed snowflake, beneath a crudely printed inscription: *In Recognition of the Adoption of Toby Nowik.*

Fire engines assemble. The first one sweeps up the drive, quickly followed by a second and a third. Men and women in yellow helmets and fluorescent suits leap out in all directions.

Someone shouts, directing the operation. Someone else runs over to Erik.

'Hello. Is everyone safe? Is anyone inside the building?' The fireman faces Erik. He places both hands on Erik's shoulders then squats down and stares him in the face. 'You are in shock, but you must answer me. Is anyone in the building?'

Erik slowly shakes his head. *No one.* He raises both hands, wrists together, as if cuffed in penitent prayer. 'I lit the fire.'

'Sir, I need you to move towards the gate away from the heat.' To Hugo he says, 'Is this your house?'

Hugo hastily stuffs the certificate into his trouser pocket as he steps back to distance himself from Erik. It is Callie who finds the courage to reply. 'This is my dad. We are on holiday from Lancaster. We were just passing when we saw the flames. I've never even been to Bude before last Saturday. My friend Lisa is . . .'

'He doesn't want to know your whole social life, sweetheart,' interrupts Hugo, suddenly ducking to retrieve his phone and jacket. 'We're only getting in their way. Best be off. We were in the vicinity and stopped to help. It was me who rang you, in case you wondered.'

'Very well. Leave your details with the officer over there and then I expect you'll be free to go.'

Hugo and Callie march quickly down the drive towards the police car that is wedged at an awkward angle between the gate posts.

'Leave the talking to me,' hisses Hugo from the side of his mouth.

'But we should tell them about Lisa!' insists Callie.

'One thing at a time, my dear. Yes, of course, officer. Anything to be of service.' Hugo happily divulges his name, and that of

Callie and their addresses in Lancaster. He explains the reason for their winter break: *a modest family celebration as the result of an unexpected financial windfall. Lucky we were passing, officer.*

Lisa 8
That Same Night

Lisa has no idea how many miles she is from Bude. She assumes Callie must be fast asleep and, in any case, Callie doesn't drive so she wouldn't be able to fetch her from the middle of nowhere. Lisa walks alone in the moonlight along the country lane between the hedges.

Whatever happens I won't accept a lift from anyone – whatever was I thinking going with that stranger? He may have meant well, but what do I know? And what was up with his mother? Had she lost her mind? So creepy to think I was asleep in the same room as her. Glad those dogs kept quiet. One day, I'll have a dog. Not a collie though. A spaniel maybe, or golden retriever. Nothing too small and yappy.

I wonder if Callie likes dogs. She must be pretty sick of me by now. Probably glad to be rid of me, like everyone else is. She'll have fun being pampered at the Starcliff without having to put up with me and all my problems. It was the tatty laces that did it. Just the thought of them cramps my stomach up. And that sickly candle smell creeps me out, but I can't work out what it is. Not normal candles; more like the sort for scaring mozzies. But that man gave me my son, helped me to feed my little one. Did I give my baby to him? I can't be totally sure but knowing me, I probably did. So stupid. If I could only see him; my baby, not the man with the laces.

What day is our train back to Lancaster? What if I missed it already? Oops, there's something tiny, jumping. What are you doing out so late at night, little frog? I'm acting too much like my mum, worrying about nothing. Just because I'm out all night partying she gives me grief. On your way little froglet, stay safe.

What's that? Footsteps on the road. Clickety clack. Quick, I'll jump over this gate. Crouch down behind this hedge. Ouch. Shh. Stay down – click, click, click, click. My beating heart . . . Oh my word, it's an old woman in high heels, looking around and behind her as she walks, like she's being followed. I can't understand what she's saying. Foreign. German or Dutch – no wonder I don't get it. Now she's singing but I wouldn't say she was drunk. Crazy maybe. A poor tramp? Homeless. Should I go to her – offer help? But look at me. I can't help anyone. What if she attacks me? Wait. Wait. Your own troubles are enough for any day and more than enough for this night.

After a couple of minutes, Lisa climbs back over the gate and continues towards Bude, in the opposite direction from the woman. She is thankful for her comfortable boots and dry socks. As she walks, she is mulling over every detail of the past fortnight, when all of a sudden she stops abruptly.

A few metres away in the middle of the road, something shiny appears to be hovering: a horizontal silver bar, catching some light from the half moon. Lisa hesitates, apprehensive. To each side of her, the Cornish hedges rise upon their base of dry stone walls, silhouettes of blackberry thorns and fleecy seed heads of the rosebay willow-herb against the navy sky. Lisa's senses prickle on high alert. She hardly dares breath, trying to interpret the image. She smells a faint burning. *Does the shiny thing have an exhaust? If so, why is it so still? Should I run while I have the chance? I daren't go back – the crazy woman is out there somewhere.*

Lisa inches forward, curious yet alert. The light on the bar is constant, but now there is more to see. A diagonal splinter of light about the length of a knitting-needle is attached to a gleaming disc in the shape of a flying-saucer which is turning extremely slowly; tick, tick, tick, tick. She realises there is a large pram lying on its side, the old-fashioned, bouncing type with massive wheels and a solid hood. She approaches with trepidation, as if the pram is some wild, undiscovered creature, presumed dead yet merely stunned and which, without warning, could leap up and kill the innocently inquisitive. What kind of a trap might this be?

My baby! Lisa presses her hands against her womb and takes courage from her own emptiness; nothing to lose, everything to search for. She crouches beside the pram but it is too dark to see inside. Her arm brushes against the uppermost wheel and it moves faster, clicking, clacking, whirring, catching light on its spokes, a zoetrope minus the moving pictures to tell the story. Lisa heaves the pram upright and, as she does so, she scoops bedding from the road. She places a sheet over the thin mattress and over the sheet, a blanket of indiscernible colour. As she smoothes the blanket, she sees a creature quietly observing her, a small beast, a cat maybe, with pinpricks of light in its green, unblinking eyes.

'Psst!' Lisa hisses but the creature doesn't move. She stamps and there's no reaction so she crosses the road and finds a teddy bear, its emerald button-eyes catching the moon. She gathers it against her neck, comforting it, whispering into its damp ear, 'Have you seen my little one? I lost him. Did you lose him too? Tell me if you've seen him.' Piece by piece, Lisa collects items as she journeys on, filling the pram with childlike delight: a miniature silver rocking horse, a pack of disposable nappies, a rag book, two rattles and a muddy teether, which Lisa finds only because she treads on it.

The smell of burning is increasingly intense. Lisa lifts her nose to the sky and inhales. Ahead of her, the sky is glowing orange-red, an eerie dawn without a sunrise, the Northern Lights shimmering in the south; a beauty lanced with fear.

The pram steadies Lisa. She grips the handle, pushing it until she arrives at a layby, which is more than a mere passing place for vehicles because there is a bus stop with plastic seating fixed within a Perspex refuge. For some distance Lisa has found nothing more to add to her collection, so she rests here.

The fire is raging. Lisa can hear the mighty cracks and constant roar. A man is yelling like his life depends on it. *He wants to save somebody.* Lisa rests her head upon the pram handle and rocks gently, gentle as a lullaby. She lifts her head because emergency vehicles are heading her way, racing through the country lanes. Two fire engines with blue lights whizz by and their sirens start to wail, shocking her out of her skin.

Bonfire night. A space between contractions. A minute. Maybe two. I can't decide whether to stand or sit or lie or crawl. Blue lights ripple over the white tiles. I remember the shadow of an angel who is not an angel but an intruder melting close behind me. I hope to die but I must live for the sake of my unborn child. The arms of the intruder ripple and his torso sways. His breath is warm against my neck as the baby falls far below me, onto the lino. The sirens of the engines rushing to the Hala Estate mingle with the baby's first cry. I hear myself saying, 'I don't want it. Take it away. I can't cope with it.'

'What would I do with a baby?'

'Four nine two three,' I lie, and the angel is gone.

Lisa feels in her pocket for her mobile phone. It is difficult to see the screen but she scrolls down to 'Callie' and dials. Though the reception is weak, Callie picks up almost immediately.

'Lisa, thank God! Where are you?'

'S–sorry to wake you.' Lisa's hand quivers against her icy

cheek. She hears Callie's voice breaking up, but so welcome.

'You didn't wake anyone. I've been so worried. We've looked for you everywhere. Have you got Toby?'

'Who?'

'Don't you even know the name of your own baby? Lisa, you've got to tell me, did you take him from the big house?'

'I'm by myself at a bus stop in the middle of nowhere. I can't walk any further and I don't know what to do . . .' Lisa hears shuffling; a new voice on the phone.

'Hello, Hugo Quin speaking. Give us your location. Be precise. We are in possession of a vehicle with a driver.'

'Mr Quin? I'm at a bus stop. Not in Bude. I've been walking back from somewhere. I don't know where. There's a fire in the distance and I'm so scared.'

'She can see the fire. I think I know where she is – drive on, Julia. Yes, we *are* going to pick her up. You wouldn't leave your own daughter alone on a dark night, would you? No, don't hang up, Lisa – and don't walk down the middle of the road as you were seen to do last night. Don't do anything silly.'

'I'm at a stop. I'm at . . . a bus stop. A stop.' Lisa reels. Her eyes close.

The next thing, Hugo and Callie are dragging Lisa to her feet. Callie is saying, 'What on earth?' because of the pram. Hugo checks the pram for signs of Toby, then he clutches Lisa by the shoulders. He is shouting in her face; 'Where's Toby? What have you done with Toby?' but Lisa shakes her head dumbly because the name 'Toby' means nothing to her. Hugo rushes headlong into the field towards a pitch-black mountain of brambles, careless for his own safety, thinking only of the baby.

Julia watches the fool as she leans against her vehicle. *These people . . . someone needs to tell them what's what.* She raises her voice: 'You lot owe me for a full valet on my car, what with your horrible smoky clothes and muddy boots. You do what you want but I'm going straight back to the hotel for a shower and some sleep. And I'll deal with you later, young lady. You may think you can lure my husband away but believe me, he's a sick man and if he's hanging out with the likes of you he must be desperate. Be thankful I even let you breathe, let alone sit in my car. If *he* wasn't here to witness my actions, I'd . . .' Julia waves her fingers to indicate Hugo, who is stumbling back, agonised and scratched from his futile search.

'I demand total silence!' Hugo commands, raising both hands to the stars, expecting the very universe to hold its breath for the sake of the child.

'Don't you tell me to shut up!' Julia huffs. She retreats to the warmth of the driver's seat and slams the door. Hugo holds his fingers to his lips. Even from here the roar of the fire can be heard, mighty cracks, like trees falling in a rainforest. The girls say nothing while Hugo listens, but neither he nor they hear a baby cry.

Lisa gathers some of her new-found treasures, (the small bear, the rattle, the silver rocking-horse) and allows Callie to shepherd her to the vehicle. Hugo sits up front, trying in vain to contact Duncan. The group travel in stuffy silence. They arrive at the Starcliff. Julia parks furiously. She leaps out and tears around the vehicle to open the passenger door. She drags at Lisa's arm.

'Where is he? If you don't tell me this instant, I'll— Oh, stop your silly little girl games and talk to me before I . . .'

Lisa, who's been fighting sleep in the warm vehicle, has no idea who Julia is or to whom she is referring. She struggles to get out of the car, then leans against it for support. 'I knocked on every door in Bude but I couldn't find him anywhere. I searched all day. I really did.'

'When she says she couldn't find "him", she doesn't mean Duncan,' stammers Callie, ever the peace-maker, but wavering between who to support.

Julia squares up to Lisa, nose to nose. They are about the same height but Lisa lacks the energy to return the powerful accusatory glare of the older woman.

'Finally the truth is out! You couldn't *find* Duncan because you already had him. What did he promise you? A life of adventure? To take you skiing? You wouldn't be much company for him on a mountainside – you can't even hold your own head up on your skinny neck. I don't know why you're acting so sorry for yourself! If you create your own storm you shouldn't be surprised when it rains. Oh, for crying out loud, get to bed the lot of you.'

Julia strides across the flood-lit gravel while rummaging in her bag for her room key.

Hugo phones Duncan without reply.

'Dad, I know I've got to stay here after all but don't leave me alone with her,' says Callie. 'Sorry Lisa, but I don't know who you are. I can't be responsible for you anymore. We'll go home tomorrow after some sleep.'

Hugo leads the way, acknowledging the night-duty receptionist by raising his hand, a reassuring politician's wave. He gives the faintest of smiles, *Don't worry mate, I'm legit!* and they take the lift to the third floor.

As Lisa sleeps, Callie lies awake beneath her duvet. Hugo, fully dressed except for his jacket and walking boots, lies on top of the covers on the single bed beside his daughter. His deerstalker hat and lime-green binoculars are on the dressing table.

'Toby,' Hugo whispers, blinking back tears.

'Do you think that woman's got him? Do you think Erik's wife has Toby?'

'Monika? Yes I do. I mean, I hope so. Erik said Monika left the big house with Toby in that pram and Lisa found the pram empty. Maybe Monika called a taxi, in which case she and Toby could be anywhere in Cornwall. I hope I'm right in thinking that she wouldn't harm the baby. She loves him.'

'But Erik said she won't share him with anyone. Sometimes people do terrible things to those they love. What if she . . . ?'

'Shh, don't go there. Don't imagine the worst. If she has – you know – done that, then we'll have to handle the consequences. If she's got Toby, maybe someone will report her. It's got to look suspect. Toby's bound to be screaming and someone will hear him. I can settle him, you know. He settles for me. Let's give it thirty-six hours and if there's no news, we'll confess to the authorities.'

'What have you done, Dad? It's okay to tell me. I'm an adult now. I'm not Mum, falling to pieces over your behaviour – I can cope, you know.'

Hugo clears his throat. He is shuddering, but not with cold. Callie rests her forehead beneath her father's jaw and feels the dampness of his tears and she says nothing more.

Hugo showers before the girls wake. He has no choice but to dress in the clothes he slept in, then he nips downstairs to the breakfast room where several guests are already ordering coffee. Ignoring their quizzical stares, Hugo loads his pockets with apples and bananas, selects three croissants and picks up a small jug of milk. He marches bold as brass past the astounded staff who were about to ask *Sir* if he required a cooked breakfast.

'Family upstairs somewhat under the weather. Breakfast in bed, if you don't mind,' he chirps, rendering them aghast and immobile. Hugo waits for the lift. Suddenly the lift door opens and Julia emerges, fresh as a daisy, immaculate in trainers and a black tracksuit with pink trim. Hugo is the last person she expected to bump into. *Doesn't this man ever sleep?*

'Any news from Duncan?' Hugo asks, stepping directly in front of her.

'Nothing that will interest you,' she snaps, side-stepping.

'Hey, hey, lady. New day, new attitude. That's what I always say,' smiles Hugo, matching her moves. 'Let's dance the two-step while you break the news that doesn't interest me.'

'Very well. Duncan sent me a text. He has no idea where I am.'

'And you told him what?'

'Nothing. Not a sausage. He can rot, for all I care.'

'So where is he then?'

'Honolulu. Hawaii. Haiti. Who knows? You're his new best friend, you ask him. As far as I'm concerned he can go to hell. I'm off to the gym and then I'll book a long massage and a manicure. Afterwards I'll drive home to file for a divorce. Should have done it years ago.'

'Don't.' Hugo shakes his head emphatically. Croissant crumbs spill through his fingers onto the worn, crimson carpet.

Julia raises her eyebrows. 'Don't?'

'Divorce. It's not worth it. It's lonely and tragic and the kids live with it for the rest of their lives. Some things really are forgivable – given time. Ever seen *The Antiques Road Show*? Some bloke on it said that just because something's damaged or wrecked doesn't mean it should be chucked out, because it could still be valuable even without restoration. I once saw a woman show that bloke a lamp. It was in terrible condition. She'd paid a tenner for it at a car boot even though it was cracked right through the middle and badly glazed. The auctioneer recognised it as posh stuff by a famous designer. Poole, I believe. He told the woman it was very rare. She had tried to get it fixed but the cost was extortionate, so she was going to chuck it. It was in an absolute state but it went to auction and fetched twelve grand! The auctioneer said it is better to have a damaged article you love, rather than not have it at all. And you love Duncan.'

'Pah! Well, let me see,' she counts on her fingers. 'There's Lesley . . .'

'Who?'

'And now Lisa. And Monika. And whoever he's with this minute, because he sure as hell isn't all by his little self in his little world in his little van with his inflated ego.'

'He never had an affair with Monika. If you saw her, believe me you'd believe me!'

'Lisa, then.'

'On that one I'll admit to the occasional sniff of suspicion myself. But when one records the facts, there's no controvertible proof. You mustn't abandon the love of your life simply because you took it into your head to drive hundreds of miles to hear a bunch of rumours about Duncan that you haven't given him chance to refute.'

'No proof? Well then, explain this!' Julia unzips the side pocket of her bag and holds aloft the chameleon. Beneath the brash hotel lights, its eyes glint red.

'Ugly beast.'

'Either he bought it or he stole it or he was given it. Whatever the truth, this thing points to female trouble. Defend Duncan all you like but I'm leaving in two hours. He can have his fancy chicken fodder – *my* children deserve better.' She steps around Hugo. As she stalks off, she adds, 'I deserve better!'

Upstairs, Hugo knocks and waits. Callie, with dripping hair and wrapped in a giant bath towel, opens the door. She pounces on the croissants and eats one immediately. She pours two coffees. Together, she and her father whisper over the sleeping Lisa.

'We can't stay here another night, Dad. Too pricey.'

'You're right about that, so guess what? I'm planning to cadge us all a lift home from guess who? Duncan's wife.'

'We could offer her petrol money.'

'Diesel.'

'Whatever. It's worth you asking because I don't fancy taking the train with Lisa, but I can't just abandon her. She doesn't seem, you know, completely *well.*' Callie taps her own temple and Hugo agrees. *Not quite right.*

Much to Julia's annoyance, Hugo is waiting for her as she emerges, flushed yet immaculate from her exercise and beauty regime. He totters along beside her, arguing his case for a lift to Lancaster for the three of them. Julia has to pass through the foyer where the girls are packed, huddled and hopeful for an easy way north to Lancaster.

Julia whirls round, throwing both hands up in exasperation. 'Very well! If you can bring yourself to give me some space to get changed, I might consider taking you and your daughter, but there's no way *she's* coming with us.'

'Dad,' urges Callie. 'Don't bother. Let her go. We can take the train. Can't you see she's fed up with us?'

Lisa flops onto a worn leather armchair. She clutches her bag against her stomach and watches helplessly. Who she travels with, at what time, or whether she even goes anywhere at all – nothing matters.

Hugo's phone rings on the loudest setting and they all jump. 'Duncan!' he hisses in a dramatic stage whisper, flapping his hand to hush the women. Julia freezes, forgetting to close her mouth. The receptionist leans forward on her desk, all ears.

'Why, hello, my friend!' cries Hugo, hamming up the *everything*'s okay scenario. He stabs the phone on to loudspeaker so the others can eavesdrop.

'I'm in Lancaster. Julia's not here. I . . . I think she's left me.' Duncan's voice is hoarse. *Is he crying?*

'Lancaster,' Hugo repeats, widening his eyes for the benefit of his audience. 'How? I mean, why? What about Toby?'

'But *she's* not here, Hugo. What shall I do? There's not even a note. I phoned her work and they told me she didn't go in yesterday.'

Hugo looks at Julia. She lifts a finger to her lips: *Say nothing. I'm not here.*

'Really? Er, what a pity. Can't think where she might be.' Hugo is fluffing. Julia mouths and flaps her hands at the phone: *Make him stay where he is.* Hugo is eager to please. He coughs politely, to allow himself time to switch his tone from total confusion to total nonchalance.

'So, Duncan, what're your plans today?' Hugo shrugs to the women: *I'm doing my best.*

'I only want to see my Julia,' Duncan sniffs. 'To confess. Make a clean start. I've kept things from her, you know. She doesn't know I lost my job. I got bored. Things escalated.'

Julia is mouthing *filthy liar.* She says aloud, 'Lost your job? When? You want a clean start? Over my dead body!' but Hugo slaps his hand over the receiver and talks exuberantly so Duncan can't hear his wife.

'I'm sure she's, er, gone out for the day, perhaps to work. Perhaps she's a lady what lunches! Ha, ha! Tell you what, why don't you chill out, mate? Catch up on your sleep. Clean those drums of yours. May I suggest you give your wife a few hours' grace? I guarantee that if you don't hassle her, she'll appear and you can discuss it all 'til the cows come home.'

'I hope you're right, Quin. Am I over-reacting? I drove over three hundred miles, psyching myself to come clean. This place is empty without her. It's cold. Unlived in. I've never told her how much I hate it.'

'You hate your own home?' Hugo thinks of his own beloved sanctuary, a single room in a hotel, with its threadbare carpet and rusty balcony overlooking meadows and the M6.

'There are more germs on an operating table than in our kitchen,' Duncan says weakly.

'But isn't that a good thing?'

'I can't relax. Be myself . . .'

'You should've told her . . .'

'But why should she change for me? She deserves better. I only want her to be happy.'

Julia tries to snatch the phone from Hugo. 'Give me that thing! I'll tell him what makes me happy. I'll . . .'

Hugo spins round to avert the crisis just as Duncan says, 'What's going on? Is someone with you?'

Hugo switches off the loudspeaker. He musters a surprising level of authority. 'Pull yourself together and prepare for your wife's homecoming. Put on the heating. Rustle up some food. Sausage pasta bake is my signature dish. Have a kip. You don't want Mrs Wilde to see you in such a state, not if you want her to be happy you're home.' Hugo can hear Duncan breathing as he considers this.

After a couple of seconds, Duncan sniffs again. 'Thanks Hugo. I owe you.'

'Me? Oh, it's nothing.'

'Am I being paranoid? What if she's left for good with our girls? I'm sick to my stomach. Their beds haven't been slept in but if I phone school to check, Jules will kill me for interfering. Not trusting. It's a thing with her – trust. Hugo, I drove all night. I'm so drained. I didn't know who else to talk to so I phoned you. And Hugo . . .' Duncan is rambling, anything for company.

'Yes?'

'Money isn't everything. You know what I'm talking about.'

'I know, I know. Now do what I told you. Sleep it off. In a few hours you'll have a whole new perspective. Remember   call me anytime if you need to talk.' Hugo hangs up and bows to the women. 'Samaritans, eat your heart out.'

Julia says, 'Right, everyone settle your bill and follow me. I've decided to give you all a lift because I'm going to need you as witnesses. And that includes you, madam. Yes you, Miss E. Rimmer. I have my reasons. Come to think of it, young lady, I've got a little something for you in my car. Give me ten minutes to get my stuff together. You don't have to follow me, Mr Quin. Obviously I'm not going anywhere without you. Run along. Wait by the Kuga if you must.'

After Julia has loaded the car and all four are seated, Julia rounds on Lisa with an expression bordering on manic. She is waving the denim purse in Lisa's face.

Lisa gasps. 'That's mine. Where did you find that? How?' She reaches for it and Julia tosses it to her, with a smug expression of victory. She turns to Hugo who is strapped in beside her. 'And there you have it. Confirms all my suspicions. Lisa knows Duncan. That purse was found by *me* in *my* drive and it contains *her* bank card, no doubt dropped by *her* on one of her illicit visits to my home. Right, that's enough. Not another word. We'll stop where I choose, when I say, and only for the loo. If you want food, you can buy your own but no hanging around or I'll leave you.'

Callie glances across at Lisa, aware that Julia can see them in the mirror, so she daren't ask for the story behind the purse.

Lisa mumbles under her breath, 'He stole my baby.'

Callie quietly texts Jason to expect her this evening. I miss you. I love you xx. She hasn't yet told him this weekend break with her new 'friend' has been a disaster. He'll be so disappointed because he had encouraged her to go with it.

Hugo leans forward for his last glimpse of Summerleaze Beach. It would be a most satisfactory place to return to next summer. He imagines taking a proper dip in that natural seawater pool. He daydreams of saving the pool from certain extinction: Hugo the Superhero, the impregnable Diamondman, Pirate of the High Seas, robbing the wealthy to shower gifts upon the grovelling poor. Hugo sees the crowds, the grateful people of Bude lining the street, five deep, cheering wildly. *You saved our pool, our pride and joy!* Hugo, in full wetsuit and flippers, waddles to the concrete edge of the seawater pool and bows modestly before diving in. Though the water is icy and he won't win any medals for style, Hugo swims a full length.

Duncan 14, Hugo 10, Julia 8, Callie 4 and Lisa 9
The Snow-Bridge Collapses

Julia pulls into the driveway of Four Valleys and slams on the brakes so everyone jolts forward. Duncan's van is parked across the path, side on to the front door. It is late afternoon but every curtain is closed, exactly how Julia left them yesterday. She unravels herself from the driver's seat and stretches her legs. She won't phone Sophie and Meg yet because her mother will ask too many questions. Duncan first.

The journey had allowed plenty of time to dream and to rehearse the inevitable encounter. The gang had endured infuriating fifty mph roadworks punctuated by two breaks, the latter at Sandbach Services, where Hugo had vanished then emerged grinning, bringing hot chips for everyone. Julia could swear he'd surreptitiously wiped his greasy fingers on the car seat.

'Wait here.' Julia gets out of the car, but Hugo is already crunching over the gravel to investigate Duncan's Cave. Julia ignores him. She is beyond caring about anyone else. She flings open the front door and marches in, striding through the kitchen then the snug and into the unused dining area.

'Duncan?' Julia's call is more of a command to a naughty child to come forth, own up, face the music, as opposed to an endearing *welcome home darling*. 'Duncan? Game over. Show yourself.' She storms into their usually immaculate bedroom and switches on the light, to see clothes strewn everywhere: clean shirts crumpled on the bed, mismatched socks crawling over the carpet and, in the corner, Duncan's favourite burgundy sweater, inside out, strangling itself.

Duncan's locker drawer yawns open precariously. The wardrobe is open, with several shoe boxes pulled out, scattered and abandoned. On the chest of drawers are some 'foreign' objects: a George Cross medal; a gold pendant on a chain; a delicate filigree photo-frame; a stunning antique platinum ring set with diamonds; a collection of cigarette cards of football players from yesteryear. And a photo of a youthful Duncan laughing with Steve in Verbier, the year before Steve's death; the year before Duncan proposed to Julia; the year before Duncan inexplicably grew up. Soon after they married, Duncan began to work for D-DIT.

Julia touches each item with a fingertip, slowly, gently, as if each is a priceless object d'art for which white gloves are required. *Do not handle. These artefacts may crumble in the light.*

She draws back the curtains as the last of the low autumn sun beckons through the naked trees. *Give me air*, thinks Julia, opening the window and gasping. She hears voices and leans out, peering to her right, across the driveway. And there he is. Duncan. Slouching in the doorway of his cave; being confronted by Callie and Hugo. *Duncan!*

Julia flies downstairs and out of the house. She is running through treacle, a nightmare in which the ground threatens to suck her into itself, into some deep and lonely crevasse, yet incredibly she finds herself standing firm as she approaches her husband. He's going to get a piece of my mind! Then her world stops.

'Duncan?' she starts but his name sticks in her throat, because this is not the man who left home only last week for that oh-so-important D-DIT conference. He hasn't shaved and his cheeks have sunk like some hopeless addict. His hair is unwashed, sticking to his forehead. His jeans are shabby – and where did he get that baggy grey sweater with holes in the elbows and those ghastly trainers with such tatty laces?

Duncan raises dull eyes towards his wife.

'I made Lisa stay in the car,' Callie is telling Duncan. He frowns, nodding like he is trying hard to remember something elusive, someone's name or the way into town.

'You should have gone along with my plan,' Hugo reminds him. 'I had this great idea. Lisa could have become a nanny for Toby, paid to care for her own baby like Moses's mother. He had a nursemaid who was secretly his real mum. I thought . . .' Duncan shrugs and Hugo runs out of words.

'Tell us what you know about the fire,' Callie tries. Duncan shrugs.

Hugo adds, 'A huge and terrible thing. I thought – I thought . . .'

'Dad thought your baby had died.' Callie is possessed by a growing fortitude, a newly tenacious yet calm fury and, because Duncan acknowledges nothing, her voice rises. 'My dad almost died trying to save your baby and where were you? Why are you just standing there? Did you know about the fire? Don't you care what happened to Toby? What did his new mum do with him?'

Duncan doesn't seem capable of registering. He blinks, dazed, as if emerging from a coal cellar into searing sunlight.

'Callie, hush,' says Hugo.

'Don't hush me. What if that burning house had collapsed on you? I only just found you again, Dad, and I could have lost you and all because of him. Don't tell me to hush.'

'But Callie, Toby is *not* Duncan's baby. Tell her Duncan,' Hugo urges.

'That's enough!' Julia is clutching the small drain spout on the corner of the Cave. 'You've been drinking. You disgust me,' she adds, sounding slurred herself.

'I took a baby from his mother.' Duncan voice is caught in his gut, distant and twisted. Julia hears his words but it is impossible to comprehend her husband's confession. Her own planned speech must vent before she can accept new terrors.

'Remember not so many years back when you left me for that hideous Lesley woman? What did you see in her compared to everything I was already giving you? *You. Had. No. Needs.* You spat on me when you went with her. To what purpose? Am I not enough for you anymore? I forgave you. Me – forgave you. Never spoke of it again, like we agreed. And you promised to be faithful. How dare you pretend to be innocent when it comes to Lisa or Monika or, or Callie, or God knows who else! Mr Quin has given me all their names, so don't think you can hide your sordid, pathetic little life from me for a second longer.'

'You're not listening,' tries Hugo.

'She never listens,' says Duncan quietly. He takes a step backwards. The Cave door frames him and it is a size too large.

'What's to listen to?' Julia's lips are white at the edges. 'I have had it up to here with your fakery. And what's all that – that *stuff* in our bedroom, hey? Anyone would think we'd been burgled! Go on, take your pathetic bunch of – of so-called *friends* inside my house. Show them what an utter shambles you've made of my beautiful home. You want to throw it all away? Good. Because I'm through with you. Take your fancy little floozy, whichever one she is, and don't you ever come crawling back to me again!'

'Hellooo, there! Is everything all right? Anything I can do to help?' A voice from the foot of the drive, a woman tugging on the lead of a golden retriever. Everyone looks up but Julia is the first to react. She grits her teeth and forms a lopsided smile.

'Rae Hook, of all the interfering . . .' she seethes. Lowering her tone to locate her more refined voice, Julia calls out, 'As a matter of fact, Rae, you can do me a favour. A big favour.' She turns to the group and hisses, 'Nobody move. Not one word!' She digs her hand into her pocket as she stalks down the drive to confront her neighbour.

'I've been on a long journey,' Julia sounds like some weary mother telling her children that she can't be bothered with their needs, because she has a dreadful headache that was all their fault in the first place. 'I popped this *thing* into my pocket, so whenever I needed to feel alive – you do understand what I mean by *alive*, Rae? It means to *feel* something; to care about important stuff. And that stuff is not about glittering ornaments, or jewels, but about keeping my family together. So I stabbed these nasty little claws into my palm and, wouldn't you know, it did the trick. Kept me awake through absolute hell. Look – stab marks. We were in heavy traffic, so slow I could eyeball all the other drivers going along on their merry little way with their merry little, cheating, lying, double-minded lives and do you know what I felt? Nothing.'

She is waving her palm at Rae's face, but Rae is too terrified to avert her eyes from Julia's animated mouth. 'The pain reminded me I was still alive, see? So thanks very much to whoever lost this, what do you call it? Chameleon. And I don't care one iota what you might *think* you know about where it came from. Say what you like to whoever you like because now, Rae, I am going to give you this. You take it to the police or return it to the owners. Because, as I've already explained, my darling husband found it on the pavement and he keeps intending, but failing, because he is ever so busy with his very, very important job – he keeps *intending* to hand it in. So, since you know so much about this thing, *you* do it.'

As the chameleon passes between them, Rae's flushed cheeks drain colourless as a waxwork. Goldie whimpers, rubbing her nose into Rae's fist. Rae starts, 'I . . .' but Julia lifts her chin, turns on her heels and marches straight back to the Cave. Stranded between the wide gateposts, Rae, the outsider, hesitates. She grips the sharp chameleon hard into her hand, too appalled to notice physical pain. After some seconds she moves on, dragging Goldie up the road. *Some people are so confusing.*

'Right,' Julia says, like she is ticking off a to-do list of household chores, 'What next?'

Hugo raises a hand, a child asking permission.   'I know you said to keep it quiet, Duncan, but in my opinion, personally, I do think it may be possibly time to explain ourselves here, because it's our fault we lost Toby. And we should care . . .' Hugo's feet shuffle into the gravel, seeking the firmer ground beneath. 'Do you think Monika would hurt her own baby? And the fire? While we were driving earlier, I nearly phoned the police, but what could I tell them? What if it's already too late? I mean, the fire . . . the empty pram?'

Hugo's words excite panic in Duncan. Truth may surface. Adrenalin, like an annoying party guest who doesn't know when to leave, surges through Duncan, urging him to enjoy the sensation of fight or flight, yet he is literally petrified. His dad is no longer around to oversee the childhood terrors of *Dr Who*, to turn off the TV and say, *'This'll give you nightmares.'*

Moh and Luke and Yasin are drinking and laughing and Steve is winding them all up for another evening of boasting. 'Hey Dunc, what would you do if we were caught at the edge of an avalanche? Everyone gets hit bad. All unconscious – except you – and one of us is buried alive?'

The snow-bridge collapses. A demon yanks the white sheet and Duncan falls. The white walls of the crevasse race skywards to his left and his right. The landing takes his breathe away and there is no one to save him.

'You did what?' Julia is saying, as Duncan's earlier words catch up with her.

'He stole a baby,' says Hugo, because he can see that Duncan is unable to speak for himself.

Julia's legs crumple, forcing her to lean against the corner of the Cave. On the journey from Bude she'd meticulously planned the confrontation of Duncan, before these obnoxious witnesses, so he could not possibly deny his adulteries, but Hugo is forcing this whole thing in an unforeseen, hideous direction.

'You killed your own baby? How? Why? Oh, Duncan, what have you done?'

Hugo interrupts. 'Of course he didn't murder Toby. He loved him, didn't you, Duncan? He found him a loving home despite difficult circumstances. We weren't to know the woman was off her head. My gut says Toby's alive, that Monika took him because she's not the sort to let go. Ever. But the fire . . . the empty pram . . . we have to care. . .'

Duncan slumps to the ground. Behind him, Hugo can see the shattered dreams of his abandoned drums and symbols.

I was in a band but they all grew up.

Hugo awkwardly reaches out to stroke Callie's arm. 'What shall we tell Lisa?' Hugo says, to no one in particular, because Lisa is still in the car.

Duncan hauls himself up, standing tall, and everyone steps back because his words are suddenly loud. 'I took Toby. I sold Toby. You want to know why? I lost my job. I was bored! What do you expect me to say? His mother asked, no, she *begged* me to take her own baby. She begged! So why are you so disgusted with me, like I'm a filthy crook?' Duncan is shouting, but still he stands guard across the doorway. 'Go away the lot of you. Yes, and you can back off too, Julia! Look what you did to me, wanting all that – that – that *stuff*. I can't live like this, trapped in so many walls, with so much order. Can't breathe. I need mess. I need time. I need mountains. Sweat. Pain. Life! What is it you *need*, darling? More *stuff*? Nothing is ever enough for you. I'm sick to death of it. Sick to my back teeth.' He bares his teeth and grasps at the air with his hands, clawing; palms forward like some wild bear defending her young.

A cry from the Cave. The persistent crescendo of a newborn, livid for landing on the cold lino, furious for food, desperate to be comforted by the man he knows as a father. The open door releases the cry beyond the soundproofed walls. Duncan raises his eyebrows: *Is it me or can you all hear that?* He looks from Callie to Hugo, then to his wife who is shrinking against the gutter.

'I'll get him!' shouts Hugo, rushing forward, but Duncan knocks him back into Callie.

'He's mine!' Duncan hisses, arms wide, defending the Cave door. 'You told me he had bruises. Erik wanted to strangle him. Monika couldn't cope. *You* didn't fetch him back – I did. I returned to the Nowik house alone. Walked in. Didn't try to hide. I walked straight in through the front door and they must have heard me but they didn't even switch off the TV. Toby was alone upstairs and you were right, Hugo, there was a bruise on his cheek.' Duncan touches his own cheek. He closes his eyes. 'I lifted him,' Duncan's hands recreate the scene; he is cradling Toby. 'I held him, carried him downstairs, and then she saw me.'

'She? A woman? Who? What are you talking about? Who saw you?' Julia covers her mouth with her hand as the crying of Toby rises and wanes.

Duncan's voice hardens. 'That stupid, fat, foreigner Monika Nowik, that's who. She waddled out from the lounge. We met on the stairs. She looked up and . . .' Duncan glares at his audience the way he'd glared down at Monika. Decisive. Silent. No argument. He slows his speech to clarify every detail, so no one can dispute that his words are the absolute truth.

'She was nodding, yes, yes, and wagging her finger, warning me to move quietly. She pointed at me. Whispered, "I knew you'd come for him, Mr Simons. Let us not concern Erik. You do this thing quickly." Mrs Nowik backed downstairs. She locked herself in the cloakroom. She even flushed the toilet to mask the sound of the front door as I let us out. Us. Me and Toby. I tucked him under my coat to keep him warm and then I walked down the drive. I'd parked round the corner, out of sight, but it wouldn't have mattered if the van had been right outside the front door. She never even said goodbye to Toby.'

Duncan turns his head to the cries of his son. 'I need a minute . . .' He turns his back, opens the door and vanishes into the Cave.

Hugo, Callie and Julia listen to Duncan's insistent, '*Shh, shhhh,*' each one anxious to rush into the Cave, but fearful of who Duncan is, or how he might react to their intervention. They hear the ping of the microwave. They exchange nervous glances. The cries subside until there is an ominous silence. Several minutes pass.

Julia whispers, 'What's he up to now?' but Hugo holds up his hand to calm her. *Wait.*

After a while, Duncan emerges cradling a tiny baby swaddled in a pristine, blue shawl. He appears calm as a midwife on hospital steps, to oversee a newborn safely home. Callie gasps, for the first time truly believing. 'Is he really Lisa's?' Duncan's serious eyes are fixed upon the face of the infant. And suddenly Lisa is among them, approaching softly until she is beside Duncan, careful not to startle him, placating him in a quiet, clear voice.

'Thank you. Thank you for caring. I can tell you genuinely love him. Oh my – he is so very beautiful.' Lisa searches for the eyes of her baby but he sees only Duncan. This man her baby trusts. Lisa's arm glances against Duncan's but he doesn't move away. She is aware of the sweat through his shirt, the perspiration of his exhaustion. Gradually, gradually, she dares to lean her head against his shoulder, to see more clearly the infant face.

'I named him Toby,' Duncan says.

'That's good. Toby.' Lisa turns towards the man whose shadow had rippled across her bathroom wall.

'Toby?' says Julia, remembering. She is rigid, unsure of what she is witnessing.

'Your son. Here.' Duncan eases Toby into the arms of his mother.

Lisa receives him, cradling the tiny boy in the crook of her elbow. She raises his tiny face to her own until their noses touch. 'Hello you,' she whispers. She brushes her lips over his pale forehead and every tiny milk spot sends a shiver of delight through her. She caresses the minute hand, cold in the November air, so she envelops it within her own. She raises her head to speak, waiting for Callie, Hugo and Julia to focus on her, allowing them time to process so they won't interrupt in their confusion or anger.

Callie is astonished because the distressed young girl she'd met in Lancaster, in unwashed clothes and with matted hair, is an intelligent woman of enviable tranquillity, who speaks with confident eloquence.

'There is a time for silence. No words can change our past. If you report this to any authority they'll be forced to investigate, which will take precious time and money away from children who this very minute are being neglected, abused, damaged. Toby is my son. On my life, I swear I'd never harm him. His father was Paul. He enjoyed mind games and controlled me with violence. He's unpredictable. Dangerous. Stupidly, I chose to be with him, just to spite my mum.

'Your husband did wrong, Julia, but at least he did *something*. Whatever his motives, he was with me when I was a mess. When I rejected my son, your husband accepted him. And because he is safe, I can forgive him. Callie, I already love you. I'm sorry for your holiday, but when we met I had no idea – you didn't deserve such a terrible time. Maybe one da . . .'

Callie bursts with relief, rushes to Lisa, flings her arms around her. 'I love you too! And wow, look at your gorgeous, sweet boy. Anyone can see he's the spit of you. Those dark eyes! Oh, come on, Dad – look at him, he's so adorable. Have you ever seen such a beautiful baby?'

'As a matter of fact, when you were born . . .' Hugo starts, but now is not the time for stories. Only Julia notices that Duncan has melted back into the Cave. He can stay in there tonight. She will tidy their bedroom, but tomorrow, he can explain the whole sorry mess, every last breath of it.

Sam Martin rolls her eyes, but she is smiling. 'Very well, you win! Lisa and Toby can stay in the box room until Christmas, when you and Jason move into your own flat. If all's well, I will give them first refusal to rent the spare double. Let's take it a day at a time. See how it goes, though goodness only knows how I'll cope with a baby crying in the night.'

'He'll be right beside me, Sam,' Lisa says. 'I promise that as soon as he cries I'll be ready.'

'Now, now, I'm not expecting superwoman. We'll cope together. Can't have the poor mite homeless, especially not at this time of year. Callie, be a love and turn the heating up a notch.' Behind Sam's back, Lisa and Callie exchange glances of relief – the landlady hadn't asked awkward questions.

It is late. Jason is in the shower, singing along to Radio One. He'd only just got in from work when Callie phoned to say they'd been given a lift back from Cornwall and could he please pick them all up, including Hugo and Toby, not from the train station, but from some mansion on the other side of the city. Jason had arrived at the Wilde's place, where he and a certain Mr Quin joined forces to load the boot with a mountain of disposable nappies, bottles, formula, and baby clothes, courtesy of the generous Duncan Wilde.

Secreted beneath a pile of baby clothes, knotted into a supermarket carrier bag, is Lisa's unused and uncancelled bankcard, along with a substantial wad of twenty-pound notes – and a hastily scribbled note. As Hugo, Callie, Lisa and Toby had waited for Jason to pick them up, Duncan had written: *Ashamed about the bankcard. Legitimate money for Toby from Mr and Mrs Nowik.*

For Duncan, it never had been about the money.

On the long drive back from Bude, Duncan had left the motorway in Taunton to visit a supermarket where he'd splashed out on all manner of things for Toby. The checkout girl gazed at the baby in Duncan's arms. 'He's a boy, right? Your son is totally gorgeous! Do you need help packing? Didn't you know we provide trolleys especially for newborns? Next time just ask if you're not sure.'

'Thanks. My son? Yes. My son is beautiful. I love him with my life.'

'Your wife is so lucky to have your support, caring for the little one *and* doing the shopping. Multi-tasking! I'm so massively impressed. Not many guys would do that without a moan, I can tell you. If only there were more guys like you in this world.'

Hugo 11
I am Durus

Hugo coughs up for a taxi from Sam's place to take him home to his own room at his half-brother Iain's hotel. He's never hired a taxi before, preferring the freedom of hitching or walking, but the hour is late and, for Hugo, it has been a particularly emotional day. Hugo imagines he is Prince William returning from hospital after the birth of Charlotte. He is the proud father of a princess, a future queen. Once more the nation lines the streets five deep, waving and cheering as Hugo glides by and a Union Jack flaps from the royal Aston Martin.

The moon flickers between vertical lines of narrow tree trunks and Hugo greets the silver disc as it appears and reappears: 'Hi, bye, hi, bye, hi, bye, hi, bye.'

Iain happens to be on the front steps of his hotel, lugging a heavy tubular metal bin when he spies Hugo ambling towards him. He dumps the rubbish bin at Hugo's feet. 'Good timing. You can shift this lot to the end of the drive for me. Empty it into the wheelie bin – you know where it is.'

'Hello, Hugo, great to see you again,' mocks Hugo, propping his rucksack against the wall and lifting the bin.

'The leaves are clogging up the drains – priority job first thing tomorrow. The family from room 16 were rehoused yesterday. The snagging list is on my desk. You'll need to buy some grout to replace the cracked tiles in the bathroom of number four.'

Hugo heaves the bin as high as he can, turning his back on his boss. *I am Durus, the mighty Atlas and upon my shoulders I endure the weight of the world.* He lugs his burden to the end of the drive, where he tips the stinking contents into the wheelie bin and knocks the lid shut with his elbow. He swings the metal bin by one finger as he returns it to its place behind the kitchen door.

In his own room, Hugo brews a mug of strong, hot chocolate. His bare feet enjoy the threadbare familiarity of the faded carpet. The light is dim – one of the bulbs needs replacing – but first there is a more pressing assignment, a few essential details to record. Hugo spreads his notes over the floor, ordering and re-ordering, adding and adjusting. He reads aloud the final sentence.

'Transcribed contacts from DW mobile: total 37.'

Hugo checks his watch. It is midnight. His phone is charging but he's not yet ready to make that call. He scoops all his papers together and shoves them into a drawer. He showers and pulls on his striped pyjama bottoms and an outsized T-shirt with the word Boss in Gothic font across the chest. He knots his dressing-gown cord tightly at the waist, which reminds him of Monika, and hopes someone 'out there' will find her and help her recover from the loss of her precious house, the love of money and her shattered dreams of Toby.

Ten past midnight. *I'll never sleep.* Hugo takes his phone out onto his rickety, wrought-iron balcony. Somewhere down the corridor a couple are arguing as usual. A tawny owl screeches and dips through the fields that stretch away towards the M6. Hugo follows its shadow until it vanishes. He scrolls through his list of contacts and selects a number.

'Hello? Hello?' The woman sounds exhausted.

'Julia, my dear! I knew you'd still be awake. You must be buzzing.'

'Oh, it's you. Delete my number.'

'I will. I will. Just tell me one thing. How's my mate Duncan doing?'

'Banished to the Cave, where he belongs.'

'But you will forgive him.'

'That's not for you to know or decide.'

'He never had an affair. He loves only you. And he adores his daughters. They need their dad more than you don't need him.'

'That is utterly senseless, Hugo.'

'If you think about it, it's a lot more sensible than you kicking Duncan out of your life without hearing him out. Two wrongs don't make a right but two outs make an in – I think.'

'*You* think? Well, I've been thinking . . .'

'What?'

'I made a decision as I was taxiing you all back from Bude, for free, that I'm going to sell up. Downsize.'

'Without Duncan?'

'With or without him. I'm thinking we've got to put the oomph back into our life or we're sunk. Either way, Four Valleys is bleeding the life out of us. Last night, after seeing how that huge house destroyed the Nowiks, I'm not about to let our house destroy us. Our mortgage is a millstone, you know. Did you see that *Panorama* programme – the one with the filthy, skinny kids playing in the slums of Calcutta? They looked far happier than our girls. Also, I read an article about a German chap who travelled to every country in the world in the same battered old car . . .'

'You want to meet a German?'

'Don't be nuts. Of course I don't want to meet him but I want to live like him. Free. Like we were before we started buying so much garbage. I'm thinking *adventure*. Maybe with Duncan. Definitely with the girls.'

'Can you do that? Just take them out of school and travel the world?'

'To save my own life? Yes. To save our marriage. Of course. We'll teach them French in France and Italian in Italy and . . .'

'Send me a postcard.'

'Nope.'

'What about Toby?'

'Not my problem, but I will tell you something for nothing – I chose his name.'

'You did? But how? You only saw him for the first time today. And what if Duncan doesn't want to travel?'

'Oh, I'm sure he will. That's the good thing about being married. You know someone better than they know themselves. Duncan loves to take risks.'

'But what if . . .'

'Mr Quin?'

'Yes?'

'It's very late. Go to sleep. Delete me.'

'But . . .' Hugo hears Duncan in the background.

'Who's that, darling?'

'Shh! It's Hugo.'

'Hugo? At this hour? Why am I even surprised?'

Hugo strains his ear because Duncan and Julia are whispering, laughing behind their hands so he can't quite catch what they are saying. He smiles, delighted that his travelling companion is not languishing in the Cave, suffering remorse all alone while losing his wife and daughters. And for all her tough exterior, Julia is quick to forgive. That, at least, is her gift. She can forgive all the lies and the thieving and the juvenile urge for excitement, as long as her husband is never unfaithful.

Hugo hangs up. He scribbles in his notebook: *All records up to date and complete.*

Biography

Katharine Ann Angel was born in Kent but grew up in Malaysia, Singapore, Germany, Bath and London, because her dad was an anaesthetist in the British Army. She has lived in many places in England but since 1984 she has lived in Lancashire with her husband, Andrew. Katharine taught in a number of schools before working for the National Teaching and Advisory Service (NTAS). She taught excluded teenagers, some of whom, along with some of her foster children, inspired the short stories in *Being Forgotten*. This book led to being invited to spend a year as a guest lecturer at Edge Hill University for trainee teachers specialising in PSHCE. Her first novel, *The Froggitt Chain*, was published in 2013.

Katharine is secretary to The Creative Network in the northwest. Under this umbrella she co-leads the CN Writers' group in Preston. On behalf of the Creative Network, Katharine has been involved in setting up a festival of words in Lancashire entitled 'What's Your Story, Chorley?' She continues to speak and read her stories at festivals and 'open-write' nights. Katharine enjoys bird-watching, wild swimming and natural history.

For more information

Website: katharineannangel.com – includes contact

Facebook: Katharine Ann Angel – 'Like' this page to receive up-to-date information

Twitter: @katharine59

Angel's books can be ordered from high street bookshops or via the author's website (personalised signing on request). They are available through most eBook providers.

A few of the many books that I have particularly enjoyed:

H.E Bates: *The Triple Echo*

Aravind Adiga: *The White Tiger*

Thomas Hardy: *Far from the Madding Crowd*

Donna Tartt: *The Goldfinch*

Oscar Wilde: *The Selfish Giant*

Jonathan Safran Foer: *Extremely Loud and Incredibly Close*

Other books by the same author

For more information visit www.katharineannangel.com

BEING FORGOTTEN - Eight inspiring short stories from the point of view of real teenagers facing various social challenges. Additional material for group discussion.

Some reviews for Being Forgotten
'Fascinating, absorbing and imaginative! Suitable for KS3 and KS4 PSHE as well as KS4 English Literature.'
J.L – Secondary School Headteacher

'An invaluable asset for teachers and youth workers.'
L.P – Partnership Development Officer

'Allows pupils to explore characters and emotions.'
C.K – High School English Teacher

Google 'Eight Special Tales TES' for the *Times Educational Supplement* review.

THE FROGGITT CHAIN – a novel

Lonely and terrified, Peter Froggitt throws away the 'stuff' of his past life in a bag, but the very 'unusual' Hugo Quin finds it and using the 'clues' within, he decides to return it with spectacular results. *The Froggitt Chain* explores the issue of 21st century loneliness, despite modern communications. It tackles the powerful problem of impossibly broken generational links between a grandparent and grandchild. It opens the debate on how adults carry huge sorrows from their childhood, burdens that lie dormant for decades or perhaps a lifetime.

Some reviews for The Froggitt Chain

'Very clever writing. The most enjoyable book of all my summer reading.' R.H

'A compelling read . . . equally humorous and poignantly sad.' P.C.

'You don't want it to end because you'll miss the characters too much!' R.B

Readers' questions about The Burglar's Baby

This book reintroduces Hugo Quin. How would you describe him to someone who has not previously met him?

In *The Froggitt Chain* Hugo is a cheerful, yet socially dislocated man in his forties who lives for the moment. He has an acute mind for facts, especially history (Hugo had been a history teacher). If Hugo thinks of a number, e.g. the time being 15.47pm, he translates it into a date and imagines that he is a historical or literary character from that date (e.g. Henry VIII).

In *The Burglar's Baby* Hugo doesn't do this but is he still impetuous, with an endearing sense of humour. He is a catalyst, inadvertently resolving difficulties by forcing people to relate to each other. He loves jokes, puns and playing pranks. He doesn't mind whether someone laughs with him or at him, yet he can behave in ways that are surprisingly sensitive.

Where do your ideas for plot and character come from?

I like to write about ordinary people who act impetuously, keep secrets or struggle to cope with 'normal' life. Like many writers, I base my characters on observations of people I know, then mix up this behaviour to create a new person. My ideas for plot come primarily from my personal experience and of course, imagination. After tutoring excluded youngsters, then fostering teenagers, I was inspired to write *Being Forgotten*, giving a voice to eight marginalised young people. Some years ago, after teaching at a rehabilitation centre, I wrote a draft idea for *The Burglar's Baby* with the protagonist (Duncan) as a desperate alcoholic/drug addict. I never finished that version (thankfully!). After completing *The Froggitt Chain*, I decided to restart *The Burglar's Baby*, but from a completely fresh perspective in which Duncan is an affluent family man with a fatal flaw: he cannot mature.

In C.S. Lewis' brilliant book *The Abolition of Man*, Lewis refers to 'men without chests', men with weak moral fibre – an apt description of Duncan Wilde. Duncan ought to represent the attractive protagonist, the 'he man' of the story; instead he is weak and presents himself as more virtuous and successful than he actually is. It is the social outcast, Hugo Quin, who behaves with a greater measure of integrity and lives life to the full.

Why did you place Duncan's confession at the very beginning of the book?
I wanted the reader to be aware of Duncan's guilt about Steve's death without the overuse of flashbacks interrupting the flow of the main story. It was important for the reader to be aware of Duncan's addiction to extreme sport, to understand why he quickly tires of his affluent lifestyle. In this opening chapter, I gave Duncan a more mature 'voice' because his confession happens some years after the events in the story; but the question remains – after 'the baby', did Duncan really change or does he continue to live a double life?

How long did it take you to write The Burglar's Baby?
About two years. So many other things eat into my time, from book signings and radio, to editing a community magazine and

other work and family commitments.

What comes next? Will we meet Hugo again?

Much as I've enjoyed 'Hugo' I need to move on. I want to develop a new style and story, so right now I'm working on an adventure about some young girls from residential care homes who are forced to live in an extinct volcano/jungle in Papua New Guinea. The research is extremely structured, but great fun!

Some themes in The Burglar's Baby

- Brokenness of family resulting in loneliness and isolation
- Individual disconnection in a world which prides itself on instant communication
- Lack of fulfilment despite having all the perceived trappings of success
- Friendship, forgiveness, humour and hope

Discussion suggestions for reader's groups and book clubs

1. Duncan's confession offers the reader insight into Duncan's future as a motivational speaker but, after the terrible events related to Toby, has Duncan genuinely changed? Or might he be continuing to conceal a burglary habit?
2. Julia meets Duncan on a skiing holiday; she also replaces the excitement of youth for a family, a mortgage and a 'perfect' home. Do Duncan and Julia ever really know each other? In your opinion, why does Julia appear to forgive her husband so quickly?

3. In what ways do Sophie and Meg betray the underlying tension in their home?

4. Lisa is intelligent, attractive and eloquent. What factors contribute to her becoming dislocated and homeless? What prevents her from reporting the loss of her child?

5. Callie and Lisa become interdependent very suddenly. This scenario was based on a true-life incident of two strangers who met and, within a matter of hours, trusted each other to travel the world. Is Callie's initial positive reaction to Lisa really too impetuous? How would you describe Callie's actions?

Lightning Source UK Ltd.
Milton Keynes UK
UKOW06f1951170716

278587UK00024B/851/P